The Witch's Compass

Witches of the New Forest

Book 3

Joanna van der Hoeven

Witches of the New Forest

Copyright

© Joanna van der Hoeven 2025

All rights reserved to the Author

No part of this book may be reproduced, or stored in a retrieval system, or transmitted in any other forms or by any means electronic, mechanical, photocopying, recording or otherwise without the express written permission of the author and publisher except in brief quotations embodied in critical articles and reviews. Without in any way limiting the author's and publisher's exclusive rights under copyright, any use of this publication to 'train' generative artificial intelligence (AI) technologies to generate text is expressly prohibited. The author reserves all rights to license uses of this work for generative AI training and development of machine learning language models. Note however that the author will never, ever, ever, EVER give away or sell those rights to license work for AI.

Let's keep our human authors in business.

Published by Joanna van der Hoeven

The Witch's Compass

This is a work of fiction. Names, characters, businesses, organisations, events, and incidents are the product of the author's imagination. The setting of this book is in Burley, a real village located in the New Forest, England. The village of Burley is used as inspiration for this book along with some of the myths and legends that surround the area. The characters in this work are completely fictitious. Any of the characters' resemblance to actual persons either living or dead is entirely coincidental.

Burley is a very real, very witchy place and the author urges you to visit if you are able.

Acknowledgements

Thank you to my mother, who every week sits down and has a chat with me about the latest chapters that I've written. I cherish these moments, and knowing that she is my biggest fan, supporting me in all that I do, makes me realise just how lucky I am to have someone like her in my life.

I would also like to thank Jasmin, for helping me with the proofing and giving me feedback on the books. You truly understand the work, and that makes me so very happy. You are magick, never forget that!

Lastly, I thank the village of Burley and the New Forest for providing me with the inspiration for this book, and for the entire series. May all the stories, myths, legends, and folklore stay alive through the telling of its tales.

Dedication

I would like to dedicate this book to all the Witches who have walked the paths of magick before, and for all the Witches who follow. May your inner compass guide you, now and forever, forever and always.

This book is intended as a fictional work only. The rites and rituals, herbs, and other magickal practices are intended solely for the purpose of enjoying this fictional work. To understand more about Witchcraft and Druidry, please see the author's non-fiction works. The author and publisher disclaim any liability arriving directly or indirectly from the use of this book.

Other Titles by Joanna van der Hoeven

WITCHES OF THE NEW FOREST SERIES

Hedge Witch, Book 1

The Veil Between the Worlds, Book 2

The Witch's Compass, Book 3

Smugglers and Secrets, Book 4

NON-FICTION

The Old Ways: A Hedge Witch's Guide to Living a Magical Life (published through Llewellyn, 2025)

The Path of the Hedge Witch: Simple, Natural Magick and the Art of Hedge Riding (published through Llewellyn, 2022)

The Book of Hedge Druidry: A Complete Guide for the Solitary Seeker (published through Llewellyn, 2019)

The Hedge Druid's Craft: An Introduction to Walking Between the Worlds of Wicca, Witchcraft and Druidry (published through Moon Books, 2018)

The Crane Bag: A Druid's Guide to Ritual Tools and Practices (published through Moon Books, 2017)

Zen for Druids: A Further Guide to Integration, Compassion and Harmony with Nature (published through Moon Books, 2016)

The Awen Alone: Walking the Path of the Solitary Druid (published through Moon Books, 2014)
Dancing with Nemetona: A Druid's Exploration of Sanctuary and Sacred Space (published through Moon Books, 2014)

Zen Druidry: Living a Natural Life, With Full Awareness (published through Moon Books, 2013)

"To fear love is to fear life,
and those who fear life are already three-parts dead."

- Simone de Beauvoir

"Do the best you can until you know better.
Then when you know better, do better."

- Maya Angelou

Prologue

"They're not coming for you, you know."

The dark-haired man circled his prisoner, his eyes intent on his captive. "They had the opportunity, and they chose *her*, not you, my brother. And do you know why?"

The man being held prisoner, surrounded by swirling mists and unable to move, simply stared ahead and gave no answer.

"They saved *her* because she is one of their own. Unlike you. You will never be a part of their world." The man studied his captive, who wore a simple, small silver coronet on his dark hair, while he himself wore a large, ornate crown of clear and smoky quartz crystal. His prisoner was tall, and lean, with a gentle fire in his dark eyes. His own ice-blue eyes bored into those of his captive. "They chose one of their own," he repeated.

The man held within the mists did his best not to react, but his captor caught the slight blink and the wave of pain that appeared in those dark eyes. "It's been months now in their world," his captor said. "And yet, you are still here, languishing in your prison." He sighed. "If only you would listen to me, brother. If only you could see sense."

His captive finally broke his silence. "I will never follow you, or your ways, Lanoc. My way is the way of light, not darkness. Of hope, not terror."

Lanoc stopped his pacing. "You were ever the pitiful fool," he said, turning his back to his prisoner. "There can never be any sort of relations with *them*. They are not like us. They will decided to extend her sabbatical by one more month, which gave them until the end of September to come to a final ion. The smart thing to do was to sell the cottage, go back , pay off her mortgage, and live a happy, safe life.

fety and security were what she had craved her entire life, since her mother had gone missing. Now that her mother eturned to them through their own recently discovered kal skills, Hunter had begun to see things a little ently. She had needed to take chances in finding and ng her mother back. She had done things she had never ed of, things she had never thought possible. Whole new ns opened up for her.

safety? Her sister had nearly died, after the latest attack rtney Peterson, possibly with the aid of Alice Hardwick, ber of one of the longstanding Witch families here in . Her family and friends had also been the targets of other us magick, not to mention physical attacks such being the road in a car accident that had put both her and Jack ospital. No, safety was not something that was promised lspeth had stated that if the Hardwicks, being one of the gickal families that have lived in Burley for hundreds of id nothing to reign in their family's practice of the dark itch War would begin. Courtney, the rogue Witch from , had worked with Alice Hardwick before. And er, or Xander Hardwick as he was known, Alice's brother, had also been a part of their schemes. Three and a Druid had already been attacked. There was no ck from that. The community must be kept safe.

r wondered what her role in this would be, if she s the morning sun shone down on her back, and her rked in the earth, she felt a sort of rooting in her own e in the New Forest. She could help them. She and her

never be like us. What you do, and the example that you set, is dangerous for us all."

The man held captive in the mists merely laughed at this, causing Lanoc to turn on his heel and glare daggers at him. He looked Lanoc straight in the eye. "I will live in a world of hope, not fear. I seek a world of compassion, not tyranny. Nothing you can say, or do, will ever change my mind. For I have found the one spell, the one great magick you will never be able to wield."

Lanoc sneered. "And just what is that, my brother?"

"True love," said Aedon.

Chapter One

Hunter stepped out the front door. She looked down the road towards Elspeth's cottage, and saw Jack's jeep in the driveway. They hadn't spoken for nearly two weeks, not since that night when everything had been revealed, and Jack had told her why he had kept his actions a secret. Hunter had said that she needed time, and so that's what he had given her. Yet it was difficult to have him so close, and to keep him from her heart. She longed to run over there and throw herself into his strong embrace, look into his emerald green eyes and tell him how much she loved him. But she knew the pain of loss and separation, and had yet to decide what would happen when this was all over. Would she stay here in England, and take over her aunt's cottage, or would she return to Canada and the life that she had led, before she even knew about magick?

Just the thought of giving up her legacy made her stomach feel queasy. She knew that she truly wouldn't ever be able to give it up, now that she had begun to come into her own power. There was something about this place, about the little village of Burley and the magickal community here that beckoned to her, that made her feel at home, perhaps even more so than the place where she had grown up and spent her formative years. Burley and the New Forest had its dangers and its risks, as she and her sister had discovered time and again. But the challenges she had faced had changed her, and made her feel better able to deal with what life threw at her, for good or ill. She felt like she belonged here, somehow, as much as she belonged to her home and her

life as a university professor in Ontario, Ca[nada] was comfortable and safe, whereas her new l[ife in the New] Forest was exciting and sometimes terrifying[. She felt like] it was torn between two places.

She sighed, going to the vegetable patch [behind the] house, and began weeding. This was a sa[fe place she] could process her thoughts. She cleared [her mind for] minutes, and concentrated on the work. S[olutions often] drifted in as she worked.

Perhaps she needed to stop thinking [so much. She] considered all that she had learned abo[ut her aunt's] Hedge Witchcraft. It was all about the lim[inal space,] neither one thing nor the other but both at [once, with] blending and borders dissolving. Maybe sl[ie could apply that] way of thinking into her everyday life, no[t just magick.] Perhaps she could live in both worlds, a[nd not just] belong to one or the other. Perhaps there [was a way.]

But still, where did that leave her a[s she couldn't] physically live in two places at once. G[iving up] her job back in Canada was a huge risk. [But the] community, the history, myths, and le[gends, and] the legacy of magick that ran through [her family...] Hunter was cautious by nature, and do[ing what] was unheard of for her. Her heart ye[arned for this] place, for what might be. But she also [had] uncertainty.

It was all still so new to her. The[y had been here] for a few months now. Hunter had s[ent word to] her sister, Ryder, to come to a decisi[on about] their inheritance. By September, the[y needed to have] some sort of consensus. They were a[lready at the end] of August, and the deadline had bee[n set.]

family, her mother and sister, could aid the community here. They could help keep the evil magick at bay, and allow the community the quiet, peaceful and beneficent lifestyle that they had enjoyed for hundreds of years. If she left, after having inadvertently started all this, would that even be an ethical thing to do?

She sat back on her haunches and thought for a moment. *No, we hadn't started this,* she corrected herself. *I must not lay the blame for the actions of others upon myself. Courtney and Alice were already manipulating Jack with dark magick before Ryder and I even arrived here. No, the blame does not lie with us.*

And there was still the issue of trying to rescue her real, Fae father, which loomed over her. Would she and her mother, and possibly Ryder if she was well enough, be able to find and release him from whatever prison his brother, the despotic Fae King, was holding him in? If he was even still alive? And what if Lanoc attacked them again? Ryder was still on crutches, recovering from her injuries after the attack by Courtney and the demonic being she had summoned. What were their chances of success in the Otherworld, if they barely survived the ordeals laid upon them by members of the magickal community here in Burley?

Hunter sighed again, and blew away a long curl of red hair that had fallen free of her ponytail.

One day at a time, she thought. *One day at a time.*

***

"I hate these freakin' things!"

Hunter entered the cottage just as Ryder plopped down onto the sofa, her crutches tumbling down to the wooden floor with a crash. Her mother, Abigail, came rushing out of the kitchen. "Ryder, are you alright? Did you fall?"

Ryder sighed. "No, Mom, I'm fine. Just the crutches fell as I was sitting down."

Hunter pulled out her ponytail and went over to pick up the crutches. "Patience is a virtue," she said to her younger sister.

"Patience is a virgin," Ryder corrected. "These crutches are a total nightmare."

"Can I get you anything, Peanut?" their mother asked from where she stood in the kitchen doorway.

"No thanks, Mom. Unless you've got some sort of spell to get me back on my feet in no time at all," Ryder grumbled.

Hunter sat down beside her sister. "That might not be such a bad idea. Mom, can we do that?"

Abigail came out and sat in the chair next to the sofa. "It is possible, but there are usually risks associated with speeding up healing. The person to ask, really, is-"

"Elspeth," the sisters said together.

Their mother smiled. "Shall I give her a ring?"

"Be my guest," said Ryder grumpily.

As Abigail went to make the call, Hunter looked over at her sister. Her colour had returned, and she wasn't in as much pain as she had been before. They had nearly lost her, when her spirit became detached from her body after a vicious attack by a demon hound, the Chained Black Dog, which had been summoned by Courtney. Hunter had done a hedge riding, and found her sister's spirit at the site of the attack. She then had brought Ryder's spirit back to her body in the hospital. She had never been so worried in all her life as she had been when she saw Ryder, lying pale as death in the intensive care unit. "You must be feeling better, if you're complaining so much," said Hunter with a small smile.

"Well, we've got stuff to do, you know? Your father to save, ridding the community of those evil bitches, fighting the good fight, and all that."

"We will," said Hunter, giving her sister's hand a pat. Ryder was much younger than Hunter, being only twenty to Hunter's thirty-five years of age. Hunter reminded herself of how impatient she had been at that age, wanting to get on with her life while being held back through caring for her family when their mother disappeared. "I'm sure Elspeth can speed things up."

Ryder looked at Hunter, an eyebrow raised over her pale blue eyes. "And what about Jack? Hasn't he got some Druid mojo that he can work? Maybe we should call him over too."

"I know what you're doing Ry. And Jack and I need some time, before we decide what happens between us."

"Before *you* decide what happens between you. The poor guy's made his intentions perfectly clear. He even went after you, when you went missing. He freakin' went to the Otherworld to find you and bring you back, Hun. That guy would do anything for you." Ryder sighed and looked away. "Here you've got this gorgeous man, who is a park ranger *and* a powerful Druid, just waiting for you to choose him, and I'm stuck here, like a lump on this couch, with a love-life that's totally non-existent."

Hunter sighed and looked away for a moment. "It's not as simple as that, Ryder."

Ryder sat up and took Hunter's hands in her own. "Yes, it damn-well is, Hunter. Don't make things so complicated. Sometimes you just have to go with your heart. You're always living in your head. You've got to let that go every now and then."

Hunter smiled, and squeezed her sister's hands before pulling away. "You may be right," she said, non-committedly.

"Good news, girls!" Abigail came out from the kitchen. "Elspeth said that she *can* do something to help speed up the healing. In fact, the whole coven might be able to aid her with this endeavour. They've already been doing some work on your behalf, but a concentrated effort, in a group ritual with Ryder present, might be just the ticket."

Ryder fist-punched the air. "Yes! Bring it on."

"Hold it a minute. What are the risks that you mentioned, Mom?"

"Well, when a great healing work is performed, the person might immediately get better, but then become ill again once the effects of the ritual have worn off. It might throw off their own energy, and cause it to go out of balance."

"I'll take that risk," said Ryder.

"Hang on, Ryder. Don't you want to think about this for a moment?" asked Hunter.

"Nope. I'm good. Let's do this. When can we do the ritual?"

"Tomorrow night," Abigail said. "We'll head on over to Elspeth's cottage. Can you make it from her driveway to the ritual circle in the back garden, on your crutches?"

"I'll go anywhere if it gets me healed up faster. Maybe Jack can carry me in his strong, manly arms." Ryder turned to grin at her sister, and to see if there was a reaction.

"I'm sure he could, Ry," said Hunter, without emotion.

Ryder just sighed, and rolled her eyes.

***

Hunter began to feel nervous as the time for the ritual approached. She pulled up her energy to shield her thoughts and learning more from their mother about hedge riding and the Otherworld in preparation for Aedon's rescue attempt. Ryder was adamant that she was coming along on this mission, and so she was putting all her faith into tonight's healing ritual so that she could accompany them soon to the Otherworld.

They knew they had to act as quickly as possible with regards to the rescue, but they also did not want to do anything foolish. Too much haste would leave them ill-equipped, while too much time meant that Lanoc would be better prepared for them when they did cross the veil between the worlds.

It was a dangerous and uncertain game they were playing, and Ryder's impatience was beginning to rub off on Hunter. She too itched to get back there, and bring her father back. She was eager to learn more about her Fae heritage, and her own magickal powers as a result of her Fae legacy. She felt like the knowledge that her father held would help her to better understand herself. She was beginning to understand just what it meant to have Fae, as well as Witch blood, but she still felt like something was missing. She felt like she was slowly coming home to herself, even if she couldn't decide just yet where her home was on the physical plane. But her soul was on a quest to come home, and she knew that she must heed its call.

As Hunter entered the room she shared with her sister, she saw clothes flying out of the closet, and heard Ryder grumbling from somewhere in the depths. She dodged tops and bottoms as she traversed the room to sit at the dresser and put on some makeup. She should at least make herself presentable, she thought. Ignoring the chaos Ryder was creating in the room, she powdered her face, put on a little blusher, and a touch of mascara. If she was going to see Jack tonight, she at least wanted to look decent. Even if she wasn't sure where their relationship emotions from Ryder, as that was the last thing her sister needed right now when she was healing.

Hunter hadn't seen or spoken to Jack for nearly two weeks now. Would he be upset with her because of that? She remembered that day when she had become lost in the Otherworld, after having been swallowed up by her anger and her pride. This had allowed an opening for the spell that had been cast against her by Courtney and Alice earlier, which only exacerbated those feelings. When Jack had found her, it was his love that had opened up her eyes to what was really happening, and the influences she was under. His words came to her, and warmed her heart. *I would follow you to the ends of the earth. I have never stopped loving you. I have watched over you, day and night, every chance I could get. I will never leave you again.*

And yet, she had still pushed him away with her request for some time and some space. Had his feelings changed over the last couple of weeks? She was sure they had. All her previous relationships had always started out like that: full of love, with grand declarations and gestures, only to end up with her being left behind as the person she loved moved on to bigger and better things. Love had never lasted in her relationships. Whether it was two months or two years, she was always the one being dumped, being forgotten, being put aside for the next thing that came along. She was a novelty, with her bright red hair and green eyes, her academic mind and her determination. But novelties always wore off, and then where would she be with Jack? Stranded in a foreign country, miles away from her birthplace in Canada, and having to rebuild her life once again. *It always ends up the same, you know*, she said to herself.

Hunter pushed down her feelings and went upstairs to get ready. She and Ryder had been studying all day, learning as much as they could about working with energy, and also was heading, if indeed they still had one, she could at least look nice.

It's been two weeks, she thought. *No calls, no sign of him.*

"That's because you asked him to give you some space, Hunter," her sister called from inside the closet.

"Stay out of my head, sis."

"Stop shouting out your thoughts and emotions, Hun, and I'll at least have some sort of chance then." Ryder emerged from the closet, a couple of tops over one arm as she hobbled on the crutches to her bed. "Honestly, every day it's been the same thing. It's a wonder you don't drive yourself totally bonkers with all that thinking that you do. Have you ever tried some mindfulness meditation? At least it would give *me* a break from your thoughts."

Hunter and Ryder had discovered that their sisterly bond allowed them to speak to each other with their minds, telepathically. While this skill did not extend outside of their sisterly bond, it was something that both amused, and sometimes exasperated Ryder. "Seriously, Hun. Jack's into you. Always has been, always will be. He's not like all the other guys."

Hunter looked at her sister in shock. "And what would you know about that?"

"Hunter, that's a large part of what you've been projecting all over the damned house since the whole incident last month. I know, you're trying to keep it to yourself, but it just leaks out. I'm telling you, Jack's a keeper. You've got to stop allowing your ex-boyfriends' jackass behaviour to tar every damned man with the same brush."

Hunter turned to look at herself in the mirror. "You might have a point," she said softly.

"Yeah, I'm wise and all-knowing like that. Now, which t-shirt would be more appropriate? I can't decide between AC/DC, Pantera, or Kiss."

"Going for the vintage look tonight?"

"Yeah. Feeling some eighties and nineties vibes."

"You weren't even born then."

"Doesn't mean I can't appreciate the music, or the vibe." Ryder leaned over her bed, and studied all three t-shirts. "Kiss, I think. Might give you and Jack some ideas."

Hunter rolled her eyes and spritzed on a light perfume. After she did, she looked at the bottle appraisingly. "Isn't it nice, to be able to wear perfume outside on a summer's evening, and not get eaten alive by bugs?" she asked, changing the subject.

"Yeah, it sure is different over here in England with the bug situation. It's nice to be able to smell like something other than citronella for six months." Ryder leaned on her good leg, and pulled the t-shirt over her head, the crutches resting against her midriff. They slipped and clattered once more to floor. "Goddammit!"

***

They bustled into the car for the very short drive over to Elspeth's cottage, which was the next house along the road that led to the little witchy village of Burley in the New Forest. They couldn't risk anyone seeing Abigail, as they had to keep Abigail's return a secret. They didn't want any media attention about a woman who had gone missing for nearly twenty years and then suddenly reappearing, not looking a day older since her disappearance. It would put the entire magickal community at risk. The car also made things easier for Ryder, though she still struggled with getting in and out of the vehicle. Abigail opened the door for Ryder, and Hunter came around to offer her aid as well. Their mother had a pashmina covering her head, and sunglasses on despite the growing darkness as the sun had just set. Hunter silently passed the crutches to her mother, and then gave Ryder a hand out of the car.

The gravel crunched behind her. "Here, let me help."

Hunter stiffened at the sound of Jack's voice. She turned her head while Ryder leaned on her, and there he stood, a half-grin on his handsome face. His dark hair was swept back from his forehead, the sides neatly cut with a few silvery-grey hairs adding some character to his thick locks. His green eyes seemed to shine in the last of the evening's light. "Hello, Hunter," he said softly as he looked at her, seeming to drink her in with his gaze.

"Hello, Jack."

"Thank God," Ryder said loudly. "Come on then, get your butt over here and take me in your arms, my good man, just like Colonel Brandon does for Marianne Dashwood in 'Sense and Sensibility'." Ryder grinned as Jack came over and picked her up. She put her arms around his neck. "You're no Alan Rickman, but you'll do."

Jack gave a short laugh at that, and his face changed from handsome to drop-dead gorgeous. Hunter felt her heart give a little jump in her chest, and she turned away to close the car door. She then took the crutches from her mother, and followed Jack into the back garden of Elspeth's cottage.

Jack had been living with his sister, Elspeth, these last few weeks, as a protective measure. Though he had a lovely cottage of his own, it was on the Hardwick Estate, and for safety reasons they had all decided that no one should be on their own while they sorted through all this witchy mess, what with the physical attacks and dark magick being cast against them. Jack confidently walked around the side of the building as he carried Ryder, and then on towards the circle of trees that stood halfway down the long, lawned area. Hunter followed, and couldn't help but check out his backside with a small gulp. Damn, but the man made her mind *and* body respond in so many ways.

There were people already gathered in the ritual circle, talking and laughing with each other near a fire that burned brightly. As they approached, quiet descended upon them all, and they moved out to form a circle around the fire. Jack carried Ryder in, and as they entered the entire coven began to applaud them with pride and admiration in their faces. What Ryder had done to save herself magickally was no mean feat. They also applauded Hunter as she walked in beside her mother, behind Jack and Ryder. Ryder grinned from ear to ear, while Hunter blushed a beet red. Abigail smiled proudly at her daughters, as did Elspeth, who stood in the circle's centre by the bright fire.

"Welcome, Ryder," she said warmly. The applause faded away.

"Hey, Elspeth. Everyone. Nice to be back."

The coven members drew closer, and offered Ryder their congratulations and words of encouragement for what she had done. Hunter felt an enormous sense of pride for her sister, and reached over to squeeze her arm as she looked over at her, still held in Jack's arms. Unshed tears shone in Ryder's eyes.

A small cot had been placed near the fire, and Jack gently set Ryder down upon it. She sat and looked around at the coven, a hand over her heart and, for once, at a complete loss for words. Hunter could feel the overwhelming emotions her sister was experiencing, and she sat down next to her. "We're all so proud of you," she whispered, and hugged her sister. Abigail came up behind them, sunglasses removed and pashmina around her blonde hair. She nodded, and Hunter released her hand, moving away to the circle's edge where the rest of the coven had fanned out. She found that she was standing opposite to Jack, who regarded her from across the space. His green eyes held her own, and she felt herself blushing once again, before she shifted her gaze down to the ground. *Why did he have to been so damned good-looking?*

Elspeth placed her hand on Ryder's shoulder. "Lie down, Ryder, and try to relax." She gave the young woman a small smile, and then turned to address the coven. "We will raise energy, and then send it to Harriet. Being a skilled energy-worker and healer, she will set the energy with a healing intention, and then pass it to Ryder." She looked back down at Ryder, and said, "It is up to you whether you accept or deny this gift. Look in your heart, and listen to your intuition. Let it guide you. If it feels right, then do it. If it does not, then do not. The choice is always yours, and free will shall always reign."

Ryder looked up at the older woman. "Thank you, Elspeth," she said solemnly. She carefully lifted her injured leg onto the cot, and then lay back. The light of the fire danced across her body, and she took a few deep breaths to calm herself.

Seeing her sister lying there, injured and on her own, made a flame of anger spark into life in Hunter's heart. She pushed it down, trying to contain it. *Anger will be your ruin* her strange Fae 'ally' had said to her twice now when they had met. And he had been right. Hunter toned it down a notch, not wanting to open herself, or her sister, to any more negative energies that may be directed their way. She had already allowed that before, through her anger and pride. She was resolved not to let that happen again. Instead, she tried to allow her love for Ryder to occupy its place in her heart. She hoped she was successful.

shoulders, her long red hair hanging loose. She circled her arms around both her daughters. "My loves," she simply said.

Elspeth took a step forward, commanding everyone's attention. She looked as regal as ever, in her black dress with a lightweight, grey scarf swept around her shoulders. Her long, dark hair was streaked with silver, and her green eyes regarded the sisters, sitting together. Silence filled the circle, the only sound the crackling flames of the fire. She nodded once, and then turned to the group.

"We have convened tonight to perform a healing ritual on Ryder Williams, a Witch descended from the magickal Appleton line here in Burley. She and her sister, along with the aid of others, have met with and overcome attacks from others in the magickal community. Tonight, we strengthen our own bonds to right the wrongs that have been done, to us and the community. We do so with love and compassion, and a fierceness of will to ensure that we are all kept safe from harm. All those not in tune with our intention are at liberty to leave the circle now. All who choose to stay, do so of their own free will."

No one moved. Hunter looked around at those gathered. She had met them all previously, and smiled when she saw their friend, Harriet, giving her the thumbs up with a wink. Harriet was a close friend to Ryder, and had helped Hunter in the past to work with her own personal energy, even though Hunter had used that knowledge and twisted it with anger and pride in her misguided attempts to heal herself from heartbreak. But there were no hard feelings from Harriet, and Hunter was determined to work better with her magick.

"Then let's begin," said Elspeth. "Abigail, Hunter, Jack, please take a position with the rest of the circle." Hunter took her sister's hand and gave it a quick squeeze. Ryder's blue eyes were wide with excitement, and a soft breeze stirred her pale

She looked around the circle, and noticed that Thomas Ingham, the coven's Guardian, was looking at Ryder intently from just outside the circle's bounds. In his role as Guardian, he was to protect those who were partaking in the ritual from any external influences that might harm or interrupt them, as well as help with anything untoward that might happen within the circle. He wore a long-sleeved, dark Henley shirt and jeans, which made his short blond, curly hair stand out in the darkness. His tall, lean frame stood casually on the periphery, but the look in his eyes was intense. His blue eyes almost shone with a light of their own behind his small, wire-rimmed glasses that reflected the dancing flames of the fire. *Interesting*, thought Hunter. She had seen that light before, in Jack's eyes when he had looked at her, his energy rising.

What's interesting? she heard Ryder say in her mind.

Nothing, Just observing. It's so different, working with others, Hunter replied, carefully covering up her thought. Ryder did not need the distraction right now. She saw Thomas then step further back from the circle's edge, and begin to walk around the outside, his gaze searching for threats. Hunter could see his magickal dagger in a sheath at his belt.

The ritual began, and everyone clasped hands to cast the circle. Once it was cast, the elements of earth, air, fire, and water were invoked by various members of the coven. Doris, the elderly lady who was also into palmistry, called in earth. Harriet called in the element of air. Miranda, a goth girl who worked at Elspeth's metaphysical shop, called in the element of fire, and Michael, a pleasant Irish man in his late twenties called in the element of water. The ancestors were called into the ritual space by Rowan, Elspeth's daughter, and the Lord and Lady of Witchcraft were beseeched by Elspeth herself for their aid and blessings on this working.

"We will now raise energy, for the healing of Ryder Williams. As is customary, we will drum up the energy, and on my command, send it to Harriet. Are we all ready?"

"Yes, we are," came the soft response from around the circle.

"May it be so," said Elspeth.

Jack and Michael reached behind them, picking up their drums, or *bodhráns*. They ran their hands over the skins of the Irish handheld drums, warming them up near the fire, and then began to play them with double-headed beaters. Hunter had never seen Jack play his drum before. She knew it was a magickal item that held power for him, alongside his staff. He had used his drum, following Hunter's suggestion, to find his staff when it had gone missing after it had been stolen by Courtney Peterson and Alice Hardwick. Hunter had not witnessed that ritual, as Jack had done it in private. Watching him now, the lively drum beat seemed to make the flames dance even higher, and the light that shone on his face did things to Hunter's heart.

Jack and Michael came up to the centre of the circle, playing out their beats, and stood near Ryder. Ryder turned her head to watch them as they approached her. They played their drums over her, and Hunter saw her sister close her eyes and soak up the power of the drumbeat. Her face relaxed in the firelight, as the men swept the drums over her a few times while they played on, before moving back out into the circle and walking deosil, or clockwise, around the area. They moved on opposite sides of the circle, keeping in time with each other, the beat speeding up ever faster and faster.

Hunter saw those gathered in the circle begin to move and sway, stamp their feet and clap their hands, each feeling the beat in their own way, letting it fill them up and allowing them to raise their own energy in accordance. She saw her mother rocking back and forth with the beat, her eyes closed and a smile upon her face. As Jack approached Hunter, she pushed aside her conflicting thoughts about him, and concentrated on the task at hand. She closed her eyes, and allowed the beat to wash over her body and soul. She reached out with her energy to touch the sound, and then she rode the drumbeat deep into the earth, where the power of the land resided. She felt the energy of the New Forest filling her, and she gladly accepted it, combining it with her own. The beat carried on, as Jack continued around the circle, and still Hunter kept her eyes closed, focusing on the earth's energy and her own, golden light building within her.

The beat swept up, faster and faster. Hunter rocked with the beat, and opened her eyes. The flames of the fire had risen several feet higher, and Jack and Michael danced around the circle as they played their bodhráns. She could see a sheen of sweat on Jack's handsome features, and his grin as he allowed his energy to rise in tune with the beat. The double-headed drum beaters were a blur in the players' hands, and Hunter saw Jack's green energy rise up and surround him, swirling with small, silvery lights glinting and sparkling. It was powerful, magickal, and so wonderful to behold.

Harriet stepped forward, and stood by Ryder's side. The drums played on, reaching a crescendo. Hunter was riding a powerful wave of her own golden energy, the earth humming beneath her feet. Suddenly, Elspeth called out, "Ready… and… now!"

Hunter directed her energy towards Harriet, who stood with her arms outstretched, opening her body fully to receive the energy sent to her from the circle's participants. Different coloured energies swirled around the young woman, who smiled and took them within her. She began to glow with a pure, white light. The light increased as she took in everyone's energy, until she was so bright that Hunter had to look away. A wave of fear crossed Hunter's heart; fear for her sister if the ritual didn't work, and also fear if the ritual did work, but messed up Ryder's own energy. She tried to push down her anxiety, not wanting to send that energy out for her brave sister.

Hunter looked back up to Harriet. Everything seemed to go quiet, and the light dimmed enough so that Hunter could see Harriet's short, dark hair moving across her forehead from the energy that swirled around her. Her gorgeous curves were illuminated by a blue-white light. She suddenly seemed to transform from the happy, good-natured young woman who ran a dry goods, refill van business, to some sort of Fae goddess. Hunter now clearly saw Harriet's Fae heritage, as her form flowed and shifted from her usual mundane appearance, to an eldritch woman in shining white robes. "By all the gods," breathed Hunter softly to herself, as the last of her energy was sent to her friend.

Harriet turned to look at Hunter, a beatific smile upon her face. It filled Hunter with joy and comfort. Harriet then moved towards to Ryder, and held out her hands. A flash of brilliant white light blinded Hunter, and for a few moments she blinked, rubbing at her eyes. When she could see again, she saw Harriet and Ryder in an embrace, holding each other and rocking side to side with expressions of joy upon their faces. Ryder was standing up, and she pulled away from Harriet for a moment, before sweeping her up into a dance as the drums started again. A cry of joy came from the coven, and Hunter let out a whoop of her own. Her heart danced in joy, and she turned to look at Jack, who was watching her with a beautiful smile upon his face. He bent his head to her, and Hunter sent him a little push of her own golden energy in thanks. He gladly took it in, winding it around his own green energy like he had done before, when they were together. The ritual had been a success.

***

Unbeknownst to them all, a large, antlered figure watched them from the shadows of the treeline.

Chapter Two

Elspeth directed the ritual to close down, and the participants relaxed in the afterglow of a successful magickal working. Hunter, Abigail, and others moved up to the centre of the circle to congratulate Harriet and Ryder. Hunter gave her sister a great big hug, and then Harriet, whom she noticed had returned to her normal appearance. Hunter then saw Jack approach, drum still in hand, and Ryder squealed in delight as she moved towards him with her arms flung out to hug him. With a huge smile he lifted her up, bodhrán and all, and twirled her around in a circle before gently putting her back down again. Hunter's heart swelled at the display of affection, and she couldn't help but grin at them both.

Michael came up to them, and Hunter reached out towards him. The short, handsome Irishman smiled at her, and clasped her in his arms. "That was incredible," Hunter said to him as he patted her on the back while he held her.

He pulled away, and held Hunter gently by the arms. "It was my pleasure, Hedge Witch," he said, in that charming Irish accent. He squeezed her arms gently, before moving on to give Ryder a hug.

"These youngsters hold some incredible power," Doris said, coming up to stand next to Hunter. "It's a good thing they know what to do with it." Hunter's mood shifted instantly, as she felt slighted by the old woman's comment. She knew that she had abused her own power in the last few weeks, had used the wrong sort of energy to shield herself and build herself back up when she thought Jack had left her. It had left her open to a magickal attack from Courtney and Alice. But how did Doris find out about that? Hunter didn't need to be constantly reminded of it, especially not now. Pushing down her anger and shame, she glanced quickly at the woman before pointedly turning away and talking to Miranda, who was the closest person to her.

"Wasn't that wonderful? Is it always like this, with the coven? This powerful?" Hunter asked the young woman.

Miranda's dark, heavy eye shadow and lipstick accentuated her delicate features with a gothic twist. "It's usually pretty good, but tonight was epic," she said, her usually pale face a little flushed.

Rowan came up and joined her friend. "Hello, Hunter. Wow, wasn't Harriet something tonight?"

"It was incredible. I've never seen her like that."

"Nor I. She shone with energy, in her own power. It was beautiful to see."

"She totally kicked ass," agreed Miranda.

Elspeth called to her daughter, to start helping people indoors for some food and drink after the ritual work that they had done. Rowan nodded, and began rounding up people, ushering them back to the house. She turned to Hunter. "Coming?"

Hunter nodded. "In a little bit. I just need a moment out here, in the quiet."

Rowan studied her for a moment, and then nodded in understanding. "Take all the time that you need. You know where we are."

Hunter saw her mother and sister look towards her. *I'll be fine, sis. I just need some time to calm down, alone.*

She saw Ryder nod, and say something to her mother. Her mother gave them both a quick look with a raised eyebrow.

Hunter figured that she was beginning to understand their sisterly, magickal bond. Her mother smiled then, and waved at her eldest daughter before putting her arm around Ryder's shoulder and walking back to Elspeth's cottage with the rest of the coven.

Hunter stood alone in the now empty circle of trees. The light of the fire was quickly dying. She hugged her arms to her body, and looked up at the stars in the night sky. She thought about what her life was like, before she had known magick. It now seemed like a world away, and a lifetime ago.

She saw movement in the treeline at the bottom of the garden. She strained her eyes in the dim light, and thought she could make out a figure, standing beneath the trees. It raised its hand above its head, and then sketched her an overly elaborate, almost mocking bow, before turning and disappearing into the darkness.

Damn, she thought. She wondered if he'd had anything to do with the ritual tonight, or whether he was merely an observer. She was fairly certain she knew exactly who it was that had been watching them from the trees. Though he had yet to tell her his name, he had presented himself to her on several occasions, and had even freed her from the trap Lanoc had set when she had travelled alone into the Otherworld. Hunter still had no idea whether the Fae man was 'a good guy' or 'a bad guy', and that irked her. She liked to have clear delineations marked, so that she could form her opinions based on hard facts. Unfortunately, the fact was that even though he had helped her several times now, she still did not trust him. There was something about him that was… undetermined.

"Hunter?"

The sound of Jack's voice behind her made her jump. "Jesus Christ!" she swore on reflex, her heart thumping in her chest.

She then flushed, thinking that she had made some sort of horrible Pagan faux pas by using Christian swearing in the circle.

Jack raised his hands in surrender, a smile on his face. "Sorry, Hunter. I didn't mean to scare you."

Hunter took a few breaths, getting her heart rate under control. She shot a look back at the treeline in the distance, but the figure had vanished.

"Something out there?" Jack asked, moving forwards, his smile forgotten now as he scanned the forest edge, his body protectively in front of hers.

"Um, no. There's nothing there," said Hunter. She flushed at her half-truth, and looked down at the ground.

"Well, that's good then," said Jack, turning back to her. "So, what did you think of the ritual?"

Hunter raised her eyes to his. Her breath caught in her throat as she looked at him. She was reminded of the first night that they had spent together, out under the stars in the stone circle that he and his Druid friends had created. There, she had looked up into his handsome face much as she did now, with the stars crowning his head and the songs of the night flowing all around them. She yanked her brain back to the present, and focused on the question. "Yes. It was lovely. Very powerful, actually. I – I've never seen Harriet like that before."

"That girl is something, isn't she?" Jack grinned and shook his head. "You kind of forget just how powerful some of the people are from the old families here in Burley. You see them on a day-to-day basis, doing normal, mundane things, and then wham! You're in ritual with them and they pull off that kind of magick."

Hunter nodded. "You're the same, you know," she said, without thinking. After she had said those words, she wanted to kick herself. She lowered her head and looked at the ground. Jack cocked his head slightly and studied her. "I mean, when I first saw you using your power, back in the forest that day, when Lanoc attacked us." She looked up at him as he silently continued to study her face. "You know, when you cut through the storm? After chanting and protecting us in that cabin? You – you're like that too, you know. Park ranger by day, badass Druid by night." Hunter clamped her mouth shut. She couldn't believe she had just said that.

"And now I see the family resemblance to your sister," he said, a slow, sexy smile spreading across his features. "Here I thought you were so different from each other. It's funny, isn't it, the perceptions we make of people?"

Hunter just nodded, not able to think of anything to say. A muntjac deer barked in the distance. A tawny owl hooted in response. Silence reigned for a few heartbeats.

"Hunter, I just wanted to say that I've missed you. I know you asked for time, and I am trying my best to give you that. But I miss you," he said simply.

Hunter looked back down at her feet. "I miss you too, Jack."

There was a long pause, before Jack cleared his throat. He looked away, and said softly, "That last night which we had spent together, that was the best thing that had ever happened to me."

Her heart swelled within her. That night had been the most amazing she had ever experienced as well. Jack was not only an excellent lover, but was also the kindest, strongest, most wonderful man she had ever known. She wondered why on earth she was so hesitant to let him back into her life right now. Just as she was forming her response, he said, "But I understand why you feel the way you do. We don't know what will happen, when all this is over. You may decide to move back to Canada.

And I belong here, in the New Forest." He turned his gaze back to her, and her heart broke at the look in his eyes. "But, no matter what, I will always, *always* love you, Hunter."

His eyes held hers for a moment, before he turned and walked back to the cottage. Tears immediately sprang up in Hunter's eyes, and began to run down her face as she stood alone in the darkness of the night, her heart breaking yet again.

His words had sounded like a goodbye. And she had heard a lot of goodbyes in her lifetime.

***

Hunter went through the motions with the gathering inside Elspeth's cottage. She smiled, and tried to act like she wasn't internally falling apart. She stayed near her mother, who had nothing but love clearly written all over her face as she watched Ryder and her friends. Hunter felt the same, but other emotions were struggling against it all, and she felt like she was trying to swim upstream, battling the current of feelings that kept sweeping her away. She excused herself, and went to the washroom, *no, the loo*, she corrected herself. Once inside, she sat down on the closed lid of the toilet, brushed away the tears that began to fall, and took a few deep breaths.

Even being three thousand miles away from her past, she just couldn't escape it.

Every man you've ever been in a romantic relationship with has left you, her inner voice said. The emotions and feelings connected to all her previous boyfriends' past rejections swirled around in her mind, and she had a difficult time trying to settle them down. *And now Jack has left you too. You're on your own again, kid.* Hunter swallowed, and tried to breathe through the pain. Then she noticed something. Kid? When had she ever used that term? *Am I now losing my mind?* she thought. *Am I hearing voices? Or am I being influenced externally, yet again?* Her heart began to race at the possibilities. *Calm, calm,* she said to herself. *Stop being paranoid. Be here for Ryder,* she told herself. *This is not about you, or about Jack. This is not about your past relationships. This is about celebrating Ryder's recovery, and success. Stop being so selfish!*

She thought back to her training with Elspeth. Elspeth had always said, in a crisis or difficult time, to go back to basics. *Ground and centre,* she thought.

She heaved a great sigh, and went to the sink to throw some water over her face. She patted herself dry with a hand towel, and checked her reflection briefly in the mirror. She wiped a smudge of mascara from under her eye, and pulled herself together. Closing her eyes, she reached down energetically with her mind, down deep through the floor of the cottage, down through the foundations of the building and into the soil beneath. She breathed out, and visualised her energy as roots, spreading out into the dark earth. With every outbreath, she extended those roots. When she felt secure, she then drew in the quiet, calm, earth energy into herself with her inbreath. She exhaled her pain out through her roots, and inhaled calm, earth energies. Again and again, exhale, inhale.

After a minute of this, she felt grounded. She opened her eyes and with her right hand, she made a motion in front of her, drawing her hand down in a straight line from the top of her head to the centre of her chest. This secured and anchored the energy within her, centring herself in calm.

She glanced quickly in the mirror, and thought she saw a shadowy form behind her. She turned around, but nothing was there. Looking back in the mirror, it was gone. *Must be a trick of the light, or my mind*, she thought. *After everything tonight,*

I'm lucky I'm not seeing unicorns dancing past in a conga line, she mused.

Hunter made her way back to the party, and joined her sister in the kitchen. Miranda, Rowan, Harriet, and Elspeth were there, laughing and chatting. Ryder saw her sister approach, and shouted, "Hey Hunter! Come and check this out!" Ryder promptly untied the drawstring of her black joggers, and pushed them down her legs, revealing some lacy black underwear.

"Ryder, what the hell are you doing?" Hunter said as she drew near, trying to cover up her sister's body with her hands.

"Jeez, Hun, it's just a little skin. I'd wear less with a bikini, for crying out loud. Now just come here, and take a look!" Ryder turned to the side, to display where she had been injured all the way down the outside of the leg. Only a long, white scar showed, almost in the shape of a lightning bolt. "How cool is that?" her sister cried out. "It's like I'm Ziggy Stardust or something!"

Hunter leaned over to look. The skin had completely healed over, and it was if months had passed, not minutes. "That's incredible, Ryder," she said, amazed.

"I know!" her sister said, raising both her hands in the air and doing a little dance, with her trousers still around her ankles.

"Um, okay Ry. You've shown me. Now maybe you should pull your pants, I mean, your trousers back up." Hunter had corrected herself, because she knew that 'pants' in the UK meant underwear, and she didn't want to give her sister, or anyone else, any more ideas. Ryder's exhibitionist streak was already strong enough. Hunter looked around, and saw the huddle of Michael, Thomas, and Jack standing in the living room opposite, facing the spectacle. Michael winked, and raised his glass to the ladies in the kitchen with a silent toast. Thomas stood frozen, his drink halfway to his lips, unable to move. Jack was studying the ceiling with a smile on his face.

"No applause, please, folks," said Ryder, as she pulled her trousers back up with Hunter shielding her as much as she could. "Just throw money." A two-pound coin from the living room promptly landed at her feet. "Michael, you tight wad!" yelled Ryder as she picked up the coin and pocketed it.

"It is remarkable, the healing that's taken place," said Elspeth. "Harriet, you have excelled yourself. You have done your family proud."

Harriet smiled and shrugged her shoulders. "It's what we do. I'm just glad that it worked so well. This is the first time I've tried to do a healing like that on such a large, physical wound. Cuts and scrapes, sure, that's easy. Healing energetic or psychic wounds, that's my thing. But this? Yeah, this was good. It's given me a lot more confidence to work on that area of healing now."

"Remember, my dear, that just because it worked brilliantly tonight, doesn't mean it will always be so," said Elspeth with a knowing look in her eyes.

Harriet nodded, not taking offense. "Don't I know it." She put a hand to her heart. "I have a feeling, now, right here in my heart, that when a person is *meant* to be healed in that way, they will be. And when it's not supposed to happen, that I have to let that be." She rubbed at her chest, a thoughtful look on her face, and looked down for a moment. "I think it will be a hard lesson, when it comes to it," she said, raising her eyes back to Elspeth's face.

"The most important lessons usually are, I've found," said Elspeth.

"I don't know about you guys, but I need a drink," Ryder announced. "Whatcha got?"

As Elspeth took Ryder over to peruse the drinks, with a strict warning to be careful after such a major healing, Hunter moved over to Harriet. "Thank you so much for all that you have done for my sister. You are amazing."

Harriet smiled, and ran her hand down Hunter's arm fondly. "I'm only glad to be able to help my friends," she said.

Hunter's guilt surfaced at the way she had treated Harriet a couple of weeks ago when she, Elspeth, her mother, and sister had tried to discern whether Hunter had been enspelled by outside forces. "Harriet, I'm so sorry for the way I acted before all this happened. I should have listened to you, when you said my energy was all wrong."

Harriet waved away Hunter's apology. "Don't worry about it. Energy work is a lifetime's endeavour. Just getting to know your own personal energy can take years. You've only been here a few months, learning about your powers and your legacy. And already you and Ryder have done amazing things. Are there going to be hiccups along the way? You bet. But you're still learning. We *all* are still learning."

A twinge of resentment prickled at Hunter's heart, resentment at still being thought of as some sort of newbie. She thought that she had broken that spell completely, the one that had changed her behaviour before she had destroyed the poppet that had been part of the magick used against her, alongside the one that had been made of Jack. She then thought that maybe it wasn't magick, but her own insecurities and pride that were coming to the surface.

She smiled, and nodded at her friend. "We truly never stop learning," she agreed. Hunter was well aware that the whole ethos of academia, in which she had worked for years, was underpinned by the quest for knowledge and understanding. Sometimes, however, not all academics were open to the idea that there was more to learn and instead, assumed a position of superiority and authority rather than admit that there was work to do. Hunter could see how Harriet's statement matched with her own attitude towards learning - and no matter how resentful she felt about being labelled a 'beginner', she had to agree with her.

It was now time to apologise to Doris.

Chapter Three

The next day as Hunter was having breakfast with her mother, Ryder came down and joined them. Her hair was mussed up, and she was in sleep shorts and an Iron Maiden t-shirt. Usually grumpy in the mornings, and a late-riser, Hunter was a bit shocked to see her sister up this early.

"Hey, Ry, what are you doing up? It's not even 8am," said Hunter.

Ryder went over and sniffed the air by the coffee machine. "I know – I'm just awake, and ready for anything. Well, almost anything. I still want some coffee first." She went to find a mug and poured herself a cup.

"It's most likely the residual effects from the energy healing she received last night," said Abigail. "Just be careful not to overdo it even if you feel completely fine, at least for the next few days, my love," she advised, standing up and giving her youngest a hug. "Promise me that you'll take it easy?"

Ryder nodded, and took a sip of her coffee once she was released. "Yeah, yeah. I'll be careful. So, what have you got planned for today?" She sat down with them at the table.

"Well, I was going to ask Mom about protection magick," said Hunter. "I know that we need to find my father, and we've still got some preparations and study to do before we attempt it. At least, that's what Mom and Elspeth keep saying. So, I figure we might want to address the problem that's in our faces right now. Essentially, the magickal attacks against us by Courtney and Alice. First, we need to shore up our magickal protection."

Ryder immediately sat up straighter, her interest piqued. "Oooo, yeah, we need some of that. I'm tired of waiting here, like a sitting duck. What can we do, Mom?"

"Well, my dears, your Aunt Ivy had already placed down some permanent wards upon this cottage. But that was a long time ago. I don't know if she kept them up these past twenty years. I'm assuming she would have, to the best of her ability, but we can't be sure." Sadness came across her face. "It's been nearly a year now since she passed away as well." She sighed. "Time is such a strange beast." She leaned back in her chair, and sipped at her tea. "I can feel something is still in place, but it may be weakened and we need to strengthen it with our own magick. If each of us adds to the protection, we will be better guarded from magickal and mundane attacks, at least here in the home. Multiple layers are much more difficult to get through than a single layer, usually. As always, it depends on the magickal practitioner." She closed her eyes for a moment. "This old house still feels like my sister's energy," she said, with a sad smile.

Hunter reached out to her mother's hand, and touched it softly. "If we did that, would we not disturb, or destroy Aunt Ivy's energy? I wouldn't want to do that."

Abigail's eyes opened, and she smiled at Hunter. "Energy cannot be destroyed, but only changed in form, Poppet," she reminded her girls.

When Abigail spoke her pet-name for her, Hunter flinched. She had recently dealt with magickal poppets, being the vehicle of choice that Courtney and Alice had used against both her and Jack to change their behaviour and enspell them. Hunter swore internally, and automatically pulled up her energetic shields. She hated that her mother's pet-name for her, one that she hadn't heard for nearly twenty years, now had other memories and feelings attached to it, and extremely unpleasant ones. It was yet one more thing that made Hunter angry, and wanting to seek revenge in some shape or form. She swallowed down her hurt and anger, and tried to carry on the conversation, keeping her feelings shielded and to herself as much as possible. Ryder hadn't looked at her or said anything, and so she knew she had been successful in this, at least. She tried to breathe her anger out and down into the earth.

"So, what would happen then, if we added our own layers?" asked Ryder. "I think Thomas and I did something like that, because we needed to shore up our protection when you and Hunter went hedge riding together. I pulled up energy from inside the circle, and he did it from the outside, and together the energies blended. He then told me to push it out to the walls, and he kind of directed it all around the cottage. It was pretty cool."

"That's very well done, my love," said Abigail proudly. "Yes, you did mention that, after we returned from our hedge riding, but I'd forgotten. I thought I could feel your energy around the house in some way, along with someone else's that felt familiar and good, but was different. Now it makes sense. The energies that you raised would have blended, and strengthened the wards, much like when a blade is forged in a fire, and the metal turned upon itself in layer after layer, to make the blade stronger. As we three are all family, our energies will most likely be on a very similar wave-length, for lack of a better term. Our blood, and our magick, knows one another. It also recognises others in the community."

"That's so awesome," said Ryder. She took another sip of coffee. "I'm still not sure what *my* magick is, really. But I'll do what I can. I can raise energy, and send it out at least. As long as I don't blow up the house."

Abigail smiled at her. "Don't worry, Peanut. The two times you've discharged those incredible amounts of energy have been in times of great stress and fear, for yourself and your loved ones. It seems more like a reactionary response that you had in those circumstances. I'm not afraid of what you can do. Your magick knows what to do, I'm sure."

"Even if I don't," Ryder grinned.

Abigail studied her two daughters for a moment. "I think we should do this magickal working in a ritual. Go all out. It can't hurt. We will need some supplies from Elspeth's shop. Herbs, candles, and the like. I can make a list."

"I'll go and get them," said Hunter. She felt that she needed to be out of the house. "Ryder needs to stay indoors for a week or two, as word has gotten out in the community about her attack. If she's up and walking so soon, people might get suspicious."

"Just great," grumbled Ryder. "I'm all healed up, and still stuck here like a lump."

Abigail reached out and held Ryder's hand. "It's only temporary. Unlike my situation, my dear. Don't worry. There's lots of preparation that we need to do here in advance, and I'll need help with that. Cleaning the house from top to bottom, physically, is the place to start."

"Swell," said Ryder. "I get to clean the house. Just what I've always dreamed of." She rolled her eyes and then suddenly brightened. "Is there a magickal way to clean the house?"

"To do the physical work? No. But we can add magick to our efforts. Ivy had recipes for magickal cleaning products, such as sprays, floor washes, and the like. We can make some up right now, with what we have to hand, and enchant them."

Ryder smiled. "I'd like that."

Abigail turned to Hunter. "Will you be okay, going into the village on your own? Elspeth said we should stay together."

Hunter nodded. "I'll take extra protection with me. I have some stones already charged up."

Abigail reached under her shirt collar and pulled out a silver necklace with a small, pentacle pendant that she had been wearing around her neck. She unlatched it and handed it over to Hunter. "Take this. My mother gave it to me, just as she gave one to your Aunt Ivy. The pentacle is a protective symbol."

Hunter took the necklace and studied it before she put it on. The pentacle, a pentagram held within a circle, was surrounded by little delicate flowers and foliage. The silverwork was amazing. "I've never seen this on you before, Mom," she said wonderingly.

"When we moved to Canada, I didn't wear it. But when I came back here all those years ago to try and find your father, I brought it with me and wore it. It seems it doesn't have much effect on the Fae, but on other forms of magick I'm sure it will provide some protection. It can't hurt."

Hunter put in on and tucked it inside her blouse. "Thanks, Mom."

"Keep it, my love. And we'll have to get one made up for you too, Ryder. Unless we can find Ivy's pendant, though she may have been buried with it."

"I'd like that," Ryder said. "We haven't seen a necklace like that since we've been here, but I haven't really gone through all of Aunt Ivy's stuff, like her jewellery and that."

"We will do that, together. Sharing the memories." Ryder and her mother smiled at each other. "As Aedon used to say, *Now and forever, forever and always*."

Hunter was so glad to see them getting along, the mother and daughter that had been separated when Ryder was only two years old. She knew her sister didn't really have any memories of her mother, and so to spend more time with her and listening to her stories would be good for the both of them. "Okay, Mom. So, what do I need from Elspeth's shop?"

***

Hunter drove into the village. She would have preferred to walk the mile-long distance, but the path into the village was where Ryder had been attacked, and Hunter wasn't taking any chances. She didn't know if that beast could, or would, appear again. That being said, the road into the village was also where Courtney and Alice had caused their car accident, but Hunter ignored that thought and concentrated on her driving, keeping her awareness open. She had already said a little charm for safekeeping as she had left the house, and she had black and pink tourmaline stones in her pocket, alongside a pretty piece of flint she had found on the heath months ago. She had traced a pentagram over the steering wheel and sent out her energy before she left, asking for protection. She made the short and uneventful journey, and parked in the village car park.

She paid for her parking at the machine, and then made her way around the block to the shops. Burley was a small village, with only one high street where all amenities were located. There was also a pub, an ice-cream parlour (above which their friend, Harriet, lived), a community hall and a hotel further up the hill. Burley was a tourist hotspot, despite being so small. The famous Witch, Sybil Leek, had moved there in the 1950s, and drew a lot of media attention with her flamboyant ways. As a result, Burley became synonymous with Witchcraft, and the old magickal families that lived there grew anxious. They didn't want their secret and magickal heritage to become known, much preferring to preserve their anonymity. Eventually, the rest of the village tired of the media circus that overtook the area, and Sybil's landlord threw her out. She moved to the United States, where she became a television psychic and an astrologer, as well as writing more books on different aspects of Witchcraft. The magickal and mundane communities of Burley gave a sigh of relief.

That did not dampen in the slightest the Witchy tourism that had sprung up around the community. Tales of the New Forest Coven still abounded: a group of witches who had links to Gerald Gardner, the man who made Wicca known to the world, and who had worked close-by. There was quite a history of Witchcraft being worked in the New Forest, one which now was mostly just a magnet for those interested in seeing a quirky, New Forest village with Witchy shops and tourism. It was also a draw for historians, folklorists, and those fascinated by the occult. But the families who had lived there for hundreds of years kept a low profile, and were happy to remain under the radar as well as seeing the community boosted by local trade. Without the tourism, Burley's village life would soon dwindle, just as those of many other small villages had, until they became a small hamlet of a few houses, with no shops, post office, or pub. At the moment, it was a thriving village community simply because of the tourism.

Elspeth's shop, *The Covenstead*, was one of three Witchcraft shops in the tiny village. Hunter thought that it was the best metaphysical shop, with locally sourced items, handcrafted tools, new and second-hand books, and more. It was a Witchcraft shop, for real Witches. It was situated in a Tudor, timber-framed building. Dark and cosy inside, it had old, uneven oak floorboards that sometimes made one feel like they'd had a few too many drinks. It was also rumoured to be haunted by a small cat, but Hunter hadn't seen or felt any evidence of that yet.

She made her way into the shop, the door propped open to let in customers, as well as more light. Hunter stopped for a moment and deeply inhaled the wonderful scents that arose from the incense, herbs, and spell ingredients. There was an apothecary section in the back, with jars upon jars of herbs. Loose, stick, and cone incense lined an entire wall, while in the opposite corner stood a book nook, complete with a couple of comfortable chairs allowing the perusal of books before purchase. Glass cabinets held handmade tools for the Witch and others of varying Pagan traditions. Hunter looked around, and saw Elspeth coming out of the back with Miranda, carrying some boxes.

Elspeth spotted Hunter immediately. "Hello, dear," she said, smiling. She walked over to the counter where she had the till, and placed her box down upon it.

"Hey, Hunter. How's it going?" Miranda followed Elspeth, and plunked her box down, brushing off her hands. "How's Ryder doing today?"

Hunter walked up to the counter. "Ryder's doing great. She was even out of bed and downstairs before 8am."

Miranda's heavily made-up, dark eyes widened. "Say it isn't so! What have we done???" She brought a manicured hand with black nail polish to her heart, in mock horror.

Hunter laughed. It had been a long time since she had laughed. "I'm sure normal programming will resume shortly," she said with a smile.

"And how is dear Abigail?" asked Elspeth. She was in her customary colours of black and grey, with a long black broomstick skirt and a floaty grey top. Elegant black boots with three-inch heels completed the outfit. Her long, dark hair was swept up into a French twist, with some silver tendrils falling around her face. Hunter wondered if she would ever be as elegant, calm, and graceful as this woman who stood before her. Elspeth was in her early fifties, and exuded controlled power and self-assurance.

"Mom's good. She's the reason I'm here, actually. She's given me a list of items to get, for a ritual. We're going to strengthen the wards around the home."

Miranda held out a hand to take the list. She looked over it quickly. "Yup, we've got all this in stock. I'll get it sorted for you."

Elspeth studied Hunter calmly for a moment, before she said, "That's a good idea. We should take every precaution possible, until we decide how to handle the situation."

Hunter sighed. "How long do we have to wait, before we can do something proactive? I'm tired of being on the defensive all the time."

Elspeth smiled. In a soft voice, she said, "Not much longer, I should think. David is going to talk to the Hardwicks, if he hasn't already, and provide us with an update as soon as possible on the situation. We must give the family time to sort out their own problems first. This might just be a case of getting Alice under control, and giving Alexander a good talking to for aiding her and Courtney. Geraint Hardwick is, ultimately, the one who will decide how we all will proceed in the future. How he, as the head of the family, handles this matter will determine the outcome."

Hunter blew out a breath. She looked around, to ensure the shop was empty. She still kept her voice down. "Has there ever been a Witch War in Burley before?"

"In Burley? No, not that I know of. But Witches of the New Forest have been pitted against each other, every now and then.

There are other families throughout the Forest, in various villages and towns. Miranda, for instance, is from the Preston family line, in Beaulieu. Some families have turned on others throughout the years, for whatever reason. But that was all a long, long time ago: hundreds of years ago. Today, with the speed at which information travels, all the families are much more discreet with their magick, and know that to expose ourselves in any shape or form would forever change not only our own lives, but the entire world. That is why it is imperative that Geraint Hardwick controls his family, and sees to it that Courtney's influence goes no further."

"But what about Courtney herself? How is it that she isn't accountable to anyone?"

Elspeth sighed. "Courtney is an outsider. A rogue Witch. She doesn't answer to any of the families, though she will be stopped for the sake of everyone here. We will wait to see what information David can provide us with before we make our move. Information has always been a Witch's best friend."

Hunter nodded slowly. She could understand that, with her academic background. Knowledge certainly was power, and making decisions that were based on limited research and poor understanding could be dangerous.

"Hey, Ellie, I've moved the shelves over to the other wall now, and they're all set up."

Hunter was startled out of her thoughts at the sound of Jack's voice. He came out from the back room, wiping his hands on his trousers. He looked up towards Elspeth and Hunter, and a look of surprise crossed his handsome features. "Oh, hello, Hunter."

"Hello, Jack," she responded, trying to ignore the ache in her heart at the mere sight of him.

Jack stood still for a moment, looking a little unsure. He ran a hand through his dark hair, as he always did when he was nervous or unsettled. "How is Ryder this morning?" he then asked.

"Much better, thank you."

Jack nodded, looking at her with those green eyes. "That's good." He cleared his throat. "Well, I guess I'm off now. Ellie, would you be able to come with me tomorrow to pick up some stuff from my cottage? There are some things I also need to check on, before the storm comes. As well, Dex wants his little kitty house to sleep in."

Elspeth smiled slightly. "Dexter certainly has you wrapped around his little paw, dear brother. But I'm afraid I can't go with you tomorrow, as the plumber is coming then to finish up the final bits of the nightmare we had a few weeks ago." She turned to Hunter. "Perhaps Hunter could go with you?"

Hunter's eyes widened in shock. "I, uh, well-"

Jack put his hands in his pockets. "That's not necessary. Don't worry, I will go myself. It will be fine."

Elspeth strode over to where her younger brother stood. In a firm voice, she said, "No, Jacob, it will not *be fine*. I have said that no one is to go out on their own. In fact," she said, turning to Hunter, "you shouldn't even be here on your own."

It was Hunter's turn to look down. "Well, someone needed to stay at home with Mom, and she gave me some extra protection for the short journey here."

Elspeth sniffed. "You are still taking unnecessary risks. Abigail could have simply phoned me, and I could have brought it to her tonight." She turned back to Jack. "You will not go to the cottage alone. Hunter will accompany you. It's too dangerous for you to go to the Hardwick Estate on your own. You know that, Jack."

Jack hefted a big sigh. "I know, I know." He looked up at Hunter. "Hunter, would you come with me tomorrow afternoon to the cottage? It shouldn't take long, and I really do need to make sure that everything is closed up tight before the big storm comes tomorrow evening." He looked back at Elspeth. "Dougal's been checking the weather, and we've got a lot of rain and high winds on the way. You might want to make sure that everything out back is secure. I'll help you at your place tonight." He glanced at Hunter. "It's going to be rough out there tomorrow night."

Elspeth nodded. She looked at Hunter. Hunter then realised she hadn't responded to Jack's request. "Um, yes, okay. I'll come with you Jack. It's not a problem," she said, even though her heart disagreed.

"Brilliant. I'll make sure to batten down the hatches this evening, in readiness for the storm tomorrow," Elspeth said. She looked at Hunter. "Make sure that you do the same."

"I will," said Hunter.

***

After having driven back to the cottage with the supplies, Hunter shared what Elspeth had said regarding any possible progress David was making with the Hardwick family, and how they had to wait until David informed them of more developments. She then told them about the coming storm, and began to get the back garden secure for the high winds and rain. Abigail had just heard on the news that the storm's ferocity had increased as it travelled across the Atlantic, and was going to hit them hard. She had already gotten out the candles, batteries, and flashlights (torches, she said, as they were called in England), and was charging up all electronic items, as well as getting water readied in various containers, just in case.

The Witch's Compass

Flood warnings were in place everywhere, and a high winds alert. Travel tomorrow evening was not recommended, and warnings of disruptions to trains and other public transport were being issued. Portsmouth and other Solent ports were recalling all vessels and making them secure for the coming storm. It was early in the year for such a storm, as hurricane-force winds normally only hit the UK in the autumn and winter. It was still mid-August, which was usually a time of sunshine and hot, hazy days. Hunter sighed, knowing that with climate change, weather patterns all over the world were shifting and out of whack. She picked up another garden chair, and brought it to the shed to store it until the storm passed.

Ryder helped, though Hunter warned her to take it easy. But her sister said that she felt fine, and insisted on helping out. Abigail was making them some lunch, and when they were done the dining table was laid out with cheeses, different salads, and bread. "Eat up, girls," said Abigail. "We've got some magickal work to do this afternoon, and you'll need your energy."

The women ate and then cleaned up. Hunter asked for a half hour to meditate before the magickal working, and Abigail thought it was a wonderful idea. Ryder, on the other hand, sighed in exasperation, but went to stroll around the back garden to get some air. "Don't go near the wood," said Hunter. "Stay close to the house."

"Yeah, yeah." Ryder waved away the warning as she walked out the back door. Hunter went up to the room they shared, while Abigail sat on the sofa downstairs. Hunter sat in the little window seat that overlooked the back garden. There, she could keep an eye on her sister, as well as look out onto the beautiful beech wood that backed onto their property. She had performed her very first hedge riding in that wood, months ago. It felt more like years. It was also where she and Jack had first kissed.

Hunter sighed, and took in a few deep breaths. She grounded and centred, and tried to calm her thoughts. She and Jack were going to be in close quarters tomorrow, as they drove to his cottage to collect some things and get it storm-ready. Just thinking about that gave her stomach butterflies, and so she pushed that thought down and focused on her breathing. She, her mother, and sister all needed to be calm, and centred in their power for what they were about to do. Any extraneous thoughts could jeopardise their intention, and the execution of the magickal working.

And yet all Hunter's brain wanted to do was go over the conversation in Elspeth's shop that morning, again and again, to see if there were any indications on what Jack was thinking. She was pretty certain he had broken up with her yesterday, as his words to her after Ryder's healing ritual had felt like a goodbye. And he was certainly hesitant in wanting her to be with him when he went to his cottage. It had been awkward between them, whereas previously it had never felt as such. But the way that he had looked at her after Ryder's ritual seemed to suggest that there was still something there, she was certain. Utterly conflicted, and annoyed at herself for thinking these thoughts, she threw her hands up in exasperation. She couldn't blame Jack for ending it, when she herself had asked for time before she could make any decision about their future relationship. Why shouldn't he get on with his life? Why shouldn't he move on? Had he already moved on? Was that why he broke up with her, like all her previous boyfriends had done? "Focus!" she growled to herself.

Clouds had already rolled in and erased the beautiful, sunny morning. Hunter guessed that it was the beginning of the storm front that was coming their way. The clouds were high and hazy. She turned her attention back to Ryder, walking around the oak tree next to the house, the one that had been struck by lightning. She saw her sister stop, and peer closer towards the trunk. Ryder reached out and down into the hollowed-out, blackened part of the old tree. She pulled out a piece of wood, and gazed at it. Hunter's senses went on full alert, and she began to gather energy to her. Ryder, it seemed, could sense Hunter's unease, and looked up to the window. She smiled and waved, and held aloft the piece of wood. *I think I read somewhere that a piece of oak that had been struck by lightning could be used for protection. Is that true?* she heard her sister say in her mind.

Surprised, Hunter nodded at her sister. *Yes, yes it is! I totally forgot about that. Well done, Ry!*

Ryder grinned and made a fist with her other hand, pulling it towards her body. *Boom!*

Hunter laughed at her sister's antics. She was glad Ryder was here, and she felt a deep love, as well as a responsibility, for her younger sister. She would do anything for her.

Ryder went and sat on the lawn near the tree, playing with the blades of grass by her feet. Hunter closed her eyes for a moment, and calmed her thoughts. She took another few deep breaths, and opened her eyes to gaze once again at the wood in the distance. She longed to get back into the wood and onto the heath, to find new paths, wandering this beautiful countryside that was so different to what she had grown up with. But she quieted her mind, and pulled up her energy, focusing instead on the intention of the ritual that they were about to perform.

After ten more minutes, she saw Ryder wander back inside, and so she went to join her in the living room where their mother still sat on the couch, in full lotus position. Hunter hadn't even known that her mother could do that. Her own long legs never seemed to be that flexible, and though she had tried yoga, going for a walk or hiking were more her thing for exercise and quieting the mind. Ryder preferred more strenuous physical activity, like mountain biking, rock climbing and other similar sports. Their mother, in contrast, had always been a sort of New Age hippie woman. Hunter had always remembered her as a calming presence, and at peace with everything and everyone at their home in Canada. Perhaps her demeanour was not so much New Age hippie, but rather a relic of her Witch legacy, and the way she personally expressed her magickal soul. It certainly opened up Hunter's eyes to see her mother now in a different light.

Abigail looked at Hunter, and smiled. "Hello, Poppet. Are you ready?"

Ryder sat down on the couch next to her mother. "Let's do this!" she said.

"I'm ready," said Hunter, still flinching from the pet name. "What do we need for the ritual?"

"I've got this – a piece of lightning struck oak. Hunter says it can be used for protection," Ryder said.

Abigail unwound her legs from her lotus position. "That's brilliant, Ryder, well done. Let's get our brooms, and your magickal knife, Peanut. We are going all out today for this ritual."

Hunter groaned inwardly. Though her broom was a beautiful, thoughtful, magickal gift from her sister and mother, she still felt a bit silly with it. She felt like all she needed was a black, pointy hat and a bubbling cauldron and she was all good to go in a caricature of the typical green-skinned, wart-bearing witch. "I don't know, Mom. What is the broom going to do in this ritual? I thought it was for hedge riding."

"The broom has many uses, my dear. Hedge riding, clearing energy, and protection are just some of its uses."

Hunter sighed internally, not wanting to upset her mother or Ryder, as the broom had been their gift. She went upstairs and then brought it back down. She held it awkwardly in front of her. Abigail turned, and instantly saw her daughter's discomfort.

"You know, it doesn't have to be a broom, my dear," she said.

Hunter looked at her mother questioningly. "What? I don't get it."

Abigail came to her daughter's side. "Look, here. If you put your hand through the bristles there, and hold on, and then with your other hand here on the handle, you can untwist the handle from the bristles, and have a stang instead." Abigail demonstrated, and pulled apart the handle from a cleverly positioned socket, hidden by the decoration and the tops of the bristles.

"No way," breathed Ryder, coming in close. "I didn't know it could do that!"

"Most brooms can, in this part of the world," their mother said with a small smile. "I'm sorry that I forgot to tell you. It's kind of a New Forest thing, really. In other parts of the country, the bristles hide… other things."

"Oh my god, like what?" asked Ryder, leaning in closer to take a look.

Hunter laughed. "You don't want to know," she said, chuckling.

"No, I really do!"

Hunter cleared her throat and glanced at her mother before turning back to Ryder. She had studied Witches and folklore for many years, as a side interest to her career as a History Professor. "Well, traditionally it's said that in some places, the end of the handle, hidden by the bristles, is carved into a phallic shape."

Ryder's jaw dropped, and she took another look at the base of the handle. Disappointed to find that it wasn't one of those, she turned to Hunter. "Why the hell would anyone put a dick on a broom handle?"

"Some would say that it represents the union between woman and man. The handle, being phallic, and the broom bristles, being feminine. The handle going into the bristles, and all that. The union that brings forth life."

"Oh!" said Ryder, finally getting it. "That's just weird."

"Different things mattered to people at different times in history, and in different places," said Hunter simply. "Sex and fertility were a big thing for our ancestors. And, in all honesty, still is today in our culture."

"Does your broom have a schlong?" asked Ryder, looking at her mother.

As Hunter bent over laughing, Abigail held a hand up to her throat. "Goodness, no, Ryder!" She blushed a little. "Mine is similar to Hunter's. Though mine comes apart into a plain walking stick, as opposed to the stang."

Hunter looked more closely at the forked staff she now held. Forming a slim, Y shape at the top, it was decorated with roses and oak leaves, acorns and ivy. "It's beautiful, Mom. Thanks, this feels better." Hunter held it in her hand. It was not dissimilar to a thumbstick, a smaller forked walking stick that was traditional in all rural areas across Britian. The thumb would be placed in the centre of the fork, for extra grip. Though Hunter's was a little taller than usual, it suited her five-foot-ten height. "Plus, I can take this with me wherever I go, and not look like a lunatic."

Abigail laughed. "That's the idea, Poppet. Now, shall we get started?"

***

The ritual went well, and the women successfully added their own energy to the old wards that the cottage still held. This was a new experience for Hunter, and it felt good to take part in the work. The energy was channelled through Abigail's broom, Hunter's staff, and Ryder's magickal knife. The piece of lightning struck oak had also been charged with their energies during the ritual, and the two sisters went into the loft to hang it from the rafters as a protective talisman. As soon as they had strengthened the wards and set the talisman in place, Hunter felt safer. She *knew* that their magick would protect them. She immediately began to devise a plan to do the same for the car, the back garden, and so on. Abigail agreed, and they spent the rest of the day warding various parts of the property, and their vehicle. Abigail made sure that they stopped at the forest edge, however, because that was "where wilderness reigned, not us," she had said.

Hunter agreed. That night, she slept better than she had for weeks.

Chapter Four

The next morning Hunter awoke feeling refreshed. She stretched in her cot, and looked over to where Ryder still lay asleep on the bed. Though it was a fairly dark morning, she felt happy and lighter. The magick that they performed the day before had really worked, and Hunter felt at peace, here in the sanctuary of her home.

That is, until she remembered that she was seeing Jack this afternoon.

Her phone buzzed, and Hunter saw that it was a text from Jack. It read, *I'll pick you up just after I finish work, around 3pm today. I'm on an early shift.*

Hunter simply replied, *Okay.* She couldn't think of anything else to say. She cursed her own social awkwardness. She also hated text messages as it was difficult to understand what people really meant, and she couldn't see their faces or get any sense of emotion from them, unless they elaborated or used emojis.

She sighed, and went to have a shower to wash her long, red hair. Afterwards, she let it air dry into ringlets, and ran some oil through it to stop it from frizzing up in the humidity. Already she could feel the approaching storm in the air. The wind hadn't yet picked up, and so the air felt stuffy and hot. She put on some denim shorts and a lightweight, peasant blouse. She still wore the pentacle necklace her mother had given her yesterday. She also decided to wear the beaded necklace that Ryder had given her last month. She would finish off the outfit with her leather ankle boots that were down by the front door.

She went light on her makeup, as in this heat she would probably sweat it off in no time. Just a little powder, blush, and lip gloss were all she applied, before giving a gentle spritz of her favourite perfume. She went out into the hallway, and saw her mother's door was still closed. Hunter made her way downstairs, with Ryder and her mother still asleep.

It was 9am when her mother came down, shortly followed by Ryder. They both looked tired. "Are you alright?" asked Hunter.

Abigail smiled, and put the kettle on for tea. "I'm fine, my love. Just a little tired from the ritual and the magickal energy we raised yesterday. Nothing some tea and a scone won't fix."

Ryder sat down at the table, still half asleep. Hunter looked at her sister. "And you, Ry? You okay?"

Ryder sat there for a moment and looked at her sister. There were no dark circles under her eyes; she just appeared sleepy. "Mornings are no longer my friend."

Hunter smiled. "Glad to see you're back to your old self again, sis."

"Mmmph," was all Ryder said.

Hunter poured her sister some coffee, and popped some toast into the toaster for her. "So, Jack's picking me up this afternoon. He asked me to help him check on his cottage, and make sure everything is ready for the storm," she said, trying for a casual tone.

Ryder immediately perked up. "You're seeing Jack today?"

"That's what I said, Ry," said Hunter, pouring herself another cup and then handing over the toast to her sister. Their mother placed some butter and jam on the table.

"That's nice of you," said Abigail.

"He actually asked Elspeth first, but she was busy," Hunter said, hoping her voice sounded calm.

Ryder ignored her sister's words. "So, are you guys back together now?"

Hunter sighed and sat down at the kitchen table. "No, Ryder, we are not back together. We are not anything right now."

"How come?" her sister asked. "I thought everything was cool after he went and saved you in the Otherworld."

"He didn't *save*, me, Ryder. He helped me find the way out."

"Same difference."

"Anyway, he made his feelings pretty clear after the healing ritual the other night."

"Really? What did he say?" asked Ryder. Abigail simply sipped at her tea, leaning against the kitchen counter, listening to the conversation.

Hunter looked down at the table, at a loss for words. "Well, you know, it's not really what he said, but, you know, the way he said it."

"Which waaaaas?"

"It was pretty clear to me that it was over. He knew that I couldn't commit to anything, as I still haven't decided where I'm going to be, come the end of September. He knew where his place was, which is here, in the New Forest."

"That doesn't sound like anything," said Ryder, wrinkling her nose as she thought.

"Trust me, Ry, I know what I'm talking about." Hunter stood, and took her cup with her upstairs to their room, where she could sit in silence while she processed her thoughts and emotions.

Meanwhile, back in the kitchen Ryder turned to her mother, a smile growing on her face. "Know what, Mom? This might be just the thing they need. You know, that 'forced proximity' trope that's in so many romance novels? I'll bet after being together like that all afternoon, they won't be able to keep their hands off each other. They love each other. They were meant to be together."

Abigail nodded and smiled. "I think you may be right."

***

Hunter spent the rest of that morning studying up on Fae lore, and then they all had lunch together. Ryder was still trying to draw her sister out regarding Jack, but Hunter ignored all her attempts. Hunter volunteered to wash up, and took her time with the dishes. She cleaned the entire kitchen afterwards, though it didn't really need it, but keeping herself busy seemed like her best option instead of fretting over when Jack would arrive. She then tidied the living room and dining room, before heading upstairs to the bedroom.

"Chill, Hunter," said Ryder, as she sat on the bed reading a book. "You're getting all hot and sweaty, and making me tired just watching you."

Hunter caught a quick glance of herself in the mirror. Her sister was right. Her hair was now clipped up in a messy bun, and bits were sticking out all over the place. A sheen of sweat covered her face and collarbones. She went to the bathroom to wash her face, and then reapplied her makeup back in the bedroom. She took down her hair and shook it out, adding a light serum to the ends. Once again, she spritzed some perfume on, and called it good.

"Much better," said Ryder from where she sat. "This weather is totally shitty. The humidity is murder."

Hunter looked out the window. The low pressure was indeed bearing down on them. They had heard reports coming in that the storm may arrive earlier than expected. She hoped it wouldn't take her and Jack too long to secure everything.

Just then the doorbell rang. It was only 2pm, but Ryder bounced out of the bed and ran downstairs to answer. Abigail came out of the kitchen with a cup of tea, and smiled. Jack was there, still in his park ranger uniform. "Hi, Ryder. Abigail. I'm so sorry I'm early, but we've had word that the storm's coming in even quicker than predicted. Is Hunter ready, by any chance?"

Hunter was making her way down the little staircase, and called out, "I'm here. Yes, I'm ready to go." As she came into the living room, she saw Jack smile at her.

"Good, let's go then. Oh, and thanks for doing this. It's much appreciated."

How polite and civil, thought Hunter.

The poor guy's nervous around you, Hunter. And it's all your fault, you know.

I don't think that's what it is, Ry. He just doesn't really want to be with me.

From across the room, she saw her sister roll her eyes before turning to Jack. "You two kids have a good time, and be safe."

"Call us if there's any problems," said Abigail, waving them out.

"We will," said Jack. He waited for Hunter to pull on her boots, grab her bag, and her keys. He nodded at Ryder and Abigail, and went out to his jeep.

Hunter followed, her nerves twisting inside her. Jack went around to her side of the jeep, and opened the door for her like he had always done previously. This old-fashioned gesture made Hunter's heart go mushy, and she tried not to blush as she got into the jeep, with Jack closing the door for her. She fished in her bag for a hair clip, and twirled her hair up into it as Jack had the top down. She didn't want her hair to explode in the wind. Jack climbed into his side and started up the vehicle, pulling out of the driveway and heading down the road, away from Burley.

"I got off work early today, because we had finished securing everything and Dougal knew that I needed to get to the cottage. I haven't been there for weeks, and need to check that everything is still as I left it, and that the garden is secure. I really hope you don't mind, Hunter."

Whenever Jack said her name in his English accent, it gave her heart a little thrill. She pushed that down, and simply replied, "It's no problem."

"With the little bit of extra time, would you like to come with me to check out the stone circle?" Jack glanced at her briefly, and she could see concern on his face before he quickly turned his attention back to the road. "I don't know, I just have a bad feeling that something's happened. Maybe a stone has fallen over, or something."

Hunter breathed in a deep, calming breath through her nose, hoping he wouldn't notice. The stone circle had been a magickal place for them, where they had spent their first night together, lying out under the stars and talking until the early dawn. It was a beautiful and romantic memory. Hunter steadied herself. "Yes, of course, Jack. It's no problem." She immediately berated herself for her repetition. She sounded like some sort of robot. She tried to minimise the damage. "It's a great place," was all she could think to say.

Jack gave her a small smile as he kept driving. "Dougal's got the short end of the stick, as he's on duty today and this evening when the main brunt of the storm is due to hit. I offered to stay and help, but he told me that he's got it covered. It's great to have him on my team. He's a good man."

Hunter nodded. Dougal, the tall Scotsman, was a close friend of Jack's, and even though Jack was his boss, they treated each other as equals. Dougal had helped Hunter out when she had gotten drunk at the pub after seeing Jack and Courtney together, and had saved her from making a complete ass of herself. He was a good man, and had gotten her home safely. "That he is," she agreed. She desperately cast about for something to say. "I guess that everyone is on high alert at the station because of this storm?"

"Yes. We've spent the last couple of days taking down any trees that could cause injury or damage to people or structures. This storm, coming at this time, could be very detrimental to the forest. When the trees are in full leaf, as they are now, they catch the wind something rotten. It causes them to fall over, much more than would normally happen at this time of year. In the winter, when the branches are bare, the wind can go through them more easily, and we don't have as much of a problem."

"I never thought of it that way. I guess climate change has caused more problems than most people realise."

"It does at that."

They drove on in silence for a few minutes. Hunter looked out the window at the rolling countryside. She loved this place, this quintessential English heathland, farmland, and forest. It made her heart happy, even as the rivers, forests, and hills of where she grew up in Ontario made her feel the same way. *Maybe it's not an either/or situation,* she thought to herself. *Maybe a heart can be happy in two places at once. Liminality.*

"So now that you've been here a few months, what do you think of the area?" asked Jack, almost as if he had read her thoughts.

"I love it," she said, and immediately wished that she had used some sort of filter. "Um, it's beautiful, really."

"It is at that. Burley, and the New Forest, is truly a magickal place like no other."

"It's where you heart lies. It's in your blood and in your bones," said Hunter.

"It certainly is." He looked over at her, an intense look in his eyes. "It's also in your blood, Hunter."

Hunter swallowed, and then looked away. "Yes, I guess you're right. I wonder how many generations the Appletons go back here, in this area. It would be interesting to investigate the family tree." There. She sounded less emotional, and more interested.

"I asked Elspeth that a while back, and she thinks it's pretty much as long as the Caldecottes have been around. She thinks that there's always been strong ties and friendship between the families."

"Really?" Hunter was intrigued, but didn't want to seem too eager. "She's never mentioned that to us before." She looked over to Jack, who just grinned his cheeky grin.

"Did you ask her?"

"Um, well, no, I haven't."

Jack glanced at her again, still smiling. "Well, there you go."

He turned off the road onto the long, gravel driveway that led to his small cottage. It had originally been the old gatehouse for Hardwick Manor but had been converted a good few decades ago, when the driveway for the manor had been shifted to branch off from a new, main road that led into the village. Since then, the cottage was on its own, in a little-used part of the estate. Jack had bought some of the land around it from the Hardwicks when he had moved in, to create a small garden and also a stone circle set out away from the property in a little woodland. They drove up to the tiny cottage, and Jack parked the jeep in the driveway. As Hunter was unbuckling her seatbelt and taking down her hair, he came around the front of the vehicle and opened the door for her. "Thank you," said Hunter, as she clambered out of the truck.

"My pleasure," said Jack.

He's just being polite, thought Hunter. She watched as Jack lifted up the soft top of the jeep, to cover it from the rain should it start early. He then went up to the door and unlocked it. He waved a hand at her to stay back while he went in first. Hunter knew exactly why Jack did this. The cottage had previously been broken into a couple of months ago, and he wanted to ensure that everything was safe before Hunter entered. He poked his head in the door, stepped in a few paces, and looked around. He then closed his eyes, and stood still for a moment.

"Is everything okay?" asked Hunter, trying to peer around him.

Jack opened his eyes. "Yes, sorry, Hunter. Just checking the energetic wards. They're still in place." Hunter looked at him questioningly. "You know, from when we laid down the protective wards together that time after the break-in?"

"Oh," said Hunter, feeling foolish. "Yes, of course." That day had been a special day for her, and very much a special night.

"Please, come in," said Jack, holding the door open for her. Hunter entered, and gave a sigh at the nice, cool air that awaited inside.

"Can I get you a glass of water? I think that's all I have at the moment, as we cleaned out the fridge before I went over to Ellie's place."

"No, I'm good, thanks,"

"Okay. Well, I'm just going to gather a few things, and put them by the door so that I don't forget them. Then we can see what needs securing out back, and quickly check the stone circle."

"Okay."

Hunter wandered slowly around the living room. It felt different, with all of Jack's plants gone. His place was always very minimalist and clutter-free, but it felt a little empty without all the greenery he normally surrounded himself with. As a Druid, she supposed it was what made him feel at home. She walked the few paces across the tiny living room to the window, and looked out. Everything seemed fine, though the grass lawn by the back patio needed a trim.

Jack came out of the bedroom, with a cloth bag of items in one hand, and Dexter's little cat house in the other. It made Hunter smile, to see the six-foot-two tall, dark, and handsome man still in his park ranger's uniform, carrying a soft, fluffy, little grey house for his cat. "I think I've got everything," he said, laying down the items by the front door. "Shall we head out back?"

Hunter pushed down her feelings, and simply said, "Yes, let's." She followed him out the door and around the side of the cottage to the back patio. There, they picked up the chairs and placed them in the little shed next to the cottage. Together they carried the glass-topped table, and after pulling the top off the base, placed that securely in the shed. Jack checked the few trees around his property, to see if they had been weakened in any way and posed a threat to the building. He declared it all good, locked up the cottage, and turned to Hunter, running his hands through his dark hair. "Okay, just the stone circle left. Just give me a minute to shore up the wards around the property, and then we can go."

"No problem."

Hunter watched as Jack moved to the middle of his back garden. He closed his eyes, and Hunter could feel that he was grounding and centring. She then saw green energy begin to flow up from the earth and around his body, like it always did when he was working magick. It swirled around him, and then slowly drifted out in a shimmering green cloud of light. As it swept past Hunter, she felt a warmth coming from it, and her energy reached out automatically to touch it. A burst of golden sparkles glittered through Jack's green energy. He opened his eyes in surprise, and then smiled. The green and golden light settled all around the periphery of the property, and into the cottage walls. "Thank you, Hunter," he said softly, an intense look in his eyes.

Hunter shivered under that gaze; her stomach suddenly full of butterflies. "You're welcome, Jack," she said quietly.

They stood like that, looking at each other for a few heartbeats, before Jack swallowed and looked away. "I - I guess we should go check the stone circle, now."

Hunter blew out a breath that she didn't know she'd been holding. A gust of wind suddenly whipped through the garden, and they looked up to the skies. Low clouds were swiftly moving in, and the wind was picking up. Jack's face looked worried for a moment. "Let's be quick," he said. He waited for Hunter to join him, and they made their hurried way down the garden to the little gated fence at the bottom, and then followed a path to the woods.

"I don't know why, but I feel anxious about the stones, for some reason," Jack confided as they hustled along the path. They got into the shelter of the wood, and continued on their way.

"I trust your instincts, Jack," was all Hunter said.

Jack gave her a quick glance, before turning to focus on the path again. "And I yours, Hunter," his voice drifted back to her. The wind was still picking up, and some leaves began to fall around them. As they came out into the little clearing where the stones stood, Jack stopped dead in his tracks. Hunter nearly bumped into his back, but managed to stop herself just in time.

"Oh no," he said softly.

Hunter thought she heard a low growl coming from the treeline near to them, which encircled the little clearing where the stones stood. She tried to peer through the trees to their right, and only caught a shadow, perhaps a stag, as it appeared to have antlers, slipping away into the trees. Jack did not seem to notice. He stood for a couple of heartbeats longer, silently surveying the area in front of him before he then moved.

He strode into the circle of stones, and Hunter came out of the woods behind him. She forgot all about the strange stag, as she too was frozen in shock when she saw what had happened.

The stones had been covered in graffiti and paint.

"Oh no, oh Jack," she said softly, following him up to the edge of the circle. "I'm so, so sorry for what has happened here."

Jack strode into the circle. He couldn't speak, he was so overwhelmed by the damage to the sacred site. Upside-down pentagrams had been painted over every stone, and red paint thrown at them to drip down like blood. He quietly took it all in, even as Hunter watched from the circle's edge. She saw his jaw clench, as anger rose within him. She could almost feel his energy radiating out in hot waves, and saw his green light start to crackle around him. Hunter had only ever seen Jack angry once, when his staff had been stolen, and this was similar, but even more so. After everything that Courtney and her accomplice, Alice, had done to them, it seemed like this was the final straw.

Small patters of rain began to fall down upon the stones.

Hunter watched, with wide eyes, as Jack's energy grew brighter and brighter around him. He held his arms out to the sides, and tilted his head back to the skies. Hunter could feel the energy that he was drawing from the earth, the trees, the skies above. It shimmered around him and began to swirl clockwise, increasing in speed and ferocity. "Brighid!" he called out to the skies. "Lady of Justice, Lady of my heart! I call upon you, Great Brighid, Brighid the Mighty!"

A thunderclap sounded, and Hunter nearly jumped out of her skin. The wind tore through the little clearing in the wood, and the rain began to come down in earnest.

"Lady of the Sacred Flame! Lady of the Holy Well! Warrior for Justice, as well as for Peace, I call to you now, as your dedicated servant! *Adjuva Briggitta!* O Brighid help me!"

The energy grew and grew, and Jack's green light shone out, encompassing the whole area. His face was as Hunter had never seen before, and it frightened her a little. She knew he held power, but his quiet demeaner often belied the fact. Seeing him now, well and truly angry and calling upon his goddess, was something entirely new for her.

A hum began to fill the space, a strange resonance that filled Hunter's body and soul. With shock, she looked around the clearing, and saw a blue-white light begin to form next to Jack. Lost in his supplication, he didn't seem to notice as he stood, arms wide and calling to his Lady.

"Jack," Hunter said, her voice barely a whisper at the sheer power that surrounded them. Her words were lost to the wind, and her heart nearly stopped in her chest as the form of a woman coalesced within the light. She stood tall, almost as tall as Jack, in a blue dress with a green mantle. Her red hair swirled around her head, and the light seemed to emanate from her brow. Jack stood as if frozen in time. Indeed, all the world inside the stone circle seemed frozen in time. The rain and winds stopped, the leaves and trees stopped swaying, everything was frozen in place around the two who stood in the circle.

The woman turned to Hunter, who was still standing on the circle's edge. Her gaze was like fire, searing into Hunter's soul. She nodded at Hunter, and then raised her hands high above her head. The light and energy from her brow arced upwards, and she dropped her hands down to her waist. As she did so, the energy spread out across the stone circle in a kind of muffled shockwave, erasing all the damage that had been done to the stones. Hunter felt the energy pass through her harmlessly, but still rocking her on her heels. The goddess, for Hunter could clearly see that was what she was, then moved forwards and touched Jack lightly upon his forehead. He unfroze, and lowered his arms, blinking. His eyes found Brighid, and speechless, he dropped to his knees before his goddess.

"Rise, my Druid. You called, and I have come."

Jack rose up with wonder on his face. "My Lady…"

Brighid smiled. "I have granted you this. The slate has been wiped clean. And now you must fill this space once again with healing energy."

"How, my Lady?"

Brighid looked over to Hunter. "The Witch, Daughter of the Forest, will know." The goddess beckoned Hunter forward with an outstretched hand.

Hunter, absolutely terrified, suddenly felt her feet shifting forwards. Her breath coming fast, she could only stare wide-eyed at the goddess who called to her. As she came up to stand before Brighid, she felt her knees beginning to buckle and her body begin to shake. Brighid smiled, and put a steadying hand on her shoulder. "All will be well, Hedge Witch. Just sing a song of healing for this place, and all will be well."

Hunter cast a quick glance at Jack. He looked at her with an intense light shining in his green eyes, almost like they were green flame. "Please, Hunter," he said. "Sing for us."

Hunter didn't even have time to think. She simply began to sing, a medieval English song that she loved, called 'Summer is Coming In':

Summer is a coming in,
Loudly sing, cuckoo!
The seed is growing
And the meadow is blooming,
And the wood is coming into leaf now,
Sing, cuckoo!

The ewe is bleating after her lamb,
The cow is lowing after her calf;
The bullock is prancing,
The stag cavorting
Sing merrily, cuckoo!

Cuckoo, cuckoo,
You sing well, cuckoo,
Never stop now.

Sing, cuckoo, now; sing, cuckoo;
Sing, cuckoo; sing, cuckoo, now!

As she began to sing, Jack's voice wove in, turning the song into a round as it was meant to be. His voice was husky and low, and complemented her clear soprano. Hunter had never heard Jack sing properly before, not like this. As the merry melody flowed from her, supported by Jack's voice, golden light filled the space. Other voices began to join them, flowing from the land and the trees around the area. Hunter looked about as she sang, but could not see anyone. Still she sang on, as the light filled the area and her heart filled with love. The union of all the voices raised in the merry song healed the space of all trauma, and filled it with joy. When the end of the song came, one by one the voices faded, until silence filled the area.

"It is done," said Brighid, before she faded away from sight. Hunter and Jack stood there, unable to speak, to think, to move for several long heartbeats. Time then unfroze in the circle, and the outside world came rushing in. The heavens had opened, and rain came pouring down on them, the storm crashing all around.

Jack looked around in shock. Hurricane force winds rushed through the trees. "Hunter! We've got to get to the cottage! It's not safe out here!"

Hunter looked all around them. The sky had gotten considerably darker, with a weird yellow light to it. How much time had passed while they were visited by a goddess? "Jack! Let's go!" she cried.

Jack grabbed her hand and together they ran out of the circle, and through the wood. "You know," said Jack, breathing heavily as they raced through the trees, "we've got to stop meeting like this."

Hunter laughed in spite of herself, wiping the water from her eyes. "And miss all the excitement?"

They broke free of the wood and pounded down the path towards the cottage, the rain falling in sheets around them and the wind howling. They could barely see the cottage for all the water that was falling out of the sky, carried on the strong winds. They made it to the door, and Jack fumbled briefly with the key before he managed to unlock it. He gently pushed Hunter in first with his hand at her lower back, and then followed, locking it swiftly behind him.

They stood in the small living room, dripping wet, looking at each other.

"Well, shit," said Jack, a wry grin on his face.

Chapter Five

Hunter laughed and wiped the water from her face, reminded of the last time Jack had said those two words when he had fallen into a pile of horse manure in her cottage garden. It felt like ages ago now. She looked down at herself, and realised that she was thoroughly soaked, right down to her underwear. Her hair was plastered to her head, and she felt like a drowned rat. "Well, that happened," she said.

Jack checked his watch. "By the gods, Hunter, it's 7pm."

"What?" Hunter went up to him and grabbed his arm, checking for herself. "How is that even possible?"

"When you're with a goddess, anything is possible," Jack's soft voice said at her ear. Hunter felt goosebumps ripple down her skin, and let go of his arm, moving a step back.

"Sorry -"

"It's okay, Hunter. That was incredible, wasn't it?" he asked. "I'll go and get some towels."

"Okay. We should probably head out as soon as possible."

Jack stopped halfway to the little bathroom, and turned to look over his shoulder. "We're not going anywhere in this," his said, gesturing to the small window and the storm outside. "There's no way I'm driving in this storm. It's too dangerous."

Hunter looked out the window. He was right; it was too dangerous. "Okay. That makes sense."

Jack turned and went to get the towels. Hunter wrapped her arms around herself as she began to shiver. Jack returned, bringing a large, blue bath towel and put it around her shoulders. "You're shivering, Hunter. Are you cold?"

Her teeth chattered. "Y-yeah, I'm a little c-cold," she managed.

Jack's arms immediately went around her. "You're soaking wet, cold, and in shock, Hunter. We've got to warm you up." He picked her up and brought her to the bedroom. He sat her down on the bed and grabbed a blanket, throwing it around her shoulders. "Are you going to be okay for a minute or two?" he asked, kneeling in front of her with concern in his eyes as she sat on the bed.

"Y-yes. I'll be fine."

"Okay. I'm going to draw you a hot bath, while we still have power. That should warm you up nicely."

"O-okay."

She heard Jack move into the bathroom, and then the water running. She looked around the small, tidy bedroom. It hadn't changed at all since they'd last spent the night together there. She pushed down those memories, and pulled the blanket closer to her.

Eventually Jack came back into the room. "Alright, in you go," said Jack, picking her up from the bed and carrying her to the bathroom.

"I can walk, Jack," she said, but still enjoyed being in his arms.

"And I can carry you," was all he said in reply. He put her down next to the tub, and pointed at a stack of dry towels on the rack. "Here are some towels for when you get out. I'll find you something to wear and leave it on the bed in the bedroom. Will you be okay to get into the tub yourself?"

Hunter looked at the beautiful, claw-footed, old Victorian tub. "Yes, I'll be fine," she said, suddenly feeling shy in front of him.

"Okay. I'll call the families and let them know we're safe." He turned and closed the door softly behind him.

Hunter stepped into the deep tub, still shivering. As she slowly sat down in the deliciously hot water, a moan of pleasure escaped. She slid further down, allowing her whole body right up to her chin to be immersed in the water. She lay there for around ten minutes, just enjoying being warm. Jack checked on her by calling through the door after the first few minutes, and she determined that she was fine. She closed her eyes for a moment, and thought back to what had happened in the stone circle. *I met a goddess!* she thought, her eyes opening in wonder. Suddenly, the lights went out and it all went dark.

"Hunter?" She heard Jack's voice on the other side of the door. "The power's gone out. Hang on, and I'll get you some candles."

Not knowing what to do, Hunter stood up and tried to reach for a towel. She couldn't manage, and had to get out of the tub to do so. She was working in total darkness, as there was no window in the little bathroom. She had just finished climbing over the edge, and was blindly reaching for a towel when Jack re-entered the bathroom. She straightened, and looked at him in surprise.

Jack came in, carrying two taper candles in brass holders in one hand. As he saw her standing naked before him, he froze in shock. "Oh! Hunter, I- I'm so sorry. I thought you were still in the tub." He still didn't move a muscle.

Hunter didn't know what to say. Finally, she said, "No, no I'm not."

Jack swallowed visibly. "You are stunning."

Hunter felt her skin heat under his gaze, and reached out to grab a towel. "Um, thanks, Jack." She wound the towel around herself.

Jack finally managed to move, and shook his head as if coming out of a daze. "I - I'm so sorry. Here." He placed one candle on the counter by the sink, and the other on the closed lid of the loo. "I'll leave you to it." Hastily, he left the room, closing the door behind him.

Hunter felt a giggle rising up, but managed to push it back. She grabbed another towel and began to dry her hair as best she could. "May I use your brush, Jack?" she called from the bathroom.

"Of course, Hunter. Be my guest, and use anything you need. I've laid out some clothes for you in the bedroom. I'll be in the kitchen, trying to get something going on the propane stove."

Hunter picked up Jack's brush and began to pass it through her damp hair. It felt strangely intimate, as she had never shared a hairbrush with a man before. She knew the power that hair held in connection to a person, as her own hair had been used in a spell against her by Courtney and Alice. That Jack trusted her with such an intimate item spoke volumes.

So what is this between us? she wondered.

She wrapped the towel tight around her, and made her way to the bedroom, holding one of the candlesticks and leaving the other to burn safely in the bathroom sink. Behind the closed door, she pulled on a pair of navy joggers and a grey sweatshirt that Jack had left out on the bed. They both had the National Parks logo on them. They were a little long and loose, but they were warm and dry, and that was all that mattered.

She came out and went to where she had put her bag on the sofa earlier, and began to rummage around in it, looking for her phone. She wanted to call her family, to make sure they were alright. "Your mum and sister have gone to Elspeth's place, to ride out the storm together," Jack said as he poked his head out from the kitchen. "I called them, and everything's fine. I doubt you'll get a phone signal now."

"Oh, thanks." Hunter turned off her phone to save the battery, and looked around the room. "Is there anything I can help you with?" she asked.

"Nope. Just finished heating up some tinned pasta. I've found a nice bottle of red to go with it."

Hunter smiled at his joke. Why was it so easy being with him, and why did she feel so at home when he was near? Why was she making things so difficult? *Because I have to protect myself. I won't go through that again. And he had already declared his intentions, very clearly, the night of Ryder's healing ritual. He had already said goodbye.*

Jack came out of the kitchen, carrying two plates heaped with tinned spaghetti. He was wearing jeans and a chambray shirt. He placed the plates on the little coffee table, and went back into the kitchen. He came back with cutlery, and two glasses of red wine. Carefully he placed them down on the table. "See? I wasn't kidding when I said I had wine to go with it. If you'd prefer some water, I can get some. In fact, I'll get some for both of us. We haven't had anything to drink for hours now."

"Okay," said Hunter. She picked up her plate and cutlery, and placed it on her lap, waiting for Jack to come back. She discovered she was famished.

"Here you go," Jack said, placing two large pint glasses filled with water on the table, next to the wine. "Eat up," he said.

They spent a few minutes in comfortable silence, just eating in the dim candlelight as the storm raged around the cottage. Full darkness had now fallen, and Hunter was glad they hadn't tried to drive back to Burley. She thought of all the storms that she had been through since she had arrived, most of them magickally induced. "I'm glad that at least this storm is a natural one," she said into the silence. She thought about all they had yet to accomplish. "I wonder how many more storms await?"

"I would weather any storm with you, Hunter," Jack answered quietly.

Hunter barely managed to swallow down her last mouthful of spaghetti at his words. *What did that mean? He can't say goodbye one day, and then say something like that.* "We have been through a lot, Jack. You don't have to be so nice, and say things like that. I don't blame you for making your choices. I don't blame you for anything." She put down her plate and picked up her glass of water, drinking half of it down in one go.

Jack placed his empty plate down on the table next to hers. He cleared his throat and said quietly, "What choices, Hunter?"

Hunter put down the water and picked up her wineglass. She leaned back on the sofa, and took a deep swallow. "You've made it perfectly clear that your home is here, in Burley. And I still don't know where I will be, come the end of next month. You made your choice, Jack, and I respect that."

Jack turned to fully face Hunter. "Hunter, I have no idea what you are talking about."

Hunter sighed, not wanting to face him. She stared off into the darkness. "It's okay, really. I was expecting it, in all honesty. I can't have you wait around forever while I try to come to some sort of decision about whether or not to stay here." She felt Jack's hand lightly touch her arm, but refused to look at him.

"Do you think that I chose to leave you, Hunter?" Hunter couldn't form the words to reply, so she just nodded and took another sip of wine. "Hunter, I meant what I said after the ritual at Elspeth's place. I will always, *always* love you. I have not left you. I have never left you. Not when I was trying to find out more about Courtney and Alice's spells, not when I was trying to divert attention away from you, and not even when you went to the Otherworld on your own to try and find out more about your father. Hunter, please, look at me." Hunter turned her head to look at Jack. "I *never* left you," he said.

Tears sprang up in her eyes, and she swallowed back a sob. She turned her head away. Had she read the situation completely wrong? Again?

"Hunter, I know that you have some very big decisions to make. And that you have asked for space. Though it has been killing me to do so, I've given you the space that you need. Do you remember when we sat out on the back patio here, and talked about how we were going to move forward? One day at a time, and simply enjoy every moment we had together? Live this life we have been gifted, one day at a time?"

Hunter nodded, recalling that first day she had come to see Jack's cottage. "Yes, I remember."

He brushed his hand along her arm. "I still wish for a happy ending, Hunter. But I will take whatever it is that you have to give, day by day, moment by moment. All I want to do is to be with you, now, and also forever. You have changed my world, Hunter. You have been a beacon of light to me, helping me to shake off the past and see a beautiful, magickal future. I have made mistakes, we both have, but one thing has never changed, and that is my love for you."

Hunter took a deep breath, and shifted on the sofa to look at him fully. *He's playing you, kid. He'll say anything to get you into bed again.*

Shocked at that thought, Hunter recoiled slightly. *Where the hell had that come from? And what is this 'kid' business again?*

"Hunter? What's the matter?"

Hunter shook her head. "I – I don't really know. Sometimes I have these strange thoughts, like there's a voice in my head that isn't mine."

Jack leaned forwards and grabbed Hunter by the shoulders, pulling her towards him. His green eyes looked fiercely into her own, and then his gaze shifted to look over her head. "Shit," he swore softly. "Hunter, I think someone is casting against you again."

Hunter's eyes widened in shock. "What? But – but I'm protected now. We set wards around the cottage, and also here, and I'm wearing my mother's protective pentacle. This – this can't be!"

Jack's eyes unfocused as he held her tightly in place, still looking over her head. "There's a dark shadow near you." Hunter tried to turn and look, but was held tightly in place. "It's not directly on you, but hovering nearby, waiting for its chance," said Jack.

"Oh god," said Hunter, her voice trembling.

Jack's voice was soft, almost dreamlike as he looked past her. "It's watching, and waiting, and speaking to you, isn't it?"

Hunter suddenly remembered seeing the dark shadow in the reflection of the mirror at Elspeth's cottage, after they had done Ryder's healing ritual. "I – I saw it, at Elspeth's," she said. "In the mirror. I looked away and when I turned back, it had disappeared. I thought it was a trick of the light. Or a trick of the mind."

Jack's eyes came back into focus, and looked intently into hers. "That was no trick, Hunter. This is real, and it must be dealt with."

"But what is it?"

The Witch's Compass

Jack gently released her. "I'm sorry," he said, only now realising how he had been holding her. "Please, forgive me. I didn't mean –"

"It's okay, Jack. Thank you."

Jack blew out a breath. "I don't really know what it is. I guess now we have to find out where that's coming from."

Hunter turned away and shakily picked up her wine glass, taking another sip. She wanted to be rid of this thing, whatever it was. A strong gust of wind rattled the window nearest to them, and she jumped, spilling some of the wine on the joggers she was wearing. "Damn," she said, trying to catch the drips.

"Don't worry about it," said Jack, picking up the glass and putting it down on one of the empty plates. "Hunter, when did you start to have these thoughts?"

Hunter thought back to the first time. "At Elspeth's was when I first noticed the thoughts. Just before I saw the shadow in the mirror."

"And you warded the house since then? And received the necklace talisman?"

"Yes."

"But it's still here. It came through the wards that we had placed on this cottage. And the newly strengthened ones I set around the perimeter of the land here too, before we went to the stone circle. I don't understand how it could come through all of our wards. Unless…" Jack looked away for a moment, sadness on his face.

"Unless what, Jack?"

He turned to Hunter. "Unless this thing is emanating from *you*, Hunter."

Hunter recoiled. "What? What do you mean?"

"Hunter, I know that you are afraid to make any big decisions right now. You have your reasons, I know. When you are ready, if you are ready, I hope that you will share them with me. But for now, I think we perhaps need to consider that this is a demon of your own making."

"I'm not really following you, Jack." Hunter's heart began to thump in her chest. She could feel her breath quicken in fear.

Jack reached out and took her hand. "Easy, it will be okay. Hunter, take a deep breath. I won't let anything happen to you."

Hunter closed her eyes and took several deep breaths, trying to ground out the fearful energy she felt rising in her. She could feel some of it sinking down into the earth beneath the cottage, and her heartbeat returned to a more normal pace. Her eyelashes eventually fluttered open, to find Jack looking at her with those gorgeous green eyes.

"Hi," he said, smiling at her.

Her heart melted. "Hi," she said back with a small smile.

Jack nodded. "Okay, here is how I see it, Hunter. I think that perhaps you have created some sort of thoughtform. It is a skill that some Witches have. You can create a type of magickal being, simply through the power of thought."

"Thoughtforms. That sounds familiar," said Hunter. "I think I briefly read up on that a while back. I – I didn't believe it, in all honesty," she said, looking down and feeling the heat rising in her cheeks.

"I wasn't so sure myself, but this feels like it may just be such a thing. What do you think?"

"I don't really know, Jack."

Jack still held her hand, and now he squeezed it. "Hunter, despite what I have kept trying to tell you, that I love you, you still believe something different. Your mind, as a Witch, has power. It is what allows you to ride the hedge, do your magick, and use your intuition. Something, somehow, is making you think something other than what is right in front of you. Look deep down, Hunter, and try to see what that is." He let go of her hand, to give her the space she needed.

Hunter nodded silently, and took a deep breath. What was it that was causing her to not see what was right in front of her? She looked at Jack, and could clearly see the love that he held for her in his eyes. All of his words had come from the heart, and there was no deception in him whatsoever. So why had she believed otherwise? She closed her eyes, and looked within.

A voice sounded in her mind, a voice that sounded like the goddess Brighid, from the stone circle earlier. *You allow your past to dictate your future.* Hunter's eyes popped open. "Oh – oh no," she said softly.

Jack inched a little closer. "Hunter, what is it?"

Hunter looked straight at him. "It's me. It's always been me." Her world felt like it had tilted, and tears once more swam in her eyes.

"What do you mean?"

"My past. All of my previous relationships - I have let them dictate my future. I have carried and projected that onto you." She blinked, and tears fell down her cheeks. "They all leave, Jack. Every man I've ever been involved with has always left me. I was a novelty, a trophy, or something else to them, and when that novelty wore off, they left me. They left, or they cheated, or both. And I believed that you would, too."

Hunter briefly saw anger flash in Jack's eyes, but he controlled it. "Hunter, I mean what I say."

Hunter nodded. "I know, Jack. It was me. I believed so much in that story, that I created a thoughtform from it. I let my past dictate my present, and my future."

Jack reached out and gently took Hunter's hand again. "Hunter, we all do, to some extent."

Hunter shook her head. "But I believed in it so much, that I created something with that power; something that was of me, but which had, or has, its own agenda. Jack, how do I get rid of it?"

Jack studied her face for a few moments. "I think you will know how best to do it, Hunter. I believe in you."

Hunter felt Jack's green energy encompass her in a safe embrace. She accepted it, and it stoked the fires within her. She looked a little deeper within herself, and uncovered another layer of false beliefs. "Jack, my mother's disappearance was what perhaps started it all. She left. She left us, to go and do what she needed to do here in the New Forest all those years ago. And she never came back. I think – I think that is part of the root cause in this belief pattern."

"She didn't *leave* you, Hunter; she would never have wanted to willingly leave you like that. But she needed to try to find your father. She had - she *has* her own destiny as well. And your mother is now returned to you, Hunter. Through your strength, and your magick, you found her again. You and her are much alike, and not just in looks. You share many magickal talents, and you are both strong women."

"Strong, and sometimes foolish," Hunter said, with a wet, tear-soaked laugh.

"We are all fools at times," said Jack. He leaned in, and gently cupped Hunter's cheek with his hand. He wiped away a tear with his thumb, and looked at her with such love in his eyes that Hunter's heart felt like it would burst.

"Jack, I'm so sorry."

Jack leaned in and rested his forehead against Hunter's. "*Mo grá,*" he said softly.

Hunter pulled up her energy, and she softly addressed both the shadowy thoughtform, and her own past in the silence of the room. "I release you." She felt a small breeze ripple through the room, making her mind and body feel a little lighter. She and Jack sat like that for a few moments in the flickering candlelight, before Hunter gently pulled away. She looked into his eyes, and said, "Jack, can you check to see if it's truly gone?"

Jack pushed himself back, and looked over her head, his gaze soft and unfocused. He sat there for a long moment, his eyes searching on the etheric plane. He came back to himself, and then smiled at her. "I don't see anything now," he said.

Hunter gave a great sigh. "I think that this is something that I will have to keep working on. I don't feel like it's a 'one and done' thing. I must be strong and sure in my course, somehow. I can't let this thing return to destroy my life. And I must not allow myself to unintentionally create new ones."

"I believe in you," said Jack.

"I know," said Hunter. "Now I must believe in myself."

There was a long silence between them. The storm still swept around the cottage, even as Hunter's emotions raged within her. *Sometimes, you've got to think with your heart, not your head,* she thought. *Listening too much to my thoughts has created a magickal being, and I must be more careful.* Hunter recalled that her sister was always telling her that she lived too much in her head. It would seem that she was absolutely right.

Hunter gave a long, shuddering sigh. She felt emotionally wiped out. "Excuse me, Jack. I just need to freshen up," she said.

"Of course," said Jack. He stood up and cleared the plates, going into the kitchen. Hunter went to the bathroom, where the candle still burned in the sink. She quickly used the facilities, and then went to wash her hands. She was struck by an idea, and just went with it, without overthinking it. She remembered that Brighid was a goddess of fire and water. She carefully lifted and placed the candle on the closed lid of the loo, then washed her hands and splashed her face with cold water. Afterwards she turned on the cold-water tap, filled up the sink, and then picked up the candle, holding it close to the water. "Thank you, Brighid," she said, touching the base of the candlestick to the water. "Lady of the Water and the Flame, I give you my thanks." A little flash of white light arose from the sink before fading away into the darkness. Brighid had heard, and had accepted her thanks.

Hunter then let the water out of the sink, and replaced the candle inside it to burn out safely. She let herself out of the bathroom, and saw that Jack was in the kitchen. She could hear water running, and so she went to help.

Jack stood by the sink, washing up the plates and the little pot he had used to cook the pasta. There was a breeze coming through the partially open window, to air out the room from the fumes of the propane stove. Hunter picked up a dishtowel and stood next to Jack, drying up the dishes he placed in the rack. He glanced at her and smiled, and went back to his washing up. They worked together in the kitchen, by the light of a single candle in companionable silence.

Hunter's thoughts began to wander to when they had last been in this kitchen. It was the start of that special night they had spent together, and made love for the first time. She felt her body react, but she pushed those feelings down. Jack let out the water from the sink, and moved around her to pick up the dishes she had dried so that he could put them away. Hunter was totally distracted, and she wasn't paying much attention to what she was doing. She placed the plate upon the counter, or she thought she did. The plate slipped from her grasp, and began to fall to the floor. Jack reached out with lightning quick reflexes, and dove for the plate before it hit the ground. He fumbled it slightly, and took a step further in to catch it properly, finding himself on one knee right up against Hunter. "Jack, I'm so sorry! I –"

Hunter looked down at Jack, who half-knelt on the floor with the plate in his hand. He was so close to her, and he slowly lifted his gaze, tracing it all along her body until his eyes met hers. At the look in his eyes, Hunter's heart skipped a beat. Jack slowly, so slowly, lifted himself from one knee, and stood up, his face inches away from Hunter's body the entire time. Without looking, he placed the plate on the counter. The air felt electric around them, and it wasn't from the storm outside. Hunter literally felt her body tingle from the energy that surrounded them. Her energy reached out to his on instinct, and met his coming towards her. Jack stood to his full height, and looked down into her eyes. No more thought was needed. No more words, no more careful evaluation, no more living in the head.

As one they came together in an explosion of pent-up emotion, their bodies almost slamming into each other in their hurry to feel each other. Jack's hand immediately went to Hunter's still-damp hair, and he tugged her head back gently to kiss her deeply. She fell into the embrace, letting go, letting it all go. It was time to go with her heart.

Her hands ran up Jack's chest, feeling his long, lean muscles. She entwined her arms around his neck, and then ran a hand through his dark hair. Her body cried out in joy at feeling him so close to her, their energies wrapping around each other, his green to her gold, mixing and melding as they were destined to do, now and forever.

Jack's tongue teased her mouth open and she moaned softly as he thrust into her mouth, hungry for her. She pulled his head closer, and savoured the taste of him as if she had been starved for months.

Which she had.

Jack reached down and put his hand up the sweatshirt she was wearing, feeling her naked breast. Her underwear was still drying out in the bathroom, and so she had nothing on underneath the clothes that he had given her. It was now his turn to moan softly as his hand cupped her softness, and then he shoved the sweatshirt higher, bent his head down and latched onto her, his other hand now on the opposite breast. Hunter had both hands in his hair, and she threw her head back as a wave of pleasure rolled over her. "Yes!" she cried.

Jack moved over to give attention to her other breast, and Hunter's knees began to feel weak. He seemed to sense that, and rose, sweeping her up into his arms and carrying her to the living room. "We are not going to make it to the bedroom," he said with a growl that made Hunter's entire body tingle with delight. He sat her down on the sofa. "I want you, Hunter. Here. Now."

"Yes, *mo grá*," she said, knowing how these two little Irish words affected him.

His green eyes flashed uncannily for a moment as the leash on his powers momentarily slipped in his desire for her. Seeing that only turned on Hunter even more. He pulled the sweatshirt off her and tossed it to one side. He then gently pushed her back and grabbed her sweatpants, tugging them off and throwing them across the room. He stood over her, placing his body between her legs, and looked at her deeply, drinking her in. "You are magnificent," he said, his words thick with lust.

Hunter's body was on fire with her need for him. But still he stood before her, fully dressed. Slowly, she watched him lower himself down before her, until he was on his knees, his eyes on hers the entire time. He reached forwards and pulled her hips to the edge of the sofa, and then gently placed a cushion to her back before pushing her to lean back and relax against it. He

The Witch's Compass

then placed his hands on her knees and widened her legs slowly, his eyes still on hers, before he moved in to feast.

Hunter threw her head back in ecstasy. Jack immediately found her most sensitive spot, and sucked gently upon it at first, then harder and harder. His tongue circled her, playing with her, and Hunter's body began to writhe in response. Jack kept a firm hold on her, his hands moving up from her knees to her thighs, keeping her in place. She obeyed, and he circled her entrance with his tongue, making her cry out in pleasure. Seeing her response to that, he brought his mouth back up and laved at her again, while his hand slid down along her thigh before gently stroking her soft, wet lushness below his mouth. Hunter groaned in pleasure, her hips moving of their own accord. Softly, Jack inserted a finger deep within her, and made her cry out again. Slowly, in and out, while his tongue played with her, he continued. He added another finger, and then lifted his mouth away from her, instead bringing his thumb to rub against her sweet spot. Hunter had never before felt anything like it, and it soon brought her right over the edge into oblivion.

When she had returned, she found Jack now standing, and unbuttoning his trousers. His shirt had already been thrown off. He pulled off his trousers, and then leaned in to kiss her once more. She could taste herself on his mouth, and she shivered with renewed expectation as he pulled away with another intense look in his eyes. "Wait right here," he said. "Do not move a muscle."

He went into the bedroom and came out with a little packet. He took off his fitted boxers and pulled the condom out of the packet, rolling it onto his length. Kneeling once more between her legs, he pulled her upright and placed her on the edge of the sofa, facing him. With his hands around her hips, he slowly pushed himself into her in one long, smooth stroke, giving a sigh of pleasure as he did so.

Hunter held onto his arms and cried out. His hard length pushed all the way into her, and they were joined. Jack watched her as he moved in and out, expertly pushing his hips forwards in total control. "Hunter," he whispered as he watched her, her head thrown back and lost to the sensations.

Hunter's legs then reached up and wrapped around his waist. She pushed her body close to his, her arms around his neck as she kissed him deeply. He continued to thrust into her in long, smooth strokes as their tongues swept across each other's. When Jack thrusted with more force, hitting a sensitive spot within her, she withdrew from the kiss, her head thrown back once more, crying out again in pleasure. Jack's hands tangled in her hair, and she lowered her arms to the seat, holding onto the cushion for dear life and he drove her onto a wave of exhilaration.

Just before she went over the edge once more, he withdrew and pulled her off the sofa, forward into his arms. He kissed her, and then gently turned her around so that she knelt in front of him. Behind her, he cupped her breasts and leaned over her, pushing her chest and arms onto the seat of the sofa. As she leaned over, he entered her once more, gently at first, in long, smooth strokes. Hunter moaned with pleasure as he continued thrusting deep inside her, all the way to her core. Her feminine muscles were stretched to their limit, tingling and clenching around his length as his hips pushed back and forth, his chest now against her back and pinning her in place. His hands rans down her arms and held hers against the cushion, and still he continued to thrust, every movement bringing Hunter immense pleasure.

Hunter could feel herself coming to a climax once again, and her breathing increased until she found she was panting. Before she went over the edge, Jack pulled out once again and turned her around to face him. "I want your eyes on mine this time," he said, and lifted her onto the sofa, settling himself on top of her.

He held himself up with one arm and entered her, his other hand running up her body to cup her breast. His finger gently circled her nipple, and then he gave it a light pinch. Hunter gasped in delight, her legs wrapping around his waist, willing him deeper into her. He obliged, lowering himself onto her, now reaching up and gathering her hands in his, holding them gently above her head, keeping her in place as he brought her to the edge once again. He looked deep into her eyes as she approached, his strokes and his breath coming quicker. His green eyes on hers, he called out her name as they fell apart together, a green-golden light flashing all around them.

After a few moments, when Hunter could see again, she saw Jack raising his head from where he lay on top of her. "I love you, Hunter," he said softly.

"I love you too, Jack."

Chapter Six

They went to the bedroom to rest, and then made love again. All throughout the night, they loved and explored each other's bodies, bringing pleasure as they had never done before. When Hunter woke up again after a short drowse, she sat up and noticed light coming in through the window. The storm had passed. She had dreamt in her light doze, and the word *compass* drifted through her mind. She wondered what that meant.

She had worked in a Witch's Compass before, a traditional type of circle-casting that centred the body among the four directions, above, and below. It could also be used to hedge ride, and travel between the worlds on the etheric. But why was she thinking of that now? Her thinking was fuzzy and thick with lack of sleep, and endorphins still rushed through her system from the night's lovemaking.

She felt a kiss on her shoulder, and turned towards Jack, who sat up behind her on the bed. "It's early yet," he said, his hands tracing down her arms. "Come, lie back and rest with me."

Hunter smiled and leaned back, snuggling up to his chest. She ran her hands down his long, lean body. Jack gave a short laugh. "Rest, Hunter, I said rest!" he grinned at her. He kissed the top of her hair, and then let his head fall back upon the pillow. Soon his breathing became long and even, and Hunter fell asleep curled up in his arms, wrapped in the sanctuary of their love.

***

When next she woke, sunlight filtered through the bedroom window. Hunter heard movement, and opened her eyes to see Jack entering the bedroom carrying her clothes that had been drying out. He put down the clothes at the foot of the bed and then lay down beside her, wrapping her up in his arms and holding her close to his body. "Morning, Hunter," he said softly as he kissed her neck.

"Morning, Jack." She smiled as she recalled their lovemaking from the night before. It had been incredible.

Jack pulled away gently and sat up to look at her, placing his arms on either side of her body and smiling. "I think it's fair to say that kitchens are a dangerous place for us to be in together."

Hunter gave a small laugh. "The things you learn about some people," she said.

Jack leaned in and kissed her. Their passion began to heat up again, but Jack eventually pulled away with a soft groan. "I've brought you your clothes, but some are still a little damp. Please feel free to take whatever clothes you need from me. In fact," he said with a smouldering look, "I really like how you look in my clothes."

"I like wearing them," said Hunter, sitting up with a smile. "But I prefer to be wearing nothing at all."

Jack's eyes flashed once again with that green fire, which indicated that he was near to losing control over his energy. "You're a dangerous woman, Hunter," he said, and pushed her back down to the bed to make love to her once again.

Afterwards, as Hunter lay in his arms, he said, "I'm so sorry, Hunter, but I *am* working today. I'm on the afternoon shift, however I should go in early, after that storm. They're going to need all hands-on deck today, to make the forest safe once again for visitors."

Hunter reached up and stroked his face. Jack's stubbly beard had grown back in, and she liked it. "I understand. I should go home and check on my family." Jack kissed her once more and then lifted himself up and off the bed. He pulled out some clothes for work and began to put them on. A memory from yesterday suddenly came back to Hunter. "Jack, do stags growl?"

Jack froze, his trousers halfway drawn up his legs as he looked at her quizzically. "That's quite the non sequitur," he said.

Hunter smiled. "It's just – I thought I heard a growl yesterday, as we reached the stone circle and saw the damage. And then something with antlers disappeared into the shadows of the forest."

Jack pulled up his trousers and thought for a moment. "They might make something that sounds like a growl during mating season, but it's more of a roar, which is why we have the term 'roaring stags'. The roaring kind are the red deer, and we do have a small herd near Burley, though fallow deer are much more common. The fallow bucks sound more like giant pigs grunting, than growling or roaring. To me, red deer sound more like cows than anything else. But you may have heard a half-roar, or something. However, it's too early for mating season, for the deer rut. Maybe it was a 'practice roar', I'm not really sure. Wildlife is always surprising you in one form or another." Jack held his hand out to Hunter, and helped her up from the bed.

"Interesting. I hope I get to see the deer rut. It starts next month, right?"

Jack nodded. "That it does. I hope you'll be here to see it too." He pulled her close towards him. "I love you," he said softly.

Hunter rested her head on his shoulder, feeling his long, hard, lean body against hers. "I love you too, Jack. I will always love you."

***

They dressed quickly, and Jack drove Hunter back to her cottage. It took longer than expected, because downed powerlines on the little lane near Jack's cottage meant that they had to go all the way around the Hardwick Estate to connect back onto the main road. As Jack pulled into Hunter's driveway, he said that he would call her later that night. He drove off to Elspeth's cottage just down the road, to drop off the things he had collected from his cottage, as well as to check on his sister before driving into the village to pick up some breakfast, and then heading in to work. Hunter had watched as he pulled out of the driveway, waving at him before she unlocked the door and went into the house. She toed off her still-damp boots, ran a hand through her wild hair, adjusted the sweatpants and t-shirt of Jack's that she was wearing, and went into the kitchen to have a cup of coffee.

Two beaming smiles greeted her as she walked in.

"Morning," said Hunter carefully as she made her way to the coffee machine.

"Morning," her mother and sister said, in perfect unison. Hunter poured herself a cup, and sat down at the table, reaching for the milk. She added some to her coffee, then leaned back and took a long, slow sip, closing her eyes as the taste rolled over her tongue. When she opened her eyes, her mother and sister were still watching her, with those huge smiles plastered across their faces.

"What?" asked Hunter, knowing exactly what they were thinking.

"You tell us," said Ryder.

Hunter sighed, and took another sip of coffee. "Ry, your interest in my love life is a little disconcerting."

"What love life, my dear?" asked Abigail innocently.

Hunter blew out another sigh and leaned back in her chair, throwing up her hands in surrender. "Fine! Yes. Jack and I slept together. And yes, we are very much in love."

Ryder let out a loud *whoop!* and high-fived her mother, who was also grinning. "I knew it!" she cried. "That trope *never* fails!"

Hunter looked at her sister in askance, as Ryder and Abigail grinned at each other. "What are you talking about? What trope?"

Ryder rolled her eyes. "Never mind. So, what did you guys do when you weren't dancing in the sheets?"

"Having some horizontal refreshment," her mother added.

"Checking the oil -"

"Dipping the wick -"

"Doing squat thrusts in the cucumber patch -"

"Ryder!" said Hunter, turning beet red.

Abigail laughed softly and squeezed Hunter's hand. "We are just having a little fun. We love you. And we adore Jack. We are so glad you two are back together again."

"You are back together, right?" asked Ryder, looking closely at her sister.

"Yes, we are together."

"Well alright!" said Ryder, fist-punching the air. "This calls for a celebration. Shall we get some takeout for tonight?"

"Or you girls should go do something fun. You don't have to sit around the house just to hang around with me. I can see if Elspeth is free, and the two of us can have our own girls' night."

Ryder looked to her sister. "What do you say? I can call Harriet, and we can have a good time!"

Hunter looked at her sister with narrowed eyes. "You are supposed to still be healing, remember? We can't let people see you walking around, fully healed like nothing ever happened."

"So I'll bring the crutches. Big deal. At least we will be out for a change. I mean, I love this house, but I'm going a little crazy here. It's been weeks now. Going to Elspeth's doesn't count."

Hunter studied her sister. She knew that Ryder's gregarious nature longed for interaction with others, while Hunter's own introvert tendencies made her quite happy on her own. She finally caved in. "Fine," she said. "We can go out, but you have to pretend you're still recovering."

"I can do that."

"Right. I'm going upstairs to have a shower. Do we have hot water? When did the power come back on? It was still out at Jack's place when we left."

"We didn't lose power fully last night; it only flickered on and off. We got lucky," her mother said.

"We weren't the only ones!" Ryder crowed.

Hunter ignored her sister. "How's Elspeth?"

"Better, now that the plumbing problem at the shop is all sorted. We had a nice time at her place last night. It was cosy, riding out the storm with her."

"And all the kitties," added Ryder.

"That's good." Hunter decided to wait to talk to them about the thoughtform that she had inadvertently created. She didn't want to ruin the good mood. "I'll be upstairs." As Hunter climbed the narrow staircase to her room, she heard giggles from the kitchen. "Doing the dipsy doodle?" Abigail said to Ryder.

"Driving Miss Daisy?"

"Getting one's kettle mended?"

"Dipping the stinger in the honey?"

"Buttering the biscuit?"

"Doing the horizontal greased-weasel tango?"

"The greased-weasel what???"

***

It was early evening, and Hunter was getting ready to go out when she realised that she hadn't even mentioned the fact that she had met a goddess, face to face. In fact, it was only when she was working some serum into the lengths of her long, red hair did she remember her encounter with the mighty red-haired Brighid. *That's odd*, she thought, staring at her own reflection in the mirror. *How could I forget something that important?* She sighed and made a mental note to talk to her mother and Elspeth about it tomorrow, as well as the thoughtform that she had created.

Ryder was bopping around the room with her headphones on, doing her usual chaotic, clothes-being-thrown-everywhere routine while deciding what to wear tonight. Hunter watched her younger sister for a moment, a smile upon her face. They were so different, and yet, in some regards, so alike. She felt that as they grew older, they also grew closer. Ryder stopped for a moment, her hands in the air as she listened to her music, and then proceeded to headbang. Hunter sighed, and turned back to the little dresser where she sat to do her makeup.

Jack had texted that he would like to see her tonight, and so she told him she and Ryder would be at the pub, meeting Harriet. He said he was in dire need of a pint and that he would meet her there. Feeling confident and a little sexy after their love-making last night, Hunter decided to ramp up her makeup a little, and went with a darker eyeshadow after highlighting her brow bones. She did a dramatic cats-eye effect with the eyeliner, applied some mascara, and sculpted her cheeks with more highlighter and then a little blusher. She lined her lips and then swept on a matching shade of red lipstick, and then spritzed on her favourite perfume. She studied herself in the mirror. Her eyes were bright and clear, despite not having gotten much sleep last night. Her skin was practically glowing. Hunter rolled her eyes and blew out a breath. *Might as well have a huge sign around my neck saying 'I got laid last night'*, she thought.

In the mirror she saw Ryder come up behind her. "Whoa, sexy stuff there, Hun! Nice!" her sister shouted, headphones still on. Hunter winced at the loud noise, and Ryder immediately took off her headphones. "Whoops, sorry! You look amazing, Hun."

"Thanks, Ry. I like your outfit."

Ryder did a little twirl in the mirror behind her. She was wearing black cargo trousers with a sparkly black three-quarter length sleeve top. "Thought I'd jazz it up a bit. I found this about a month and a half ago at a flea market - I mean - car boot sale in Portsmouth with Harri. Do you like it?"

"It's very you," said Hunter diplomatically. It really did look great on Ryder, with her pale skin and long, light blond hair. Hunter wished that she could sometimes pull off Ryder's edgy, yet cute look, but she was more of a boho kind of girl. "Don't forget your crutches."

Ryder skipped over to the bed, and pulled them out from underneath it. One had been wrapped around with a black, silky scarf, and the other had an electric purple, sparkly piece of fabric wound around it. "All set!" she said.

Hunter smiled. "Well, let's go then. You ready?"

"Hang on," said Ryder, moving back to Hunter and grabbing the red lipstick that she was about to put in her bag. She swiped some on her lips and gave them a smack before handing it back to Hunter. "Now I am."

"Help yourself, why don't you."

Ryder went and got her own bag from the closet, pulling it across her body. She picked up her crutches, and pretended to hobble out of the room like she had just come from the front lines. "I think that's a bit much, don't you?" asked Hunter.

"Too much? Okay, I'll tone it down some." Ryder picked up the crutches and then made her way down the little staircase. Hunter followed, one hand on the rail, the other on the low ceiling above her, which she had to duck through to fit her much taller, five-foot-ten frame.

As they came down the stairs, she saw that Elspeth was sitting with Abigail in the kitchen. "Hello," said Hunter.

"Hello, Hunter. How are you today?" Elspeth's eyes shone with knowing.

"I'm very well, thank you," she said guardedly.

Ryder slapped her sister in the back. "Oh, let go, for fuck's sake, Hunter. Lighten up. You and Jack slept together, and you're back together. Enjoy it, stop trying to hide it, or pretend it didn't happen for the rest of the world."

Elspeth nodded. "Though I wouldn't quite say it in those terms, I do have to agree with your sister. I'm glad you both are together again."

Hunter managed a small smile. "So am I. Well, we're off. We shouldn't be too late."

"Have fun!" their mother waved.

Feeling like she should get her own back, just as Hunter was pulling the cottage door closed, she leaned in and said, "Oh, by the way, last evening I met the goddess, Brighid, and also found out that I can create thoughtforms. Bye!"

She slammed the door shut and went to her little VW bug, feeling a little smug. Ryder was striding out towards the car, holding her crutches in one hand, until Hunter said, "Ry, crutches." Ryder stopped, sighed, and then hobbled the rest of the way on her crutches. Hunter grinned at her younger sister as they got into the car.

They parked up in the pub's own car park. It was fairly empty, being a Monday and still early in the evening. Hunter reminded her sister once more about the crutches before they got out of the car, and they then made their way inside. They saw Harriet at the bar, talking with her cousin, Jenny, who was pulling pints. As soon as Jenny saw Ryder, she finished up the pint and then came around the bar, giving her a big hug. "It's good to see you again, girl. Nice crutches," she said with a wink.

"Thanks, Jenny. I'm looking forward to coming back to work as soon as I can," said Ryder.

Hunter deduced that Harriet had told Jenny about the healing. "She's on the mend, that's for sure," she said with a smile. "Hey, Harriet."

"Hi all! I've got us a table just over there." Harriet waved with her drink to a nearby table, and they made their way over. Jenny followed them to get their drinks order. Hunter went for a small glass of red wine, and from then on she was on soft drinks, being the designated driver. Ryder ordered a rum and Coke.

"I'll be back in a moment with your drinks," said Jenny, giving Ryder's shoulder a little squeeze before she left.

"So, how have you been?" asked Harriet.

Ryder grinned openly at her. "Hunter and Jack are back together. Last night they made the beast with two backs."

"Ryder!" said Hunter, shocked.

Harriet laughed out loud. "Nice! It's about time you two got through all that angst, worry, and other stuff. You were meant to be together."

"I still don't know where I'll be, come September," grumbled Hunter.

"I do," said Ryder. "You'll be here with me, living it up in jolly old England."

Hunter shook her head. "I don't know. I've got a life, and a career back home."

Ryder grimaced. "No, you just have a career back home. You didn't have a life. You never went out, and after your last dirtbag boyfriend, you haven't even dated. And that was two years ago. Now you've got friends, a helluva hottie boyfriend, and," she leaned in close to whisper, "magick."

Hunter thought about that for a moment. Her sister's candour was refreshing, and did put things into a perspective that her often muddled and over-thinking mind never could. "Hmm. You might be right."

Ryder placed a hand to her heart, and took on an air of surprise. "Be still my beating heart! I got one on the professor!"

Harriet laughed, and then turned her gaze to the door. Walking into the pub were Jack and Dougal. "Well, look who's here."

Ryder sighed. "That's a lot of tall, hot, and sexy park ranger action to handle in one go," she said, looking at both men in admiration.

Harriet snorted. "Jack, maybe, but Dougal? Come on."

"Dougal is totally hot," said Ryder, gazing at the Scot. "He's tall, built, and that accent. Och, aye," she said, in a passable imitation.

"Not my type," said Harriet, turning away and picking up her drink. "He's always got his eye on the ladies."

"Only one lady, really," Hunter said playfully.

Harriet rolled her eyes. "He's just being nice. It's his way."

Ryder chimed in. "I'm digging the new beard thing he's got going." The women studied the two men, who now saw them and waved, making their way over. Jack's tall, lean frame and dark hair made Hunter's heart sigh in appreciation. Dougal came up behind him, his even taller, broader frame almost blocking out the light. His short, flame-red hair was mussed up, and his stubbly beard did indeed accentuate his face nicely.

"Hello, ladies," said Jack. He leaned over to give Hunter a kiss on the lips. It made her tingle all the way to her toes. "You look wonderful tonight," he said softly to her, his green eyes flashing with desire. He then straightened, and turned to the group. "Can I get you a round?"

"We just got our drinks," said Harriet. "You go and order yours."

"Ye hens sure? How about some food?" asked Dougal in his thick, Scottish accent.

"I ate before I came out," replied Harriet. Hunter and Ryder nodded to indicate that they had as well.

"Well, I'm famished," said Jack. He turned to Dougal. "Come on, let's order some food and a pint." The men made their way back to the bar. All three women watched their retreating backs.

"There is nothing I would not do for those who are really my friends. I have no notion of loving people by halves; it is not my nature," said Ryder with a sigh.

Hunter turned to her sister in shock. "Did you just quote Jane Austen, from *Northanger Abbey*?"

Ryder nodded, her eyes not leaving the men at the bar. "Got all the books for free on my e-reader. Did you know that old, out of copyright books like those are free to download? It's awesome."

"But people alter themselves so much, that there is something new to be observed in them for ever," said Hunter with a smile, quoting from her favourite book, *Pride and Prejudice*.

"Okay, enough of the chick-lit," said Harriet. "So, you and Jack are back together? Nice. I want every detail."

"Which you won't get," said Hunter, taking a sip of her wine.

"She's so tight-lipped when it comes to that. Come on, Hunter. This is what us girls do."

"No, Ryder, it is what you do. Not me."

Her sister rolled her eyes. "Fine, fine. So, what else happened then? Anything interesting?"

The men were coming back to the table with their pints. "Um, I'm not sure I really want to talk about that in public either," said Hunter uneasily. She leaned in close. "It involves some pretty powerful stuff."

Harriet waved the men to hurry over. They came to the table with curious expressions at Harriet's insistence. Jack sat next to Hunter, and Dougal eased his large frame down into a chair next to Harriet. "How's my girl?" he asked her.

Ryder openly swooned when he said the word 'girl' in that accent. "Oh, say that again, Dougal."

"I'm fine," said Harriet. "And I'm not your girl."

"Aye, you are, you just don't know it yet," he said with a wink and a smile.

Once they were all settled, Harriet closed her eyes and subtly waved her hands once in the air before her. She then opened her eyes. "There, we can talk now."

Hunter looked at her quizzically. "What did you do?"

Harriet smiled. "Look around." Hunter did, and saw that the few people in the bar seemed a little fuzzy, almost like they were under water. The noise was muffled too. "It's a glamour, a privacy, as we call it in our family. Makes people not take any notice of you, or hear you, when you want some space."

"That's so cool," Ryder breathed. "Can you teach that to me?"

"Maybe, I'm not sure. It might be something from our Fae blood."

"Neat. Maybe Hunter can do something like that then, with her background."

Hunter raised an eyebrow. "I've got enough stuff on my plate right now, Ry."

Harriet smiled. "Don't change the subject. You have something interesting and amazing to tell us. What is it?"

Hunter looked to Jack. He smiled at her and nodded, squeezing her gently on the knee. "Well, yesterday we saw a goddess. Brighid."

"No fucking way," said Ryder, her eyes wide.

"Yup. Jack's stone circle had been vandalised, and he, well, he summoned her, is that the right term?" She looked at Jack for confirmation.

"Invoked," he said with a grin. "I'm not really sure how I did it, but I was just so angry at what had happened, that I called out to my Lady, Brighid the Mighty. And she came. It was… just amazing, really."

Ryder reached out across the table and slapped Hunter's arm, barely missing knocking over her wine. "Why didn't you tell us that earlier?" she admonished.

"Because you were too wrapped up in my sex life," she said simply.

"Mackie's seen Brighid a couple of times too," said Dougal softly. "He doesn't remember much about it, apart from her 'presence', as he calls it."

Hunter nodded. "I almost forgot about it too, today. It's the weirdest thing."

Jack chimed in. "I think it's a way for the gods to help us, or influence us, in our lives, without us becoming totally obsessed by the encounter. I mean, we met a goddess, face to face yesterday. My mind should be utterly blown apart by that encounter. But the memory faded quickly, for some reason."

"I'll bet I know what that reason was," said Ryder with a wink. Hunter wanted to punch her on the arm, but she didn't want to lean across the table to do so, afraid of spilling their drinks.

Jenny came towards their table. She stopped halfway there, and looked around as if lost. Squinting her eyes, she then smiled, making her way over to them. "Damn, girlfriend, you should let me know when you're going to pull out a glamour," she said quietly, putting down two huge plates of food before Jack and Dougal. "Can I get anyone anything else?"

"No thanks, Jen. We're good for now. Sorry about that," said Harriet.

"No worries," Jenny replied, heading back to the bar.

"Do you ladies mind if we eat?" asked Jack, even as Dougal dove into his food.

"Not at all," said Harriet. "Go for it." Both men went quiet as they attacked their plates.

"I guess you've been working hard today?" asked Ryder, as she watched them shovel food into their mouths.

"Mmm hmm," said Jack, his mouth full of potato. Hunter smiled at him. Both he and Dougal were still in their dark uniforms, and they smelled of pine, earth, and sweat. It was not a bad combination. In fact, Hunter found it quite sexy.

"Is Mackenzie in town at the moment?" asked Ryder, taking a sip of her drink. Hunter pulled her mind back to the conversation at hand, taking another sip of her wine.

Dougal spoke around the food in his mouth. "No, he's at uni, doing his extra classes this week and the next as well as exams. But he might be back at the weekend, if he's not spending it in the library." He swallowed. "That boy," he said, shaking his head. "He really needs to get a life."

Ryder looked over at Hunter pointedly and grinned. Hunter ignored her, instead turning to Harriet. "Harriet, what do you know about thoughtforms?"

"Thoughtforms? Some. Why?"

"I think I created one accidentally."

Harriet leaned back. "Wow. That's incredible. Well, to be honest, it really shouldn't surprise me. You're quite the powerful Hedge Witch."

"I'm still learning. It's all still so new to me."

"Yeah, but with your Fae heritage, you're a bit of a powerhouse. So, tell me about this thoughtform."

Hunter looked around the table. The men were engrossed in their meal, but Jack looked up and winked at her with his mouth full of steak and kidney pie. Hunter sighed. "Well, I noticed that I began having some thoughts that were not my own, if that makes any sense. And then I saw a dark shadow over my shoulder in the mirror at Elspeth's place, the night of the ritual. Jack saw it too, last night. He thought it was a thoughtform. It kind of makes sense. I realised last night that I had let my past dictate my future so much, that I was sabotaging everything. I only noticed it when those weird thoughts popped into my head, with terms like 'kid' which is something that I've never said to myself. I released it immediately when we discovered it, and Jack says that he can no longer see it."

Harriet leaned back in her chair, and looked over Hunter's head. Dougal stopped eating long enough to look at Harriet, studying her face intently for a moment, before blushing slightly and downing half of his pint in one go. "There's nothing that I can see emanating from you, Hunter. But that's not to say that it might come back, or that you create new ones."

Hunter sighed. "That's just it. How the hell do I stop this? I've no wish to create something like that again. My life is already overwhelming at the moment."

Jack reached out and squeezed Hunter's arm. "You'll know, Hunter."

Harriet nodded. "Being aware of this ability is probably the biggest step to controlling it. It's an advanced practice, and not all Witches can do it. My mother, for instance, can create thoughtforms, but I can't. She created a thoughtform to protect the house, and another one to guard the herb garden from the rabbits, deer, and other animals who would eat it all up." Harriet grinned. "She gave them names too. Laurel and Hardy."

Everyone chuckled at that. "So, what do I do?" asked Hunter.

"Just be aware. And experiment. If you're going to intentionally create a thoughtform, Mom says that it's important to give them a timed duration for their existence, otherwise they can carry on even after the Witch has died, for example. You need to make sure that there's some sort of statute attached so that the energy dissipates should anything happen to you. And as for creating one unawares? Probably best just to be aware of your thoughts, so that it doesn't happen again. Maybe even ease up on the thinking. Be more zen, mindful, live in the moment, and all that."

Hunter groaned inwardly. Her problem was that she was too inside her own head. And now she had to be super-aware of her own thoughts? It all seemed like a new burden to bear. Jack's arm snaked around her shoulder. He leaned in close to her ear. "You can do this, Hunter. I know you can. *You* know you can."

Hunter nodded, feeling buoyed by Jack's confidence. The conversation then turned to village life, and Hunter enjoyed listening to all the local gossip. After a time, Ryder said, "Right, well, I need the loo," as she popped up from the table.

"Ryder, your crutches," Hunter reminded her softly.

"Oh, yeah. Pass them to me, will ya, Dougal?"

"For the lady," he said, handing her the crutches. Harriet waved her hand, and the room came back into clear focus. Ryder then made her slow way through the tables towards the bar. When she reached it, she turned right to walk past the stools that lined the bar to head to the toilets in the back. Hunter watched her sister as the conversation continued. It was only as Ryder limped on her crutches past the bar that Hunter saw someone she recognised. "Oh no," she said softly.

Xander Hardwick stood at the bar in jeans and a white shirt, his light brown hair falling artfully over one eye and a glass of whisky in his hand. He was watching them.

"What's up now, lass?" asked Dougal, as he turned to look where Hunter was watching.

"Shit," said Jack, and he moved to stand up.

Ryder approached Xander, unaware of him as she kept her eyes on the floor in front of her. Xander turned around and leaned lazily against the bar railing, a smirk on his face. She still hadn't noticed him, as she was intent on staying upright with her unwieldy crutches. Suddenly, a nearby chair moved forward a few inches all on its own, catching one of her crutches and causing her to stumble forwards a few steps, putting weight on both her legs before catching herself.

At the same time, Dougal quickly swiped his pint glass off the table and onto the floor where it landed with a loud crash, causing the customers in the pub to turn his way.

Xander Hardwick watched Ryder with interest on his handsome face. Her head turned towards the bar, and when she saw him, she froze. He then faced the group at the table and downed his drink in one shot, his eyes on Hunter the entire time, before turning around and placing the empty glass on the bar. Meanwhile, as everyone in the pub applauded Dougal's clumsiness with his dropped pint (as was customary in pubs), Xander walked out of the bar and into the night.

Ryder looked back at Hunter, guilt on her face. *I'm so sorry! I never even saw him!*

It's okay, Ry, thought Hunter. *Don't worry about it. No one else saw it. Dougal distracted everyone.*

Ryder nodded, and picked up her crutches. She then made her way to the back, keeping up the act.

Hunter placed her hand on Jack's arm, as he moved to follow Xander. He looked down at her, and she shook her head. Blowing out a frustrated breath, he sat back down. Jenny came over with some rags and a bucket. "Dougal, between you and Jack, you're costing me a fortune lately in glasses," she sighed.

Dougal bent down and helped her clean up the mess. "Sorry lass," he said softly. "I'll pay for the glass too."

Hunter went to help. "Xander Hardwick was there, and he was trying to catch out Ryder. Which he did," she said softly to the bartender.

"Oh crap. I didn't see him. Brett must have served him as I was pulling pints down the other end."

"It's okay, Jenny, really. It's not your fault."

Jenny nodded, her lips in a tight line, before she spoke. "Those Hardwicks are really getting on my nerves. I can't ban them from the pub, because they've done nothing wrong, at least in the mundane sense."

Dougal spoke softly as he put the last fragment of glass in the bucket. "There's nought you can do about that, lass" he said. "It's not your fault he is a royal prick."

Jenny stood up, followed by Hunter and Dougal. "Either way, I'll get you another pint," she said to him, patting his arm lightly before moving away. Hunter and Dougal sat back down at the table.

"Damn," said Harriet softly. "That sonofabitch is now going to tell his family."

"So?" said Dougal.

Harriet looked worried, and spoke softly. "It's just... well, *we* know what's gone down here, with Ryder being attacked and all. And Courtney and Alice know the truth too. But the rest of the Hardwick family? How much do they know? Alice and Xander might be pulling the wool over their own family's eyes. And now Xander's got 'evidence' of sorts. He'll tell them that Ryder wasn't injured. They will think we're faking this, and setting them up for a fall. And if, on the other hand, the Hardwicks are all in this together, gone dark and all, they will just be extra pissed off now."

Hunter was still trying to get used to the dynamics between the magickal families here in Burley, let alone those of the mysterious Hardwicks themselves. "You can't know everything," she said softly. "You couldn't have known Xander was there."

"But still, I'm so sorry. I should have thought that when we're in a privacy glamour, we can't see out very well, just as people can't see in. I should have scanned the area before Ryder left the table."

"It's okay, Harriet. It's not your fault."

Harriet just shook her head and looked at the door where Xander had gone.

"I wonder what David said to Hardwicks, and what's going on there," said Hunter softly. "We could really use some information."

"Maybe it's time we ask him," said Jack, his face set impassively.

"On it," said Harriet, whipping out her phone and sending a text.

***

Police Constable Hart said that he would meet them at the sisters' cottage in an hour. They finished up their drinks, and made their way to the car park in the back. "Much as I'd love to hear what you've all got going right now, I'm puggled," said Dougal. When they all looked at him questioningly, he elaborated. "I'm done in. It's been a long day."

Jack nodded and clapped his friend on the shoulder. "Come in a bit later, tomorrow. Have a lie in."

Dougal rubbed the back of his neck. "Normally, my pride would say no, but I'm no eejit. I'll see you around 11am."

"No worries," said Jack. Dougal gave them a wave, and headed off to his truck. "I'll follow you ladies to the cottage," said Jack.

"Okay," said Hunter. She, Ryder, and Harriet piled into the VW, and Jack climbed into his jeep. They drove back to the cottage, where Elspeth and Abigail were watching a film. As they entered, Abigail looked up and smiled. "David phoned, and said he'll be here any minute," she said.

Hunter gave a small smile back. "Okay." She turned to let the others come through, and watched Jack as he took off his work boots in the porch. He straightened and smiled at her wearily, running a hand through his dark hair.

"You're tired," she said, reaching out to him.

"Yeah, I am at that," Jack said, drawing her close. "But we need to know what's going on." He kissed the top of her head just as they heard a car pulling up in the driveway. They turned to see PC Hart getting out of his police car. He looked up at them for a moment and nodded, before reaching into the back and grabbing his hat. He placed it smartly on his head and walked up to the door. "Hello, Hunter. Jack. May I come in?"

"Of course," said Hunter, pulling away from Jack. "Can I get you anything to drink?"

"A cup of tea would be heaven right now," said David, smiling down at her. His blue eyes twinkled, and his dimple showed as he flashed her a grin.

"No problem. Please, come in and sit down." Hunter went in, followed by David, with Jack closing the door behind them. David took off his hat as he entered, and greeted everyone. He pulled up a seat from the dining table, placing it next to the sofa and seating himself. He then noticed that Ryder was moving around without her crutches. "Miss Williams, I thought you were still healing," he said with a piercing look. His entire countenance had changed.

Ryder just grinned at him. "The coven did a massive healing ritual for me the other night. It was so awesome. All I've got left is the scar. Wanna see?" She started to unbuckle her belt.

"I don't think that's necessary," said Hunter, quickly moving up and putting her hand on her sister's shoulder. "Enough people have seen it already."

Ryder sighed. "If only that were the case," she said longingly.

David cleared his throat. "I – um, I'm glad that you are feeling better, Miss Williams," he said formally.

"Please, it's just 'Ryder'," she said, flopping down on the couch.

"Alright, Ryder. And how is everyone else?" he asked, looking around the room. Everyone nodded, with a chorus of 'good' and 'fine' answering him. "Excellent." Hunter came out of the kitchen with a cup of tea. She knew how he took his tea, from their afternoon at the teashop a while back. "Thank you," he said, smiling at her again.

"So, David, what information do you have for us?" asked Elspeth, taking a seat next to Ryder on the sofa.

David took a large sip of his tea, sighed, and then put his cup and saucer down on the side table next to him. "Geraint Hardwick is in a difficult position. He doesn't want to believe that Alice and Alexander have any involvement in all this, and it will be difficult to prove as there is no hard evidence. He is, however, worried about the influence that the outsider, Courtney Peterson, is having on both of them. At least, that's what he says. Whether he's lying, I have no idea. Geraint is a very difficult man to read. He said that he has noticed a change in Alice's behaviour specifically, but he cannot and will not say whether there is anything evil at work. He says that he cannot speak for Miss Peterson."

"So what happens now?" asked Hunter softly, sitting down next to Elspeth on the other side of the sofa. Jack pulled up a chair next to her, and Abigail sat in the recliner.

"My grandfather said that protocol must be followed in these types of situations. We must give the Hardwicks an entire moon cycle for them to sort out any problems or difficulties that they might have. If, at the end of the cycle, there is still a threat to the community from them, then it will be dealt with accordingly."

"What does that even mean?" asked Ryder, scowling.

"It means, my dear, that the families will have to take sides in this dispute, and see that justice is served," Elspeth said.

"But isn't that what he's here for?" Ryder asked, waving at David.

"Yes, and no," he smiled down at her. "At the moment, I'm here to see that protocol is being followed. After that, my role is as a mediator, should that be required. If things still escalate, then those who have the power will see to it that the harm is negated, and the secrets of Burley stay safe."

"I still don't get it," said Ryder.

Elspeth's eyes were grave as she turned to Ryder. "He means that we, the magickal families, will take matters into our own hands to protect our own and our secret."

Ryder's eyes widened. "Is that even legal?"

Elspeth smiled grimly. "There are no longer any laws against Witchcraft, my dear. Those were lifted over seventy years ago."

Abigail nodded sadly. "We must protect our own, and our way of life," she said to her daughter.

Hunter leaned back, unable to comprehend all this. "Doesn't this all sound a bit... Machiavellian?"

Elspeth nodded slowly. "Yes, it is, Hunter. But after I learned from Jack what had happened to his stone circle, combined with the other vandalism we've seen on buildings in the area, as well as the attacks on animals and livestock, it's becoming a very real and problematic situation. This is all on top of the attacks against both you and your sister. This must be taken seriously, and dealt with swiftly. The media and the police are already too interested in the stories that are currently circulating."

"And we can't let anything happen to you or Ryder again," said David, looking at Hunter. He then turned to Jack. "What happened at a stone circle?"

"The stone circle that I and my Druid Grove created on my piece of land next to the Hardwick Estate had been vandalised. Reversed pentagrams and red paint splashed all over it, to look like blood."

"Do you have any photos?"

"No. It was cleaned straight away." Jack didn't offer up any more information.

David sighed. "It's a very difficult position. I believe you all, but there is very little hard evidence to point directly at the Hardwicks, and Miss Peterson. The vehicle that ran you off the road? Yes, it was found on the Hardwick Estate, but there were no fingerprints found. Of course, gloves could have been worn. The break-in of your cottage, Jack? Again, no evidence or fingerprints. The ritual site in the abandoned building you described before, Jack, along with your stolen item? You got rid of all the evidence, not knowing who I was and that I needed it in my special role here in Burley. And your stone circle, again, no evidence. The attack on Ryder? No witnesses, only her testimony that she heard Miss Peterson's voice, which would not be enough, given the condition she was in at the time."

"What about the poppets that had been made, to enspell Jack and Hunter?" asked Ryder.

"I destroyed them," said Hunter softly. "I had to, in order to fully break the magick." Jack simply nodded beside her.

David sighed, and picked up his tea again, taking a sip. "Well, you can see my predicament. I don't have hard evidence to present to Geraint Hardwick about his children's behaviour.

Miss Peterson is rogue, and so if any hard evidence does show up, then I can act, but as of yet, I don't have any at all."

"What *would* you do to Courtney?" asked Ryder, very interested.

"I asked my grandfather the very same thing. He said that what usually happens is that the rogue Witch, who attacks the magickal community, is removed from the place and banned from ever returning."

"How does that work, then?"

David looked at Hunter with sad smile. "I'm afraid I can't tell you. As part of the special force, we too need to keep some of our secrets, in order to do our job correctly. Just as I am sure that the families will handle this situation in their own fashion, if mediation does not work."

Hunter spoke into the silence that followed. "I understand that we need to protect our own," she said slowly, "and that we've also gained in power since this all started. But does that now mean we have to go on the attack? Will this be a full-on Witch War?"

David shook his head sadly. "Honestly, I have no idea. I am doing all that I can, to protect you and the community. But ultimately, it is up to the families, and the heads of families, to decide what is right to protect their way of life. In the end, my main role is to protect everyone as best I can, offer mediation, and clean up any messes that may be left behind, to keep Burley's secret safe."

Elspeth nodded. "Thank you, David."

"What if something else happens in the meantime?" asked Ryder.

David studied her for a moment. "You mean, if you or anyone else gets attacked again?"

"Yeah. Are we supposed to just suck it up?"

David shook his head. "No, you have every right to defend yourselves. If anyone is attacked again, then it is within reason to seek retribution. But call me first."

There was silence as everyone took this in.

David finished his tea, and stood. "I wish I had more to say, or more that I could do right now. Jack, did you want to formally file a report on the vandalism at the stone circle?"

"No, I don't think it would help anything, and as I said, all evidence has been wiped clean."

David nodded. "I'll make a note of it, but also that you didn't file a formal report. Please, call me if you change your mind." He glanced briefly at Hunter, and then nodded to them all. "I have a lot of paperwork to fill out for our special files, which my grandfather will be helping me with tonight. This hasn't been part of my usual police training," he said with a wry smile. "I'm still learning too. I'll bid you all goodnight. Stay safe."

"Hey, David, can I get a lift with you?" asked Harriet.

"Are you going back to your place?"

"My parents', actually. We're kind of sticking together right now; everyone that's been involved in this ordeal, that is."

"Good idea. Hop in, I'll drive you there."

Hunter stood, and saw them both out. "Thank you, David. We appreciate everything that you are doing."

"Thank you," he said, with a soft look in his eyes. "Good night, Hunter."

"Good night, David. See you, Harriet."

After David had left, Hunter decided to talk about the thoughtform that she had created. Elspeth and her mother listened intently. She related what Harriet had said about thoughtforms at the pub, and they agreed that the advice was sound.

Elspeth looked intently at Hunter. "Remember, this, Hunter. As a Witch, everything that you do, everything that you think, is a spell."

There was silence as everyone absorbed this information. After a few moments, Abigail then turned to Hunter. "So, tell us all about meeting a goddess!"

Hunter relayed what had happened, and her mother's eyes shone with excitement. "Oh, how wonderful for you! I am just so pleased for you, my love. That was incredible."

Elspeth nodded in agreement. "Extremely well done, Hunter and Jack." Hunter blushed at the praise. Elspeth then sighed, and stood up. "Well, it's time for tea, and there are cats to feed."

Before Jack and Elspeth left, Hunter managed to grab a quick kiss from Jack on the porch, as Elspeth made her way to his jeep. "I'll come by tomorrow," Jack said, a hungry look in his green eyes.

"Okay. Take care. Have a good sleep, and rest, my love," she said, stroking his dark hair and looking at his tired face.

"I will, *mo grá*."

Chapter Seven

The next morning Hunter woke early. Once again, she had dreamt of a golden compass, and woke with the words, *the Witch's Compass* in her mind. She quickly and quietly dressed in the room she shared with Ryder. She then went downstairs and grabbed some books from the dining table, bringing them into the kitchen as she made a pot of coffee. As it brewed, she went over what David had told them last night.

The fact that they had to wait an entire moon's cycle before anything could be done both annoyed and reassured her. She seriously hoped that now that the head of the Hardwick family knew what was going on, that he would stop it, if he himself was innocent. No one really knew just how far down the path of darkness the Hardwicks, as a whole, had gone. And dealing with Courtney, the rogue Witch, was going to prove as big, if not an even bigger challenge. A shiver rolled down her spine, and she hugged her arms to herself. She hated waiting, but the start of a Witch War troubled her even more. She looked out the kitchen window and drank in the sunshine, to ward off the dark spectre that seemed to loom over them all.

Once the coffee was brewed, Hunter sat down with her books and began to do some research. The Witch's Compass, a part of traditional Witchcraft that differed from Gerald Gardner's modern Wicca, had a multitude of uses. As she had used it previously, it could be invoked in ritual to centre oneself in the world, between the four directions, above, and below as part of grounding and centring. But it wasn't just a simple grounding

The Witch's Compass

and centring exercise, or a way to cast a magick circle, for lack of a better term. It could also be called in and used as a guide to the Otherworld, helping one to map it out and journey there to seek answers. However, she also discovered that it was not only a doorway to the Otherworld, but also a doorway to one's soul.

Hunter found this fascinating. The landscape of the Otherworld could be mapped out with the aid of the Compass, as well as the map of the soul. Given that she had powers that she sometimes couldn't control or understand, this seemed like a beacon of light to her. If she could better understand herself, her soul, and her journey, perhaps she wouldn't do things without conscious awareness, such as creating thoughtforms that impacted her life in negative ways. Through the Compass, she could have better control not only over her magic, but also her own life.

As well, she discovered that the directions were not only related to north, south, east, west, above, and below, but also *centre*. This felt like something that was really important to her and her journey in Witchcraft, and Hedge Witchcraft in particular. She had never before thought of *centre* as being a direction.

The compass could also incorporate the four Celtic fire festivals that marked the turning of the year, or the greater sabbats as they were known in many traditions of Witchcraft. Therefore, there would be eight directions, as well as above, below, and centre. This would centre her firmly in the natural cycles of the land where she now found herself, deep in the New Forest of England, as well as in her own body and soul.

The many-faceted elements of the Compass could also be seen as parts of the World Tree, or the *axis mundi* that was prevalent in different mythologies. A shamanic element of riding the World Tree could be found in Norse and Celtic cosmology and traditions, with different worlds being placed along the tree which one could access.

Hunter recalled Elspeth describing the broom, staff, or stang as a representation of the World Tree. As such, Hedge Witches like herself and her mother could use these tools to ride the World Tree, crossing the veil between the worlds. But now that symbolism took on an even deeper meaning, if worked within the Compass. The tools were not only used to travel to the Otherworld, but also to travel along the meridians of the soul. In doing so, one could better understand one's own self, and in doing so, better understand others.

There could be many other different associations and correspondences attached to the Compass, stemming from ancient mythology to medieval ceremonial magickal practices. Although interesting, Hunter felt that this muddied the waters, and that one's own personal vision grounded in one's own experience and environment were a much better route to understanding the different elements of the Compass, rather than introducing bits and pieces gathered from different traditions and using symbolism, names, and other descriptive elements that did not resonate or were unfamiliar. Though that may work for some, it didn't feel right for her. She didn't need long, drawn out elaborate rituals, spell working or correspondences. She preferred simple and straight to the point Witchcraft, as that was how she worked her own magick and which she found was the most effective.

Hunter leaned back in her chair, the morning sunlight streaming through the kitchen window onto her shoulders and making her red hair flame. She closed her eyes, and knew that this was something that she couldn't just think about as an academic exercise, but was rather something she had to feel and

The Witch's Compass

experience intimately in order for the knowledge to turn into wisdom.

She closed the books and stood up, with a nod of her head in self-determination. She went to where her broom lay against the wall in the living room, beneath her mother's broom which hung over the door. She detached the bristles from the handle to reveal the stang. Hunter then went to the back door and opened it, greeted by birdsong and the sight and scent of dew upon the grass. She smiled, inhaling the sweet smell and made her way through the back garden to the old, lightning-struck oak tree.

She didn't dare go too far from the house and its wards, and stayed well within the ward boundaries they had created around the property. Though she would have liked to have gone to the yew tree in the beech woods that stretched out behind their property, she thought it was better to be safe than sorry. That giant yew in the beech wood was where it had all started for her. But this old oak, which had weathered many storms, including a magickal one, and now seemed neither dead nor alive but somewhere in between, felt like a good, equally liminal place for her. As she strode towards the old oak that had been cleaved in two, she caught a glimpse of something in the trees beyond. She stopped, and narrowed her eyes. A large shape emerged, and she gave a sigh of relief. A White Hind emerged from the treeline, to walk gracefully towards her, head held high.

This beautiful white deer was Hunter's familiar. Hunter had learned that a familiar was a magickal creature that often aided a Witch in her work. She hadn't seen her familiar since the day she went bodily into the Otherworld through the portal that the White Hind had shown her. She was glad of her familiar's presence now, having been worried about when she had gone against her warnings, and proceeded to cross the veil between the worlds despite what her familiar had said about the time not being right. She wasn't sure if her familiar would abandon her after all that had happened, and after her stupidity.

The White Hind approached, and nodded her head. "Hello," murmured Hunter in the quiet of the early morning.

You have learned some lessons since I last saw you, her familiar said in Hunter's mind.

I have. I am so sorry for not listening to you.

We learn from our mistakes just as much as from our successes.

There was nothing Hunter could say to that. It was so true. *I am about to use the Witch's Compass, with my stang as the focal point and a symbol of the World Tree. I hope to better understand myself, and centre myself fully so that the work that I do is both conscious and empowered.*

The White Hind nodded. *That is a good thing. And what about the rest of your life?*

That too. In both my magickal, and mundane life, I aim to be centred, to know my own soul, and to work to the best of my abilities with that knowledge. Hunter looked at the beautiful doe for a moment, drinking in the magickal wonder of her. She then asked aloud, "Is there anything I should know before performing this?"

The White Hind stamped her dainty front hoof. *I see you've learned some humility since last we met. That is good too.*

I'm sorry, thought Hunter. *Though I was under an external magickal influence, it was because of my own pride and anger that I allowed myself to be so manipulated in the first place.*

You are already coming into a good awareness of your self. I see that love has also re-entered your heart.

Hunter smiled. There was nothing she could say to that, but only feel.

Hedge Witch, know that the Compass, when used properly, will show you many things. You will see yourself as you truly are, in all your beauty and glory, and in all your faults and errors. You are well on the way to achieving that goal, but you must still go deeper within yourself and face the ultimate truth.

I know, thought Hunter.

Within the Witch's Compass you will find yourself. You may not like what you find, but you must remember that it is you, nonetheless. What you do not like, you can change. What you like, you can enhance. You have the power.

Hunter took those words in. *Thank you.*

Go with power, and a true heart. Her familiar walked up to her, and nuzzled her arm. Hunter reached out and stroked her long neck, tears in her eyes at the beauty and wonder of this moment. The White Hind then turned and walked away into the trees, disappearing into the forest.

Hunter took a deep breath in, and slowly exhaled. She grounded and centred her energy, and then began her ritual in the usual format that she preferred. When she was ready to call in the Witch's Compass, it felt different to how she had previously used it. Now it was so much more.

She walked in a circle around the oak tree, drawing up energy from the earth and combining it with her own, pushing it out with her stang to form a magickal boundary for her work. She then stood in the middle of the circle by the oak, and called in the Witch's Compass, holding her stang before her.

Facing north, she called in the powers and associations she held with that place. She felt a line of energy emanating from the north flow into her body, a line that anchored her and held her. She did the same for east, south, and west. Anchored within the four cardinal directions, she then called in the seasonal round of Celtic festivals, grounding her in the moment and also in the history of the Witchcraft traditions. Finally, she called in above and below. She then felt her stang begin to hum with power, and she opened her eyes to look at it. The stang called from the centre. It glowed with a golden light, and she fell into it.

She found herself at the base of a mighty tree. It was an enormous yew tree, its width wider than the cottage, its height reaching towards the heavens. It was a tree of liminality, a tree that didn't die but which lived on, ever growing outwards with new shoots even as the centre became empty and hollow. Neither dead nor alive, but somewhere between the two, and encompassing everything in the cycles of life, death and rebirth.

Hunter stood in awe of this magnificent tree for a few moments, before remembering her purpose. She was to ride the World Tree, but not to the Otherworld as she normally would have done as a Hedge Witch. Instead, she was to ride the World Tree to her own soul, her authentic self, her centre. It was time to see who she was, without all the blinders that she had put in place, without the external criticisms and validations, as well as the internal monologues. She wasn't here to think, she was here to feel, to experience, to truly come home to herself. She was here to see the truth.

She reached out her hand and touched the reddish-brown bark. A yew tree was where her journey as a Hedge Witch had all started. It was the tree of death and also eternal life. Just like the soul, just like energy, it could not be destroyed, only changed in form. It was every beginning and every ending.

She felt the whooshing sensation that she sometimes felt when hedge riding, and entered into a realm of darkness. The tree had disappeared, and she was alone in the inky blackness. Panic began to rise, but she pushed it down, taking in deep breaths. She reiterated her intention to herself. *I am here to centre myself in the Witch's Compass. I am here to let it guide me to my true self. I am here to be me.*

A misty form coalesced from the darkness. It began to take shape, and slowly came into being. Hunter took another deep breath, and came face to face with her self.

***

A long, lithe, elegant man stepped out from the forest's edge where he had been watching Hunter work. He was dressed in shades of grey, and he drew down the hood of his short cloak to reveal a head of pale blond hair, which curtained at his forehead to frame his fine features. His grey eyes were intent on the woman in the magickal ritual. A small smile curled his lips as he approached.

You will not disturb her, the White Hind said to him.

He turned slowly to face the deer, who stepped out from the trees. "And what do you know of my intentions?" he asked the doe, his head cocked slightly to one side and a mocking expression on his handsome face.

Whatever they are, you will not disturb her, the White Hind repeated.

"I have only ever helped this little Hedge Witch," he said smoothly, before turning back to study Hunter. She stood in the circle of energy that she had created, with visible energetic lines running through her body from the four cardinal directions, the seasonal round, as well as above and below, her stang glowing with power from the centre. She was held in place by this energy, her face quiet and serene. He began to walk around the edge of the circle, looking at her from all angles. "She is impressive."

Leave her be.

Witches of the New Forest

The man stopped and turned to the familiar once more. "Or what, *Bán Fianna*?"

A flash of brilliant light appeared by the White Hind, and next to the familiar now stood a tall, red-haired woman. "Do not intrude on this ritual, Finnvarr. This Daughter of the Forest is under my protection. The fate of many, yourself included, is reliant upon her success."

Finnvarr's arrogant smile faded at the sight of Brighid. He bent his head, and spread his arms wide in acknowledgement, before stepping back and disappearing into the trees. Another flash of light and the goddess too was gone.

***

It was strange, to see her self, standing in front of her. She was unsure what to do. Then, her self spoke.

"Who are you?"

Hunter was taken aback by the question. It was one she had been about to ask her own image, standing in front of her. She took in a breath, deepening her resolve to just go with it. "I am Hunter Williams."

"No, you are not."

Hunter thought about that for a moment. She was right. She wasn't Hunter Williams. Her birth father was not Daniel Williams. "I am Hunter, daughter of Abigail Appleton and Aedon of the Fae."

"No, you are not."

Perplexed, Hunter thought about it again. What answer could she give that would satisfy the version of herself that stood before her now? She ran through many different answers in her mind, but knew that all would be denied. *Damn*, she thought. *I'm falling at the first hurdle.*

"Who are you?" her self asked again.

Hunter's academic mind suddenly ceased its relentless whirring. A sense of peace came upon her, as she gave up trying to find the answers. In blissful surrender, she said, "I don't know. But I'm willing to find out."

Her self moved a step towards her, and held out her arms. Hunter took the last step forward, and gently went into the embrace. When the two touched, a golden light surrounded them. Hunter's entire being was overwhelmed by thoughts and sensations.

She was all her successes and failures. She was brilliance and intellect, and she was also martyrdom and self-centredness. She was love and compassion, and she was pride and arrogance.

She was every person in her family. She was every Witch working for the benefit of the magickal community in the New Forest. She was every woman that had ever lived. She was the earth, the moon, the stars. She was energy. She was magick.

She was also every person that had failed her. She was every Witch who had done destructive magick. She was every soul who had performed unspeakable crimes. She was greed, and pride, and much worse.

As she felt these things, the good and the bad, the beautiful and the ugly, all the constraints and limitations, the restrictions and impositions that she had placed upon herself faded away. She was open, and aware, and alive. She was a tiny dust mote in a universe so vast, and she was also the universe itself. She could not live solely to study and watch life in order to learn from it, but rather she must *be* life itself. She must surrender to each experience as being new, for she was everything, forever changing as the seasons, as the earth spun on its axis, as the galaxy rotated amongst the sea of stars. The lens of her perception shifted to encompass this world view, and she felt it solidify within her like a glowing, golden ember in her heart.

"Thank you," she said, the golden light growing brighter and brighter, until she could no longer see. She then felt the whooshing sensation of hedge riding, and the image of the World Tree flickered briefly on the periphery of her consciousness. Then she was back in her ritual space by the oak tree, and the lines that centred her in the Witch's Compass faded from view. Released, she stumbled forwards and fell to her knees next to her stang, tears in her eyes.

"Thank you," she said again.

***

From deep within the shade of the treeline, opposite to where Hunter worked her ritual, a pair of large, yellow eyes watched in silence. When Hunter came back from her working, the yellow eyes blinked and disappeared.

***

Hunter was once more sitting at the kitchen table, an untouched cup of coffee before her when her mother came downstairs. She took one look at her daughter, and knew that something powerful had happened. She gently placed a hand on Hunter's shoulder, as her daughter looked up at her with a smile. "You've seen it, haven't you?" Abigail asked. "You've seen the World Tree."

Hunter nodded as her mother sat down next to her. "Yes, I have. And so much more."

"What else did you see, Poppet?"

Though the sound of her nickname should have pained her, after what Hunter had been through, she found that it no longer did. Instead, she saw it with new eyes. The term held the original meaning that her mother had created out of love and affection, instead of reminding Hunter of the dark magick that had been used against her. Hunter was both stunned, and grateful, for this new perspective. "I saw myself, in the Witch's Compass," was all she said.

Tears came to her mother's eyes. "You have finally begun to find your way, haven't you?"

"I have come home to myself. But it is something that I must be strong in, and be vigilant with. For too long have I lived in my head, allowing my past to dictate my future. I've allowed my thoughts to run riot over my life. But no longer. I cannot think my way through life. I must feel. I must experience. I must live and I must love. I am not above, nor below anyone or anything. I simply am."

"Oh, Hunter," her mother said, rising up and embracing her daughter, kissing her on the cheek. "I am so proud of you."

"Thanks, Mom," replied Hunter, letting the love she felt for her mother flow through and out to her. She felt her mother's own energy strengthen in response.

"What's with all the hugging?" asked Ryder, standing blearily in the doorway.

Abigail pulled away and smiled. "Your sister has done some powerful magick for her own self."

Ryder rubbed her eyes. "That's good. Does that mean you'll stop being such a worrywart and just enjoy what's right in front of you?"

Hunter laughed out loud. "Yes, Ry, yes. That and more."

Ryder nodded, and then went to pour herself some coffee. "Well, thank fuck for that. So, what's the plan for today?"

Abigail stroked her youngest daughter's sleep-rumpled hair. "I think, Peanut, that while we are in this moon cycle's waiting period, we should travel to the Otherworld to find Hunter's father."

Ryder immediately perked up at that, and she turned to her mother. "Really? It's about freaking time. What will you do? How are you going to do it this time? Can I come?"

Her mother laughed. "We haven't decided on any of that just yet. Let's have some breakfast first, shall we? I'll call Elspeth and see if she can join us tonight after work."

Hunter nodded. "Good idea. We could use all the help we can get."

"What about Jack and Harriet? Surely they'll want in on this as well," said Ryder.

"Good point. Let's see if we can get them all back here tonight."

"It sounds perfect," Abigail said, smiling at her daughters. "I'll call Elspeth now, and see if she's free tonight."

***

Elspeth came over after she closed up the shop. Ryder answered the door, and welcomed her.

"Hello, my dear," said Elspeth as she entered the cottage. She wore a dark grey dress and a black lacy shawl around her shoulders. Her dark hair was plaited in a long, French braid down her back, and silver tendrils fell to frame her face.

Abigail came out of the kitchen, followed by Hunter. Hunter spoke up. "We think it's time we went to search for my father."

Elspeth nodded. "I too was thinking that this morning, before Abigail rang me. After what David said, it seems like the best use of our time."

Another knock on the door, and Ryder opened it to see Harriet there, while Dougal and Jack were pulling up into the driveway in a New Forest Park Authority truck. Harriet turned and waved at them, and then went into the house. Ryder stood waiting at the door for Jack. He came out of the truck, still in his work uniform, and smiled at her. He reached in behind his seat and pulled out a posy of flowers. He said goodbye to his friend, and began to walk up to the porch. Dougal waved at Ryder before pulling back out of the driveway and heading home. "Aw, Jack, you shouldn't have," said Ryder, as Jack walked up to the door with the flowers in his hand. "Hunter will get jealous."

Jack grinned, and plucked a daisy from the little bouquet. He tucked it behind Ryder's ear and said, "Hello, Ryder," before giving her nose a tap with his finger.

Ryder blushed for a moment, before turning towards the interior of the cottage and shouting out, "Loverboy is here!"

Hunter came out from the kitchen with a sandwich plate. She walked up to Jack and gave him a kiss. "Here, I thought you'd be hungry," she said.

Jack smiled at her and leaned in close to her ear. "For many, things, Hunter. For many things," he said softly. Hunter felt a frisson of delight as his energy gently touched hers. He then straightened and took the sandwich plate. "Thanks, I'm famished."

"Go on, take a seat. Everyone's here." Hunter followed Jack into the room. They sat down in the living room, a plate of cheese and biscuits with some fruit laid out for anyone who was peckish. Elspeth had a cup of tea in hand, and Ryder went to fetch some water for Harriet. Jack sat down next to his sister, and Hunter took the last spot on the sofa next to him. Harriet pulled out a chair from the dining table for herself, and Abigail settled in the recliner. Ryder handed over the water to Harriet, and then sat down on the floor by her mother.

"Well, here we are!" Abigail said with a smile. "I guess now you all know why."

Nods answered her from around the room. "So, you're going to go and try to find, and rescue, Hunter's father," said Harriet. "It makes sense to do it now, while we wait to see what happens with the Hardwicks."

Elspeth gently put down her tea cup and saucer on the coffee table. "Indeed. But we must also ask ourselves, are we sufficiently prepared?"

Hunter nodded. "Yes, I think we are," she said softly, but with confidence. "If we wait much longer, Lanoc will have too much time to prepare, and my father might be in grave danger at his brother's hands. If he is even still alive." She looked over at her mother, whose worried face gave away her emotions. "He most likely will be; if for nothing else, he can then be used in my uncle's plans." It still felt strange to call Lanoc her uncle, but Hunter accepted the fact and moved on. "The real question is, how should we go about getting to the Otherworld and rescuing him? We have choices to make. Do we go on the astral, or do we physically cross the veil between the worlds? Which will be more effective?"

Elspeth studied Hunter for a moment, and Hunter knew that the older Witch could tell something was different about her. Elspeth then smiled warmly and nodded at Hunter. "Which do you think would be most effective?"

Hunter looked around the room. "I think that as my familiar showed me a way to physically cross over, then perhaps that is how we are meant to travel there. When I last attempted it, she said, *now is not the time*, and I ignored her, to my detriment. But now I believe it is the right time."

"And I agree," said Abigail. "The question is, who will go, and what is our plan once we get there?"

"I want to go," said Ryder.

Abigail leaned over and put her hand on Ryder's shoulder. "I'm not so sure you're ready, sweetheart. And you've never been to the Otherworld, in any shape or form."

Ryder shrugged. "I go where Hunter goes."

Hunter smiled at her sister, her heart warming at the loyalty expressed. "I think maybe Mom's right on this one, Ry. Besides, it would be safer to have people at the portal to guard it for when we come back. You're my best link to this world, a link that I can follow, hopefully, if I need to. The last time I went through, I had absolutely no back-up plan or anything, and I couldn't find my way out. That is, until Jack found me. And even then, we nearly didn't make it out. What if Lanoc decides to attack the portal this time, after having seen how we escaped? We need you here, on this side, for lots of reasons."

Jack nodded; his mouth full. He swallowed, and looked at Ryder. "Lanoc might even try to come through, for whatever reason. And we need to prevent that too."

Ryder thought about this for a moment. "But my magick is unpredictable. I don't even know how I do it. How then can I guard the portal?"

"Because I'll be right here with you, to help out," said Harriet, smiling at her friend.

"As will I," said Elspeth. Everyone turned to face her. "I think Abigail, Hunter, and Jack should go. All three of them have already been to the Otherworld, and know what to expect. If Harriet, Ryder, and I remain to guard the portal, then our 'forces', for lack of a better term, will be evenly distributed."

"What about Thomas?" asked Harriet. "Is he around to help? Didn't he help with your last hedge riding ritual?"

Ryder nodded. "Yeah, he helped to protect us and the cottage from Lanoc, when Hunter and Mom went to find more information. He's really good too. And he can throw that magick knife like nobody's business. It's pretty cool."

"I will get in touch with Thomas," said Elspeth, "and see if he is available on the day we decide to go ahead with this. In the meantime, is there a plan for when you three do enter the Otherworld?"

The room was silent for a few heartbeats, before Hunter spoke. "As I understand it, magick seems to be about connection. Connection to the elements, connection to the gods, and suchlike." She looked at Jack at the mention of gods, and Jack nodded in agreement. "There is also connection to each other. I found Mom at the barrows because I had a connection to her. I could also see the form of my father, before he was attacked by Lanoc. I think that perhaps that is how we could accomplish our goal. Everything is connected, in some way or another. All life on this planet, in this galaxy, in this universe, is connected and interwoven in many different ways. If we narrow our focus, we might be able to find the thread that connects me to my father, like a strand in a tapestry, and follow that back to its source."

Everyone looked at Hunter in surprise, and then broke out in smiles. Ryder was grinning from ear to ear. "Damn, sis, that's pretty deep. You really have changed. Like you're trusting your gut, or your heart, instead of your head. I think this is the way to go."

Elspeth nodded. "Yes indeed. Everything is interconnected, and what Hunter says is true. If she can connect to the link with her father, then it should lead her to him."

"I found Ryder that way, when she had been attacked," said Hunter softly. "I did a hedge riding at the hospital, remember?"

The Witch's Compass

She looked to Elspeth. "You said that I was the only one that could find her. And I followed the thread that connected our souls, right back to the site where the accident happened. I didn't think about it, I just did it. I'm sure I can do something similar, to find my father."

Abigail's eyes shone with unshed tears. "Yes, my love, you can. This feels right." She placed a hand over her heart.

Everyone nodded their assent. "So, all that remains is to decide when we will perform this working," said Elspeth.

"Any evening works for me," said Harriet.

Jack finished his plate of food, and placed it on the coffee table. "Tomorrow is our last big clean-up day before things settle into a more usual routine. So, the night after tomorrow would be best for me."

Elspeth nodded. "Abigail? Girls?"

"Works for me," said Ryder with a grin. Abigail and Hunter nodded.

"Well then, it's all settled," said Elspeth, picking up her tea and finishing it. "The evening after next it is. The timing is good, as you can harness the energy of the full moon that night for your work, and the nearly full, waxing lunar energies for your preparations. The coven will be doing their full moon ritual at my place, and they can send us their prayers and blessings. Rowan isn't there to send me channelled energy like we did when you found your mother at the barrows, so we can't rely on that. She is with her father for the rest of the month. But now that we have a better idea of what we are facing, we can be better prepared, magickally speaking." She looked to Abigail, Hunter, and Ryder. "I expect you three will have a day to get ready, to choose what tools you will use, and to prepare any charms or talismans that you feel might aid you in your work. Listen to Ryder, and go with your heart on this one. You can then spend the following day doing whatever suits you best in bodily and mental preparation." Everyone agreed. "I can help my brother prepare, and get some magickal items and charms sorted, while he is busy with work." She looked over at Jack, who nodded his thanks. "Right, well, I'm off home now to enjoy a nice dinner and some wine. Jack, are you ready?"

Jack looked at Hunter. "Would you like to come over, Hunter?" he asked. "It's a lovely evening."

Hunter looked at her mother and Ryder. They nodded, and Ryder said, "Go on, get out of here."

Jack stood and took Hunter's hand, pulling her up next to him. Elspeth rose, and bid everyone good night. As they left, Abigail thanked Elspeth. "We will see you the day after tomorrow," she said. "Thank you for all your aid."

Elspeth patted her arm gently. "The friendship between our families is a bond that will never be broken," she said softly. "Good night, Abigail."

***

As the sun set, Elspeth drove them down the road to her cottage. It was a nice evening, and Elspeth told them about her day, and how pleased she was that the plumbing had been sorted in her shop. The tourist trade was very busy this year, and she was having record sales this month. When they got to the cottage and stood in the driveway, Elspeth smiled at them as Jack took Hunter's hand. "You two enjoy the evening out here. Be careful, and do not go far. The wards extend to the forest edge, and that's it," she said.

"I know," said Jack softly. "Could you please give Dexter his dinner?"

"Not a problem. Pyewacket, Grizzel, and Tom enjoy having him around. It's good to see them getting along." She waved at them and headed inside. Jack led Hunter around the house and into the back garden.

"Are you sure you've had enough to eat?" asked Hunter. Jack nodded, and silently led her to the tree circle in the garden, where Ryder had received her healing. They walked through into the ring of trees in the last of the evening's light, and came to the centre. "Come here," he said softly, and drew her to him.

The bright orb of the almost-full, gibbous moon cleared the trees in the twilight, shining its light on Hunter and Jack as they came together in a passionate embrace. Jack smelled like the forest and the scent of his own sweat: both sweet and tangy mingled with the scent of pine and earth that were on his body and clothes. Hunter loved his scent, and ran her hands over his chest, purring in delight. Jack reached up, tangling his hands in her hair, and leaned down to cover her mouth with his, hungry for her taste. He pulled her head back gently to deepen the kiss, and pressed his body to her, holding her close.

After a few long minutes, Hunter pulled away, breathless. She looked around, and then back at Jack, who encircled her with his arms. "Jack, we can't – not out here."

Jack smiled at her. "And why not, *mo grá*? There is no one to see us here."

Hunter's heart beat rapidly in her chest, and she took a few breaths to calm down. She remembered something from when she and Jack had been in his stone circle a few months before. "That's not entirely true," she said, looking at him. "We have been watched before, in the stone circle; the owl, remember?"

Jack only hugged her closer. "No one can get through Ellie's wards here, Hunter. And especially not in this circle, if we cast our magick about us. This circle is a sacred place, and is already full of power. If we do not wish to be seen, we shall not be seen."

Hunter blushed slightly, and looked down. "So, um, if its sacred, wouldn't what we are doing be... sacrilegious, in some way?"

Jack chuckled softly. "Wrong religion, Hunter. Making love is an act of worship. Love is natural. Sex is natural. We are following our hearts, and exploring our love. There is nothing sacrilegious about that, in our way of life."

"So, your sister won't mind?"

Jack shook his head, still smiling. "No, she wouldn't. This circle is full of energy, which is why it is so powerful. It has its own energy, after having been worked in for so many years. Any act of love performed here will only strengthen its energy."

Hunter nodded. "That's a beautiful way to think about it."

"Love is beauty, and beauty is truth. What is in our heart is all that matters, and that what we do is true to ourselves."

"Come here," said Hunter with a grin, pulling Jack's mouth back to hers in the growing twilight.

Chapter Eight

The next day Hunter and her family charged up the tools that they would use that evening. Abigail, like Hunter, has removed the bristles from her broom for this venture, and now had a walking stick to take with her. Hunter empowered her stang with energy, and Ryder did the same for her magickal knife. They went through other tools that they had in the cottage, debating their various uses and weighing up whether any of them were important enough to bring, or whether they would simply encumber them on their journey. In the end, alongside some magical talismans and amulets that they wore, they decided that their previously chosen tools would suffice.

Abigail also decided to brew up some potions. Hunter and Ryder worked with her in the kitchen, watching and learning. They made a potion with the herb, eyebright, to provide them with clear sight and to help prevent any misdirection or fairy glamour. Abigail also showed them how to brew up a potion for luck, with clover and basil.

Finally, they made amulets of protection with the wood of the lighting-struck oak to carry with them. Hunter quickly went over the various methods she had learned were used by Witches for protection, and decided that the Norse Younger Furthark runes would be the simplest and most effective for them in this work. Though each rune held great meaning, they were still easy to use magickally, and so she opted for them in her work. She had studied the runes previously in an academic sense, for one could not study the Viking Age without touching upon the runes. However, putting them to actual use was something totally different.

As such, Abigail, Hunter, and Ryder now had amulets with the runes *Týr*, *Úr*, and *Reið* carved into them: justice, strength, and journeying. For herself, Hunter had found a piece of wood from the lightning struck oak which had a hole where a knot had been, that offered a perfect place to loop a leather thong through it so she could wear it around her neck. She spoke a charm over the amulet, and empowered it with her own energy before putting it on. Abigail and Ryder had pocket amulets instead.

They also gathered some food and drink into two backpacks for their journey. They had no idea how long they would be gone, for they knew that time worked differently in the Otherworld. What seemed like an hour or two could be the better part of a day in this world. Hunter explained that clocks, watches and mobile phones didn't work in the Otherworld, so they would have no means of telling time other than by going on instinct. She said that she would try to keep track, and did a quick, rough calculation so that they wouldn't be leaving those guarding the portal out there for days. She estimated every hour there was the equivalent of around five hours in this world, and so she vowed not to be there for over two or three hours in Otherworldly time for this first venture. They realised that they might not be successful on the first go, and that multiple attempts might be necessary before they even found out where her father was, if he was still alive. But Hunter didn't allow those thoughts to deter or sway her from trusting her instincts. She felt, in her heart, that she could quickly follow the thread that connected her to her father, and hopefully would be able to rescue him straight away.

They spent the following day in restful quiet. Hunter refused to worry about everything that could go wrong. Instead, she meditated and once again performed the Witch's Compass, to settle herself firmly in her own power and in her own self. Abigail also meditated, and Ryder read a book for a bit, before giving up and settling down on the sofa to watch some films. Harriet came by early, and sat with Ryder to keep her company.

After they ate dinner, Hunter decided that she should wear comfortable, practical clothing that didn't garner too much attention. She slipped on her black leggings and long-sleeved t-shirt, to be paired with her hiking boots. This outfit was simple, unrestrictive and, if her assumptions were correct, would blend in with the darkness. She plaited her long, red hair into a braid down her back and pulled a lightweight, grey scarf around her shoulders.

An hour before sunset, there was a knock at the door. Ryder waved Elspeth and Jack into the cottage. Elspeth wore dark, slim-fit denim jeans tucked into low-heeled boots with a flowing, black blouse. Jack wore a slate grey, long-sleeved t-shirt, dark cargo trousers, and his hiking boots. He had his magickal Druid staff with him. Hunter entered the living room and waved at them, before going up to Jack. She kissed him softly, and smiled up into his face. Elspeth gave them some room, and greeted Abigail and Ryder.

"You look beautiful, Hunter," said Jack, his eyes on her face for a long moment. "And... different. Has something happened?"

Hunter smiled up at him. "You were probably too tired, and then... a little too busy to notice the other night, but yes, something has happened. I tried something different with the Witch's Compass the other day. It was a life-changing moment."

Jack studied her intently, and then smiled. "I'm so happy for you, Hunter. You seem... at ease."

Hunter gave a small laugh. "Well, as much as is possible before I head to the Otherworld to find the father I never knew I had."

Jack smiled and kissed her again. "I have every faith in you."

"You always have. And I thank you for that. I will tell you more about it all, later."

"I'm glad that this time we are going to the Otherworld together." He leaned in for a gentle, yet sizzling kiss that made Hunter's body light up.

"Okay, you two, knock it off. Or get a room," Ryder's voice carried from the kitchen where they were gathering the foodstuffs.

Hunter ignored her sister as she finished the kiss, smiling all the while, and then said, "I'm glad you're with me too."

Jack smiled down at her and nodded. Then, letting her go, he leaned his staff against the wall next to the door. Hunter took his hand and led him into the living room where everyone was gathering. The talk ended and everyone looked at her expectantly. She swallowed once, and began. "I think that the best way forward would be to head out onto the heath. I will call to my familiar, if she isn't waiting already, and ask her to lead us to a portal. How does that sound?" Heads nodded around the room.

"Oh, I forgot to say, Thomas can indeed aid us, and is on his way," Elspeth interjected. "He should be here any minute."

As soon the words had left Elspeth's mouth, there was a knock at the door. Hunter answered, and saw Thomas standing there, tall and sleek in black jeans and a dark t-shirt beneath his button-down dark denim shirt. It appeared that everyone had similar thoughts when it came to dressing for this adventure. "Hello, Thomas," said Hunter, waving him in. "Thank you so much for helping us tonight. Again."

Thomas nodded and gave her a small smile. He pushed his small, wire-framed glasses up along his nose, and said, "It's my pleasure." He entered the room, and said a soft greeting to everyone. Hunter noticed as he moved that he carried his magickal knife at his waist. *Good,* she thought.

"Hey, Thomas, how's it hanging? asked Ryder. Thomas smiled and replied that he was well. Hunter noticed that the smile he gave her sister was somewhat different to the one he offered to the rest of the room. She smiled, having her suspicions confirmed.

Hunter turned to Thomas. "I was just saying that I think we should head out onto the heath, and hopefully my familiar will show us the way to a new portal. I have a feeling that the previous portal that I used will be watched, now that Lanoc knows where Jack and I have physically gone through, although that portal seemed to be able to shift, and move closer to us when we needed it most. I'm afraid I still don't understand all this portal business. But choosing a different one *feels* right. At any rate, I'm sure my familiar can help us answer that question. She showed me the way last time, and knew when and where to go."

Thomas nodded. "That makes sense. Elspeth said that we are to guard the portal from this side, while you three are on the Other Side?"

"That's correct," Hunter affirmed. "We will try to keep track of the time, so you won't be out there for too long. But don't be worried if we are gone for ten hours or more. Time works differently over there. It might even be fluid, going either slower or faster, and my calculations worthless. I'm sorry, but I really don't know how long we will be gone. I should have asked, will you all be okay with spending the night out on the heath? I know you all have your own lives to live…"

Everyone in the room either nodded or gave their assent. Hunter sighed in relief. "I will try to not let us be gone for too long."

"How long until we should start worrying?" asked Ryder, concern creasing her brow.

"I will try to keep it within the ten-to-fifteen-hour range for you, but that is relying on my calculations, based on my one previous attempt, and as I said, time is fluid in the Otherworld. I'm sorry that I can't be any more accurate than that with my estimate." Hunter looked to Elspeth, to see if she had anything to offer.

The older Witch nodded. "Most of the myths state that time moves slower there, but we can't be one hundred percent sure of that."

"And what if you don't come back in that time frame?" Ryder asked, voicing the concern that others had, but did not speak aloud. "What if, say, you're not back by dawn?"

"Honestly Ry? I don't know. I'm not going to pretend to know what to do in that situation. I think that you will have to decide what you think is best."

Abigail spoke up from where she sat. She too wore dark colours, having borrowed some dark jeans and a blouse from Hunter. "I would prefer you all to remain here, should we not come back. I wouldn't want to lose everyone if we fail."

Ryder shook her head, her long, straight blonde hair falling forwards. "Nuh-uh, not gonna happen. If you, Jack, and Hunter get caught, I'm coming to get you. And if I fail, well, so be it. Better than living here without you, wondering if I could have done anything to save you."

Hunter went up to her sister and gave her a hug. "I love you so much, Ry. This is your decision to make, and yours only."

Elspeth also spoke up. "I too could not leave my brother in the Otherworld."

"Well, if you are all going, then I'm going too," said Harriet with a grin. "I'm not letting you guys have all the fun without me."

"I too would follow," said Thomas quietly.

Hunter's heart swelled at the display of love and affection from everyone in the room. She looked at Jack, and smiled. "Well, it looks like if it all goes wrong, we have a rescue party ready."

Jack smiled back, and then looked at everyone. "Thank you, all of you, so very much."

"Okay, let's get this show on the road," said Ryder, standing up.

"Ry, can you cover up your face while we're on the heath somehow? You're still supposed to be healing."

"Got that sorted," she said, pulling up the hood on her black, Metallica sweatshirt. She then threw on her small backpack and looked at her sister, waiting.

"Mom?"

"Ready," Abigail said, swirling a scarf over her head and putting on some dark sunglasses. She reached over and picked up her magickal walking stick.

"Let's go then," said Hunter. She picked up her backpack, and grabbed her stang. Elspeth hitched her own bag over her shoulder. Thomas already had a small bag slung over his shoulder, and Harriet had her cross-body bag on her. Jack's backpack was by the door.

"Okay then, let's go," said Hunter.

"Hey, Thomas," she heard her sister say as she picked up her keys and phone. "Nice outfit; love the double denim. Did you know that back home we call it a Canadian tuxedo?"

***

They locked up the cottage, gathered their gear, and were in the driveway when a Parks Authority truck pulled up into the driveway. They watched as Dougal jumped out of the truck, still in his uniform. "You're not going without me," he said, walking up to the little group.

Hunter smiled at him "Dougal, I really do appreciate your offer of help, but I fear that this might be a bit out of your wheelhouse, so to speak."

Dougal shook his head. His blue eyes narrowed as he pointed at Jack. "Jack's my friend, and although he's already tried to give me the slip today, after telling me yesterday of your plans, I'm still behind him all the way."

Jack went up to his friend, and clapped him on the shoulder. "Dougal, you truly are a good friend. I know how much you care, about me, and about everyone here. But this is really something for those with magickal powers, and you could be in grave danger."

Dougal still shook his head. "Nay, I won't take no for an answer. Although Mack's the lad with the magicks, I can still help. I want to help, in any way I can." He looked at them all, holding them with his gaze for a few moments. "You'll have to use your powers against me, if you're wanting to stop me."

Silence greeted this statement. Hunter tried another tactic. "Dougal, if everything does indeed go wrong, we will need someone to inform David and others in the magickal community of what has happened."

"Nope, that's nay gonna work either, lass. I've told Mackie to do that for me, should it all go tits up. He'd come too, but he's been sitting exams today for his summer course in Portsmouth.

He'll be here tomorrow. So, you're stuck with me. Where Jack goes, I'll go too." He then gave them all a cheeky wink. "Plus, he's my boss, and tomorrow's payday. I want to make sure I get my money."

They all had to laugh, and Jack turned to Hunter. "Well, my love?" he asked. "What do you think?"

Hunter moved up and gave Dougal a hug, which caused his face and neck to redden even as he hugged her back. She pulled away and looked into his eyes. "It would be an honour to have you with us," she said. "Can you stay with those who are guarding the portal? Any help would be appreciated."

Dougal nodded. "I'll do whatever I can."

"Thank you," said Hunter, tears glistening in her eyes at his loyalty.

"Very well, shall we move on then, everyone?" asked Elspeth. "The evening is coming on, and we want to make sure we use our time wisely." Hunter nodded, and began to lead the way across the road and out onto the heath.

She followed her instincts, and chose a path that was different from the two others she already knew. She was certain that if they got lost, Jack would know where to go, as he knew this area like the back of his hand. They walked for a couple of miles as the blackbirds and nightjars sang around them. As they moved in the soft evening light, Hunter felt a pull in her solar plexus to take certain paths, and she followed that feeling until they came out into a large patch of gorse. The path looked like it wound through the gorse, but the way was blocked. Standing in front of the large, prickly bushes stood her familiar.

"Oh, wow," said Ryder softly.

"Hello," said Hunter softly. The White Hind nodded her head at them. "We think that we need to find a new portal, as the previous one may be compromised. Can you show us the way? Do you know where we need to go?"

The deer looked at her. *Yes, I can show you the way. There is a portal, one where he cannot go, one that is used by those who seek to protect this land. You may use this portal, if you so choose.*

Hunter nodded, and looked back at her group, relaying the information. Everyone nodded in agreement. Hunter could see her sister's face beaming with excitement beneath the hood. "Yes, please," Hunter said to her familiar. "We will try that portal."

Follow me, was all the white doe said.

They followed her silent footsteps into the gorse bushes. The flowers had all finished blooming last month, and Hunter found that she missed their coconut scent. She carefully avoided the spiky branches after Jack had warned them that they needed to be careful, as each prickle could leave a tiny end piece embedded in the skin, which could cause irritation and even infection. They all took care, coming out of the patch of gorse unscathed and continuing to the woodland beyond.

The sun was nearing the horizon when they finally came to a small clearing. In the centre of the glade, a small mound of earth lay. It looked like a tree had been uprooted, but there was no fallen tree in the area. As he approached, Jack spoke softly. "What in the name of… why would anyone uproot and take a tree all the way out here?" He leaned on his staff, and looked to Dougal. "Have there been any other incidents like this lately?"

Dougal scratched his head. "Nay, I've not heard of anything like it. Maybe the odd Christmas tree in December, but those are cut, not pulled out of the ground. I've not seen anything like this."

"Do not get too close," warned Elspeth. "Not until we are certain of this place. It feels… it feels like it is imbued with very old magick."

They all turned to look at Elspeth. "What does that mean?" asked Ryder. Elspeth shook her head, unable to elaborate, her gaze taking in the area.

Hunter's familiar spoke in her mind. *The Witch is correct. This is a very special place, a place of power for the New Forest.*

Meaning what? asked Hunter silently.

Those who wish to protect these lands and people may use this place.

Hunter repeated the information to everyone. They all walked around the mound of earth, keeping a safe distance, not wanting to touch or disturb it. "This is so weird," said Ryder, with a little shiver. "I don't know, but it kind of creeps me out."

She feels the power too, said Hunter's familiar. Hunter nodded wordlessly. She stood in thought, wondering what their best course of action was.

The sun is setting. Now is the time, the White Hind said.

Thank, you, Hunter said to her familiar. *I really appreciate all that you have done.* Her familiar nodded at her. Hunter then took a deep breath. "It is now time. Are we all still in agreement? Are we ready to go?" she asked. Everyone nodded. Those that were to remain behind placed their bags near the centre of the clearing. They then stood in a circle of five around the three that were about the use the portal. Hunter wondered what she should do, as she couldn't see the portal anywhere. Would they need to perform some kind of ritual? Suddenly, as the sun touched the horizon, a beam of sunlight came through the trees and shone upon the ground next to the loose earth. A silvery, shining portal appeared.

"Hot damn," breathed Ryder in awe.

Hunter looked around at everyone. "Let's go." She turned to her sister. "Love you, Ry."

Abigail went up to her youngest daughter and gave her a hug and a kiss. "We will be back as soon as we can, Peanut. I love you."

"I love you too, Mom," Ryder replied, her eyes glistening with tears. She moved up to Hunter. "Love you, Hun. Stay safe," she said softly.

Harriet moved up to her friend and put her arm around Ryder's shoulders for support as she said her farewells to Abigail, Hunter, and Jack. "Good luck, everyone. You've got this."

"Go with the blessings of the Lord and Lady," said Elspeth, moving up to give them all a hug.

"We will be careful," said Jack softly as he hugged his sister. He looked at Thomas over Elspeth's shoulder, and saw him nod. Jack nodded back in unspoken thanks.

"Lang may yer lum reek," said Dougal.

They all turned to him questioningly. "You want them to reek?" asked Ryder.

Dougal sighed, and then simply said, "Good luck."

Hunter looked to her familiar. "Will you come with us?" she asked.

The white doe shook her head. *Where you are going in the Otherworld I cannot easily follow. I am not suitable.*

Hunter nodded, though she was disappointed. "Thank you for showing us the way," she said softly. Her familiar turned and disappeared into the darkness of the trees.

Hunter took a deep breath and approached the portal, Jack and Abigail moving silently behind her. She turned to them with a small smile. "Here we go," she said, gripping her stang tightly. "Remember to keep moving through, and hopefully we will come out the Other Side." She then stepped through, the bright white light flashing all around her.

***

As the group stepped through the portal, one after the other, a silence descended upon the little clearing in the wood. As Jack went through and the last flash of light from the portal flared, the beam of sunlight faded as the sun went below the horizon. Those that remained behind stood still, hoping and wishing the best for their friends and loved ones. Finally, Elspeth broke the silence. "Right, we need to be vigilant. Thomas, can you set up a protecting circle and ward this place? Ryder, Harriet, can you help? Dougal, can you keep an eye out for anything that seems unnatural, or out of place, from both within and outside of the circle that they are casting? You know this forest better than any of us." Dougal nodded. "Good. I will invoke the Lord and Lady to watch over us, and also tune in to the energies and blessings that the coven might be sending our way this night." She reached into her bag and drew out a loaf of bread and a bottle of wine.

"Oh, great, I'm famished!" said Dougal, moving towards her.

Elspeth held up her hand. "Sorry, Dougal, but this is an offering to the gods and the spirits of place, to ask for their aid in this work that we are doing here."

Ryder came up to Dougal with her bag, and reached in. "Here you go, big guy," she said, pulling out a couple of sandwiches. "Hope you like peanut butter. The other one is cheese and pickle."

Dougal accepted the sandwiches with a smile. "Thanks, lass."

They made their preparations, and then settled to wait in the growing darkness.

What they didn't know was that something else was watching and waiting with them.

***

As Hunter moved through the veil between the worlds, she found it was a similar experience to using the previous portal, except that instead of a shining white light once she stepped through, she was surrounded by darkness. There was a heavy, *old* energy about it. It almost felt like it could suck her in forever if she stopped moving. She pushed on as she had with the previous portal, and suddenly she came out of the blackness of the void and into a dark forest. She felt a little dizzy, and leaned on her stang to steady herself. Behind her, she felt her mother come through. She wanted to turn, but felt that she would fall over if she even moved, and so she stood still, waiting for the dizziness to pass. She felt her mother's arms around her, giving her a little hug. "Well done," Abigail said softly. Hunter felt steadier, and she turned, the dizziness leaving her, to watch the portal for Jack.

He soon followed, but as he came through he fell, landing on his hands and knees, his staff falling out of his grasp and onto the ground beside him. Hunter moved quickly to him, and knelt down beside him. "Jack, are you alright?" she asked softly.

Jack nodded, his head down. "I just need a moment." Hunter placed her hands on his shoulders, letting her love for him flow through her and down her arms, into him. Her golden energy surrounded him, and he lifted his head and smiled. "Thanks," he said. They slowly stood up together, and Hunter let go, bending over to pick up his staff and handing it to him. Suddenly, they heard a voice coming from the shadows of the trees.

"I've been waiting for you."

Chapter Nine

Hunter whirled around at the sound of the voice. From out of the trees and into a patch of moonlight stepped a figure that she recognised. His blond hair fell around either side of his face, his eyes shining in the silver light that bathed his body. Hunter's mind and body reeled at the sheer beauty of him for a moment, before she gained control of her senses. "You," she said softly.

Finnvarr stopped and tipped his head to the side, studying them. "That's not quite the greeting that I was expecting, my dear, but there you have it. Hello, Hedge Witch." He peered behind Hunter towards Abigail and Jack. "Hedge Witches, and a Druid tagging along, I should say," he corrected himself. His eyes ran up and down Jack's body. "Who is your friend?"

Jack drew himself up to his full height. "Who is asking?" he said quietly.

The Fae man smiled at him. "I am a friend of Hunter," he said, moving up to her. Hunter took a step back, and Jack growled, moving closer. The man tutted. "Now, now, there is no need for that. Hunter and I go back quite a way. In fact, I seem to remember you now, from that night of song," he said, studying Jack appraisingly.

Jack's face looked perplexed, but he still moved forward to stand protectively in front of Hunter, both hands gripping his staff. "Who are you?" he asked again.

The Fae man looked up at Jack, his lips quirking up into a small smile upon his handsome features. "Your guide, of course."

Silence greeted his response for a few heartbeats. Then Abigail spoke up. "You – you seem familiar. Have I met you before?"

Finnvarr leaned to one side, to peer around Jack and get a better view of Abigail. He then stepped away from Jack with a slight sneer, before turning his attention to Abigail. He took her in with his gaze, and Jack began to move to protect Abigail. Finnvarr waved his hand dismissively, and rolled his eyes. "Stand down, Druid. I mean no harm. I do know this delicious creature. In fact, I spent quite some time with her." Abigail looked at him, not understanding. He smiled at her, all charm. "We found you in the forest, *Cailleach Fál*. We kept you safe."

Dawning realisation fell upon Hunter. "You were the one who found my mother's body, when Lanoc trapped her spirit. You kept her body safe."

The Fae man inclined his head graciously, and then looked Hunter in the eye. "Indeed, Hedge Witch."

"Why?" Hunter asked bluntly.

The man looked heavenward before closing his eyes for a moment, as if his patience was being tested. "Is it a crime to do a good deed?" he asked her.

"Why didn't you take her body back to where she belonged?" Hunter persisted.

Finnvarr rolled his eyes now in exasperation. "My dear, if I had done that, she would probably be six feet underground by now. In your world, the body cannot last long without a soul."

Hunter remembered how her sister had been so near to death, when her soul became lost after the accident. She nodded. "So, you kept her where exactly?"

Finnvarr smiled once again. "Here." Hunter gave him an annoyed look, and he elaborated somewhat. "In the Otherworld."

Jack glared at the man. "You still haven't answered my question. Who are you?"

Finnvarr gave him a predatory grin. "It is only polite to introduce yourself, first."

Jack blew out a breath and shook his head. "Names have power."

"That they do."

Abigail moved forwards. "How do you know Hunter's name?"

Finnvarr smiled at Hunter. "As I said, we have met several times before."

Jack looked at Hunter. "Is this true?" he asked with concern.

Hunter nodded. "Yes, although I don't think I remember all of them properly, or at least, I didn't at the time. I think the first time I saw him was at the pub, when we were singing karaoke. He was part of the group that came in, who I mentioned to you after the accident."

Jack nodded slowly. "And we all thought that you had imagined that, because of the concussion." He turned to Finnvarr. "When did you meet again?"

Finnvarr openly smirked. "Why does that upset you so much, Druid?"

Hunter sighed. "You won't get much information out of him, Jack. I've already tried. Before everything kicked off when I attempted to go to the Otherworld on my own, I was out walking in the forest to relax, and came across a burial mound. He came to me there, to offer me some advice." Hunter smiled ruefully. "And he was right. I should have listened to him, but in my pride and anger I did not. He was also the one who saved me when I got caught in Lanoc's trap in the Otherworld."

Jack's brow furrowed for moment, before he spoke. "I remember now. You said that you had some help from those in

The Witch's Compass

the Otherworld. I did as well; a Fae woman helped me to find you much quicker than I could have on my own."

Hunter nodded. "There wasn't time to go into much detail, as we were running for our lives. And then Ryder got attacked, and everything became so messy, it – I don't know Jack. I just didn't really think about it again."

Abigail came up and put her hand on her daughter's arm. "The Fae have ways of making us forget certain things, Poppet, if they so wish. Don't you worry. Just keep your wits about you, and you will be fine. You've already handled yourself well, so far."

Finnvarr gave them all a charming smile. "She has indeed. Very well." He then looked up towards the moon, and said, "So, my little ragtag group. Time is short. What will you choose, *Cailleach Fál?*"

Hunter pursed her lips for a moment. She looked to Jack, who simply said, "It is your choice, Hunter. Do what you feel is right."

That's just it, thought Hunter. *I don't know what is right.* She hefted a big sigh, and blew a curl out of her eyes that had fallen free from her long braid. "He has helped me, twice now," she said as she weighed the circumstances. "And last time, you said 'just this one time', as you freed me. So, what has made you change your mind, to make you willing to help me again?"

Though something flashed behind his eyes at her question, Finnvarr smiled that charming smile, which made Hunter's hormones leap up in response. She pushed those thoughts down. *It's Fae glamour,* she reminded herself. *Do not fall for it.*

"Because, as I told you before, I wish you to succeed in this matter. We are allies."

Hunter tried to recall their last conversation at the barrow. He *had* said that before. She had asked him three questions, and it seemed like he was bound to answer with three answers. She wondered if she could do something similar now.

Finnvarr seemed to be able to read her mind. "Ah, ah, little Hedge Witch. You have already asked your questions, more than three. There's no need to be greedy. I might have more time for you later, afterwards." Jack made another low, growling sound next to Hunter, which Finnvarr ignored. "I can be your guide, if you wish that from me. All you have to do is ask."

Hunter tipped her head to the side. Despite this Fae man's offer of help, it felt like some sort of trap nonetheless. "Do you even know where we are going? And why?"

Finnvarr smiled. "I have a good idea."

Jack reached out to Hunter. "I don't trust him, my love."

Finnvarr looked at them both. "Well now, isn't that charming. But the Druid doesn't understand the world like we do, Hedge Witch. He is not of our blood."

Hunter wondered how he knew, and then remembered the short conversation she had had with the Fae woman, before this strange Fae man had then rescued her. The woman at the edge of the forest had told her that the Fae knew their own, and Hunter had understood perfectly well what she meant. She would be able to tell a Fae from a human easily, with her half-Fae heritage. But did that extend to knowing what they thought, how their minds worked, and what their motives were? Hunter didn't think so. But she knew herself, and her own growing powers.

She hooked her stang in the crook of her arm, and unslung her small backpack. She reached in to grab the eyebright potion. Straightening, she took off the top of the little glass bottle, and looked their would-be guide in the eye as she downed the potion. The final drops she placed on her eyelids, so that she was covered internally and externally from Fae glamour, as her mother had taught her to do when they had made the potions together. When she opened her eyes and looked at him again, he was still achingly beautiful, but she felt less under his power than before. Without hesitation, she walked up to him and moved right into his personal space. He did not move. She stood before him, inches away from his face, looking deep into his grey eyes. She and the Fae man were almost of matching height, with him only being an inch taller.

Being so close to him was electric. She could feel energy radiating from his body, probing and searching her own, which she kept close and guarded. His eyes held secrets that she could never fathom. His scent was like wet leaves and sweet sunshine. She searched within her heart for a sign, as her mind could not help her with the dilemma she was facing. She already had all the facts, and they did not make the decision whether to trust him any easier. To her eyes, he was still as beautiful as ever, and though he held secrets, the potion she had taken did not seem to indicate a Fae glamour being cast at this moment in time. Knowing she had one last resource to use, she pulled up her energy and centred herself, allowing the Witch's Compass to guide her.

Her familiar had been unable to be her guide in the Otherworld. Did that mean that this man was more fitting to the task? Looking within her heart, Hunter realised that yes, he was suitable, even if he wasn't to be fully trusted. His eyes gleamed with many desires and hidden secrets, to which she was not privy. But she felt, in her heart, that her mission here was supported by him. "Very well," she said softly, still only inches away from him. "In this, and this alone, I will trust you."

Finnvarr smiled, his eyes dancing with both delight and mischief. "And I you," he said.

***

Darkness was settling around the group waiting at the portal. They had lit a fire to provide some light, and Elspeth had also brought some battery-operated lanterns which were placed around the edge of the space. Elspeth had done her invocations, and the wards had been set all around the area. Dougal walked the perimeter of the clearing, on alert for anything out of place. Thomas walked further in, around the portal itself while at the same time scanning the entire area. Harriet and Ryder sat together, watching Elspeth as she now stood in front of the portal, studying it.

"Elspeth is pretty bad-ass, isn't she?" Ryder whispered softly to her friend.

Harriet chuckled softly. "Yeah, I think that's fair to say."

"Have you ever seen her, like, full guns a-blazing and all that? I mean, we saw her throw down some big magick when we did that ritual at the barrows to find my mom, but, well, what else can she do?"

Harriet shrugged. "She's not big on showy displays of magick. None of us are, really."

"Keeping it on the down low?"

"Yeah, I guess you could say that. It really has to do with keeping our secrets safe, for the most part. If someone was just walking out in the woods at night, and saw us throwing around big magick, our cover would be blown and we'd be the centre of a lot of unwanted attention, not just from the media, but probably from scientists, the military, everyone, really."

"Yikes," said Ryder, with a little shiver. "I never really thought about it like *that*. Your whole lives, and, well, like, the entire world, would be changed. I guess that would also blow the cover of other Witches, Druids, and people with supernatural powers all over the world. They'd be after them too."

Harriet nodded. "And not just the people, but the magickal and mythical beings too."

"What do you mean?"

Harriet sighed softly, scanning the treetops as the first stars came out. "Well, take the New Forest, for example. There are so many myths and legends about magickal creatures, supernatural forces, paranormal happenings – where do you think they all come from? It's not from someone's imagination. These are all real. The stories have truth to them, passed down through the years."

"So, like, the giant that Jack told us about; he's here in the New Forest."

"Yup. Yernagate is sleeping, and he's real."

"How do you know the difference between a story and reality, then? Surely there are some made-up things too?"

Harriet looked at her friend. "Us magickal folk, we can feel each other's energy, to a certain extent. The ability will vary for each individual practitioner, of course. My family are very attuned to seeing, feeling, and working with energy. The Hedge Witchcraft that runs in your family will draw your mother and sister, and most likely you as well, to the liminal folk, beings, and places here in the New Forest. And it also depends on how much time and effort you put into it too."

Ryder nodded. "Jack's seen some stuff in the forest, he told us. Because he lives and works there every day, and he's from one of the magickal families, I guess that's why he sees the other magickal creatures."

"Yup, that's pretty much how it goes."

Ryder looked back to Elspeth. "I wonder what Elspeth has seen, and what she knows."

Harriet smiled. "A lot," was all she said.

***

Hunter moved away from Finnvarr. She looked around the little clearing they stood in, the stars and moon shining brightly above them. She noticed that autumn had already come to the Otherworld, even though it was still high summer in her world. Some trees were tinged with golden and russet leaves, shining in the moonlight. Hunter pushed the thought aside, and focused on their mission. "Right," she said decisively. "Let's do this."

Finnvarr smiled and started to move towards the edge of the clearing. When Hunter didn't follow, he turned back, a quizzical look upon his handsome face.

"But first, there's something I must do," said Hunter, internally pleased that she had got one up on this Fae man. Jack and Abigail nodded, and moved close to her to protect her. Finnvarr crossed his arms, and simply watched them with an elegantly raised eyebrow.

Hunter closed her eyes, grasped her stang with both hands, and called upon the Witch's Compass. With Jack and her mother next to her, she felt that she could centre them all within its magick. In her mind, she called upon the four directions, and as she did so, a breeze blew in from each quarter, bringing energy with it for her working. She also called upon the seasonal times of Imbolc, Beltane, Lughnasadh, and Samhain: the sabbats which heralded the start of each season. This would centre them within the cycles of life, death and rebirth. She then called upon above and below, and finally, she turned to centre.

There she felt a glowing golden light envelop them, which emanated from both the stang and her own heart. All that she was, all that she had ever been, and all that she could be were drawn together in this moment to inform her in her mission. The light withdrew until it settled back within her heart, and there she explored the different threads that connected her to others. She felt the thread that connected her to her mother strongly: a bright, golden thread from heart to heart. She felt a very different and subtle thread that flowed between her and Jack, its green and golden energy soothing and supportive. She could also feel a strong thread back to Ryder on the other side of the portal. Hunter then dove deep within her heart, to try and find the thread that connected her to the father she had never known.

She felt a gentle tug in her heart, and a soft, gently glowing red-gold light made itself known to her. She inspected this thread, trying to get a reading on it, to see if it truly was what linked her and her father. Nothing concrete came to her, so she tried another tact. She tugged softly on the thread with her mind, and then felt it tug back in response, and the image of a dark-haired man being held within the mists came to her. In her mind's eye, she saw the man lift his head and look straight at her, a new hope lighting up his gaze. *This is my father,* Hunter thought. She knew this, within her heart. She felt him gently pull once again on the thread, the thread that would lead her to him. Hunter then realised that she would probably also have a thread that connected her to Lanoc, but she was not about to go there in case she alerted him to their presence.

Hunter opened her eyes. She looked around, and saw her mother standing next to her. Abigail moved closer and wrapped her arms around her daughter. "You saw him, didn't you?" she whispered in Hunter's ear.

Hunter nodded, words failing her at this moment in time. She had seen her father. Her *real* father. Her *Fae* father.

Finnvarr sighed impatiently. Abigail released her daughter, and Hunter turned to look at the Fae man who stood with his arms crossed in front of his chest, an eyebrow still raised at her. "Do you know where my father is?" she asked. "Can you take us to Aedon?"

Finnvarr nodded.

"I will know if you are lying, or leading us astray."

Finnvarr smiled a mocking smile. "How fortunate for you."

Hunter looked to Jack and her mother. "Okay, are we ready? Let's go."

***

Elspeth moved away from the strange mound of earth in the centre of the clearing. She went over to where Ryder and Harriet sat, and eased herself down next to them. Stray strands of silver hair fell around her face. "This place is most extraordinary," she said.

"How do you mean?" asked Ryder.

Elspeth shook her head. "I've never felt anything like it. It is *old* magick. The kind of magick that goes back hundreds, if not thousands, of years."

"Whoa," said Ryder softly.

"What do you feel here, Harriet?" asked Elspeth.

Harriet shrugged. "It feels like a very liminal place, for sure. I can't really tell how old the magick is here, I just get a sense of it being… protective? It's a bit ambiguous, really."

"How so?" asked Elspeth.

"Well, from what I can sense, it's neither good nor bad; it just is, if that makes any sense."

Ryder closed her eyes and tried to feel what the other Witches were feeling, but came up with nothing. She sighed, shaking her head. "My spidey-senses are a complete bust."

Elspeth smiled at the young woman. "Give it time, Ryder. You are still new to all of this, and it will come."

Ryder sighed. "I feel like time is definitely not on our side, for some reason," she said, plucking at the grass where she sat.

***

Finnvarr led them out of the clearing, and onto a little path through the forest. Moonlight filtered through the trees, and the silvery light it cast upon everything was utterly magickal. Hunter looked around as they walked, enchanted with the sight. The pale moonlight on the changing colours of the leaves took her breath away. A faint mist hung everywhere, in the cool night air.

Hunter then turned her attention to their guide, who walked a few paces ahead, his lean form moving with a grace that only the Fae could possess. His pale clothing seemed to attract the moonlight, as did his pale blond hair. He turned to glance at her, with a seductive smile over his shoulder. Hunter quickly looked away, aware that she had been staring.

Her mother walked next to her, and she heard Abigail sigh in contentedness. Hunter turned to look at her while they walked. Her mother had a beautiful smile on her face as she gazed upon her surroundings. Behind them, Jack brought up the rear, his tall presence watching them protectively. Hunter spoke softly to her mother. "You really do feel at home here, don't you?"

She could see her mother nodding in the moonlight, her red curls falling about her face. "Yes indeed, Poppet. Sometimes - I don't know - it feels more like home to me than our world on the other side of the portal. I can't explain it."

The strange Fae man's beautiful voice floated back to them from where he led. As they carried on walking, he softly sang:

It calls to you in the day,
It calls to you in the night
You seek out the darkness
As much as the light

Hunter stumbled as he finished his little song. His words reminded her of the Witch's Compass, when it had shown her everything that was good in her, as well as everything that was bad; the light and the dark. She had to come to terms with being both, and with being everything in between. Was this some sort of Fae knowledge as well?

"And what do you know of the light and the darkness?" asked Hunter, trying to draw him out.

Ahead, she heard their guide laugh softly before he answered, without turning to look at her. "That both are needed, in this World and the Otherworld."

Hunter pondered this for a moment, and then a sudden realisation dawned on her. For this strange Fae man, *her* world was the Otherworld. Pushing that thought aside, she decided to try and test him, to see on which side he stood: the darkness or the light. "And why is that, exactly?"

"You know very well, Hedge Witch."

Hunter sighed. He was an evasive fellow, that was for sure. She wondered how old he was, and just what place he held here in the Otherworld. "And when you are not leading strangers through your world, what do you do?" asked Hunter.

"Many things, my dear. Taking care of reckless Hedge Witches seems to be occupying most of my time, lately."

Hunter sighed, and gave up trying to get any information from him. They walked in silence for a while, before Hunter saw a patch of light coming up ahead. They began to move uphill, and as they approached, she could see that the forest opened out into another clearing, this one much larger than where they came through the portal.

As they stepped out into the full moonlight, Hunter gasped in awe. A large, treeless hill rose before her. The side that they could see had a long, gentle rise before the gradient changed to a steep climb, just before the summit. The path followed the ridge on this side, and was laid with white stones, shining in the moonlight. Upon the top of the hill was a stone tower, with a large standing stone next to it. "Where are we?" breathed Hunter. She had never seen anything like it. It was so eldritch and magickal.

"A shortcut," said Finnvarr, turning to look at her with a condescending smile. "If that suits you?"

"But – this place, it must be something special."

Finnvarr moved up to Hunter. She felt Jack come close behind her, in case the Fae man threatened her. "It is indeed, my little Hedge Witch."

"It's like a fairy fort," her mother said softly.

Finnvarr turned to her with a charming smile. "Indeed, that is one of your names for these sorts of places on the Other Side."

"It reminds me of Glastonbury Tor, in Somerset," said Jack.

Finnvarr turned a shrewd gaze to him. "They are similar. Well perceived, Druid."

Jack ignored the praise, and studied the hill. "Is this another portal?"

"Of sorts," replied Finnvarr. "We can use it to travel to certain places within our world. It will not take us to the Other Side. As I said, it is a short cut."

Hunter turned to their guide, dumbfounded. "I think that's the most information you've ever given us," she said with a growing smile.

Finnvarr looked at her, his eyes once again dancing with mischief. "I have told you many things, Hedge Witch. You have simply chosen not to listen."

"Will this take us to Aedon?" Abigail asked, a rising hope in her voice.

"It will take us to Lanoc's castle."

A dread suddenly filled Hunter. "And that's where my father is?"

Finnvarr nodded, still smiling. "You asked me to take you to him, so that is what I am doing."

Behind her, Jack sighed in frustration. "It feels like a trap, my love. Truly, it does."

Hunter turned to look at him. She too sighed, in resignation. "Either way, what choice do we have?"

Abigail took another step closer to the hill, rising out of the forest. "The fairy fortress, within the hill. There are myths and legends all over the country, of the faerie folk that reside within the hollow hills."

"Like Glastonbury Tor," said Jack softly, studying the slopes under the moonlight. "Where Gwynn ap Nudd, the King, rides out at Samhain and Beltane."

"There is truth in the old stories," Finnvarr said simply, before he began walking up the path. "Though this is not *his* hill, it does contain a shortcut to get there."

Hunter followed their guide, a deep curiosity rising within her. "So, whose fortress is this?" she asked him.

"Mine."

Chapter Ten

"Your fortress?" asked Hunter, stopping in her tracks. "Why would you have a fortress?"

The Fae man turned to her; impatience etched across his handsome features. "That is not important right now. Do you want to get to your father or not?"

Hunter bit her lip in frustration. She turned to her mother for help, but Abigail shook her head, not really knowing what to do. Jack put a hand on Hunter's shoulder, and gave it a gentle squeeze. "Your heart knows what to do, Hunter," he reminded her.

Hunter nodded, and closed her eyes. She concentrated on the thread that linked her to Aedon, and felt a gentle tug towards the hill that rose before them. Sighing, she opened her eyes and nodded. "Yes, this is the way we need to go."

Finnvarr looked at her with his usual arrogant smile. "So glad you approve." He turned and began walking up the stone path.

"Keep your eyes on him, Hunter," said Jack softly. "I'll stay with your mum."

The little group followed the Fae man in silence. Hunter wondered how long they had been in the Otherworld now. It felt like around an hour, but it was difficult to know for certain. Some minutes seemed to stretch, and others flowed past like a dream. She only hoped that she would not overrun the time estimation she had set for those who remained guarding the portal.

A breeze swept across the hill, getting steadier and stronger as they climbed. Clouds appeared and scudded over the full moon, sometimes lighting their way, sometimes dropping them in shadow. Hunter's breath became laboured, as did everyone else's with the climb – everyone, that is, except for their guide. He walked as if strolling through a summer meadow, unbothered by the wind and the steep terrain. Halfway up the hill, Hunter turned and leaned on her stang, looking back at the rest of their party. She saw her mother struggling, beads of sweat on her face and her breath coming hard.

"Stop, please. We need to take a short break," Hunter called out, to their guide. She could see him visibly sigh where he stood ahead of them, but she ignored it and turned to her mother.

"Thanks, Poppet," Abigail said with a smile as she approached. "It's been a while since I've done a climb like this."

"No worries, Mom," said Hunter, turning her gaze to Jack to check if he was okay. He looked over Abigail's shoulder at her. He was breathing hard from the climb, but he still gave her a cheerful smile in the moonlight. Once their breathing and heart rate slowed, they continued.

They took another break before the steepest part of the climb, just below the summit. The wind whipped and pushed at them, at times feeling like it was trying to blow them right off the side of the hill and into the depths of the forest below. Hunter hunkered down and kept going, hot and sweaty but also feeling a little thrill for the first time since they began this adventure. She made it to the top and looked around as she waited for her mother to arrive, followed by Jack, who was close behind and helping Abigail as best he could, ensuring that she did not tumble back down the hill.

The view was incredible. Even in the darkness, she could see the moonlight wash across the land in streams of silver. The wind whipped at her, tugging curls loose from her braid and blowing them across her face. She had to hold them back with her hand as she gazed upon this Otherworldly sight. Her heart sang. Why, she did not know; only that her soul felt free.

Unbeknownst to her, the Fae man had come up beside her. He spoke, and Hunter jumped in shock. "Magnificent, isn't it?" he said in her ear.

Annoyed that he had startled her, she refused to answer. Instead, she turned around to look at the tower that sat upon the hill. "Why is there just the tower, and no other part of a fortress or castle?" she asked.

"It is all there, my little Hedge Witch."

"Where?"

"You are in my world, now, beautiful one. Things are always more than they seem."

Hunter shivered, whether from the wind, his presence, or his words, she wasn't quite certain.

"Phew!" she heard her mother behind her. She turned to see Abigail and Jack crest the top. Her mother was smiling and looking around with delight. "Isn't it gorgeous? It's just like a dream!"

Jack eyed Finnvarr and Hunter's closeness with narrowed eyes. "Is everything alright, Hunter?" he asked softly.

Hunter nodded, giving him a smile. "Yes, Jack. Everything is fine." Finnvarr turned his back on them all, and looked out over the vista as he waited for them to recover from the climb.

After a few moments, Abigail nodded and tapped the end of her walking stick twice on the ground. "Okay, I'm ready." Jack nodded as well.

"Me too," said Hunter. She turned to their guide. "To the tower?"

Finnvarr turned and gave her his most charming smile, which triggered a deep lust in her body. She subdued it with her mind, and glared at him. He only laughed, and then turned and led them to the stone tower.

***

It was nearing midnight, and Ryder stood up to stretch her legs. One thing had been on her mind for a while now, and she turned to face Elspeth, who was now standing near the fire. She walked up to her, and looked into the flames for a moment, before she spoke. "Elspeth, you said that Courtney is a 'rogue Witch'. Just what does that mean?

Elspeth sighed. Her eyes never left the fire as she answered the question. "Rogue Witches are those who do not uphold the morals and ways of life that most Witches subscribe to, especially in today's day and age. They are also Witches who may not have been born into a Witch family, but who have studied the dark arts and found their power through these other means."

"Like how?"

"There are many ways one can attain power, Ryder. Those who follow the paths of darkness tend to make pacts, or deals, with certain beings."

"You mean, like, the Devil?"

"He's one, but there are many others. Just as there are many gods, goddesses, and beings that are beneficent, so there are others who seek to harm."

"Why the hell, if you'll pardon the pun, would someone want to do that?"

"Power," Elspeth simply said. "Many who are not born with it try to find fast and easy ways to get it. Without the benefit of having it in their blood, some seek it out through these means as a kind of shortcut, if you will. Others are just plain, bad people, who wish to do harm. I can't really explain why people choose the paths of darkness any better than that, I'm afraid."

"Does it happen often?"

Elspeth shook her head. "Thankfully, not."

Ryder mulled this over for a moment. "So, Courtney may have made a pact with the Devil, or is drawing her power from some other evil being."

"Yes, I believe so. She may also be drawing it from those she calls 'friends'."

"You mean Alice, her bestie?"

"Yes. Alice. Although she doesn't really know how to wield her own innate power, from what I have heard, she still comes from one of the five magickal families here in Burley. Courtney might be using her for her power."

"Like a big ol' blonde battery?"

Elspeth laughed softly. "You could put it that way." She looked up, and saw Dougal. "Bring Dougal here, he needs a break. I have coffee, and cake."

Ryder nodded and looked around, spying Dougal walking the perimeter near them. She went over to him, and gently touched his arm. "Hey, Dougal, take a break, okay? You're making me tired just watching you. Plus, you've been at work all day."

"It's nae bother, lass," he said, but Ryder could see in his face that he was starting to tire.

"Come on, and have some coffee. Elspeth also made cake."

"Is there anything that woman can't do?" asked Dougal cheerfully as Ryder led him to where Elspeth and Harriet now sat.

"Dougal, please, take a seat," Elspeth said, handing him a thermos flask of coffee, followed by a large piece of cake. "Ryder, would you please also fetch Thomas? And then you and Harriet can take over, while these two have something to eat and drink."

"Sure thing," said Ryder, turning away to scan for Thomas. She saw him on the opposite side of the clearing, and called to him as she made her way over. "Hey, Thomas! We've got snacks!"

She saw the tall, blond man turn and smile at her, even as he shook his head. "Thank you, Ryder, but no, I'm fine."

Ryder went up to him and stood in his way, forcing him to go around her in order to continue his rounds. He took a step to the side, but she matched it and blocked him. When he did so again on the other side, she mirrored him. "Enjoying the dance?" she teased.

Something flashed in Thomas' eyes, something that made Ryder's heart skip a beat. He then reached out, and grabbed her by the elbows. When she stiffened in surprise, he simply lifted her up and put her down to one side, and then continued on his circuit.

"Whoa," said Ryder softly, watching his back as he moved away from her. Tall and very slim, there was still a strength to him that surprised her. *Thomas is kind of hot.* She pushed away that thought and sighed, throwing up her hands in defeat as she turned to her friends by the fire.

Harriet came up to her and tossed her a thermos. "Here, at least give him this, if he won't bloody well stop," she said with a wink.

Ryder smiled, and bounded up to Thomas once again. Though he tried to remain impassive, she could see his lips quirked up in a slight smile. "At least have some java," she said, handing him the coffee.

"Thank you, Ryder," Thomas said softly, taking the flask and then continuing his rounds.

Ryder sighed again, and went back to the little group by the fire. Dougal had demolished two pieces of cake, and a thermos of coffee. He moved to stand, but Ryder pushed him down by his shoulders and spoke over his head to Harriet. "Take a few more minutes, big guy. Harri and I have got this."

Dougal sighed and sat back down, running a hand through his red hair. Elspeth handed him a bottle of water which he gratefully accepted, with thanks.

"Come on, it's our turn for a bit," said Harriet. She and Ryder began to patrol the circumference of the clearing, opposite to where Thomas walked. They were silent for a few moments, before Ryder asked, "So, how long have you known Thomas?"

Harriet looked over to where the tall man walked and caught him watching them, the firelight reflecting off his glasses. She smiled, and waved. "I've known Thomas since primary school. He was a couple of years ahead, but a nice guy. Quiet. But don't let that fool you. He's no pushover."

"I got that impression," said Ryder with a wry grin.

"I remember the other older boys, trying to pick on him in secondary school. But Thomas held his ground. One time they tried to start a fight with him in the playground. Two boys, complete idiots, both of them. They thought they could pick on someone who was weak. Did they ever misjudge! They may have started the fight, but Thomas ended it."

"Really? How? Did he use magick?"

Harriet shrugged. "I don't know. Maybe. But if so, it wasn't noticeable. I think maybe he was in some martial arts classes or something at the time. At any rate, he defended himself, and took them down quickly before simply walking away, straight to the Headteacher's office, to tell her what had happened."

"Did he get in trouble?"

"Not that I know of. The other two boys got suspended for two weeks. There were plenty of witnesses."

"Huh," said Ryder, turning away from where she was watching Thomas and peering into the dark trees that surrounded them. "Who'd have thunk it?"

Harriet stopped suddenly, and narrowed her eyes as they heard something in the undergrowth nearby. Ryder whirled around and stepped forwards, trying to get a better look. The bracken rustled, and then a large shape emerged.

A pale, scruffy pony walked up to the edge of the clearing. It stopped at the treeline, and looked at them.

"Oh, look, a New Forest pony!" cried Ryder. "Come here, cutie!" She went towards it, and saw that it was rather bedraggled. Something niggled at the edges of her mind, but she ignored it, wanting to help this animal.

"Ryder, stop!" shouted Elspeth from where she stood by the fire. Ryder turned, a quizzical look on her face at the urgency in Elspeth's tone.

"Ryder, back up to me, please," said Harriet softly behind her.

The strangeness of the way that they were all acting was warning enough for Ryder, and she stepped back from the pony. "Um, what's up, guys?"

Elspeth strode towards them, with Dougal hot on her heels. Ryder noticed that Thomas, on the opposite side of the clearing from them, had his knife out.

"Care to elaborate, Elspeth?" asked Dougal as he hurried behind her.

The Witch's Compass

"Everyone, stay back," Elspeth said sharply as she looked over the pony that stood near to Ryder and Harriet. "That," she said with grim finality, "is a colt pixie."

"A what?" asked Ryder.

"Shit," said Harriet, pulling Ryder even further back.

"What? I don't get it," Ryder hissed softly.

Elspeth walked towards the pony, raising her arms before her and crossing them at the wrists. "Begone, foul imp! Begone from this place! In the name of the Lord and Lady, begone from this place!" As she finished, she threw her arms down and out, and a wave of energy rolled towards the pony. It slammed into it, throwing it back into the darkness.

"Oh my god, why the hell did you do that?" cried Ryder, as she tried to run forwards to see if the animal was okay. Harriet grabbed her and held her back.

"No, Ryder! It's not a real pony! It's a malevolent creature, trying to lure us away for whatever reason," said Harriet as she struggled against Ryder.

At that, Ryder stopped and looked at her friend. "A what?"

Elspeth strode to the clearing's edge, and saw the pony scramble up and then run off into the night. Thomas came and stood beside her, while Dougal stood close behind. "It is gone," Elspeth said simply, staring into the inky blackness of the forest.

"Um, I'm gonna need some more information," said Ryder uneasily. "Just what the hell happened?"

The older Witch turned to face Ryder. "The colt pixie is a magickal creature of darkness, Ryder. It is an imp that delights in luring both people and livestock away from safety, and into danger."

"Fuck me," breathed Ryder as she stared at Elspeth.

"You okay?" asked Dougal, coming up to Ryder. "You look a wee bit pale there, lass. Come and have a seat." He placed a hand on her arm.

Ryder shook it off. A dawning realisation had come to her. "No, guys, the pony. Remember?"

Harriet came up beside Ryder. "What are you talking about?"

"The pony, the night of the accident." Ryder looked at Elspeth. "Remember, right before we got run off the road, a scruffy, pale pony just like that one appeared, and we swerved to miss it."

Elspeth's eyes flashed. "Yes, Ryder. You are correct."

"I think that was the same pony."

Elspeth nodded. "I think you are right."

Ryder hugged her arms to herself. "So, what does this mean?"

Everyone looked at Elspeth, whose face hardened with grim determination. "It means, we are being watched."

***

Hunter stopped at the large entrance to the tower. It was double-doored, with huge crossbeams of oak, studded with large metal roundels. It was wide enough to allow them all through, side by side, with room to spare if they so wished. She placed her hand on the ancient wood of the door, and closed her eyes.

What if I am leading everyone into danger? she thought. *Do we really need to go in here?* She looked up at the tower. Their guide simply stood at her side, watching her with his head slightly cocked to one side, considering her. She ignored him, and looked within to her inner compass and the thread that connected her to her father. She felt a slight pull, that led into the tower. *Well, we need to get in, and this strange Fae is the only one that can open these damned doors,* she thought. "How do we get in?" she asked him.

"Knock," was all he said.

Hunter raised her hand and knocked on the large door.

Nothing happened.

Finnvarr then began to laugh softly. "Oh my," he said, his eyes dancing. "You are so delightfully inexperienced, so raw. I can tell this is going to be fun."

Hunter heard Jack shifting in anger, even as she resisted the urge to punch their guide in his gorgeous face. She held up her hand to hold Jack behind her, and turned to the Fae man. "Very funny. Open the door."

"As you wish," he said with a mocking bow. He waved his hand in front of the tower, and a smaller door appeared in the stone wall, next to the larger door.

"A hidden wicket gate," said Hunter ruefully, as she studied it. "Of course."

Their Fae guide raised an eyebrow. "It would appear you do know a thing or two, my dear."

"One or two things, yes," Hunter said. "After you."

He bowed again, and then grasped the iron handle, lifting it and pushing the door open. The scent of roses and wine flowed out. He stepped within, and disappeared into the darkness.

Hunter looked over her shoulder at the rest of the group, and nodded at them with an uncertain smile, before she turned and entered into the darkness of the tower. The strange, yet pleasant scent enveloped her, making her head swim for a brief moment before the feeling settled. A flash of light appeared, and she saw the Fae man standing before her with a lighted torch. The warm glow of the flickering flames danced along the stone walls in the corridor. Hunter turned back to ensure that her mother and Jack were through. When they entered, they stopped, a look of both surprise and pleasure on their faces.

As they stood motionless, seemingly captivated, Hunter swore softly. She had realised straight away what had happened. She went up to them and reached into their backpacks for the potions of eyebright, resting her stang in the crook of her elbow. She uncorked one and placed a couple of drops on her finger, sweeping it over her mother's eyelids as she stood there, mesmerised, before placing it to her lips and pouring it into her mouth. Abigail swallowed automatically, and then looked around in surprise.

"Glamour," Hunter said through gritted teeth, as she moved up and did the same for Jack.

"You tricked us," she heard Abigail say as she swept the potion over Jack's eyelids. She heard their guide laugh softly.

"Trick? No. You humans are just... susceptible to Fae charms. There is no trickery here. Only my fortress, as it is, and as it should be."

Hunter reached up onto her tiptoes and poured the liquid into Jack's mouth. When he snapped out of it, he looked at her quizzically. "Fae glamour," she said softly. "I just gave you an eyebright potion, to counter it." She put a hand on Jack's arm, as he moved to attack their guide. "No, Jack, I don't think it was intentional."

Jack stopped to look at Hunter. "You didn't succumb."

Hunter shook her head. "No, I did not. But remember, I took the potion earlier. And, I'm half-Fae." Jack nodded at that, and turned to study their guide with a look that Hunter could not fathom.

"Are we all ready, then?" the Fae man said with his charming smile. Hunter nodded. "Very well. Down we go."

He turned and entered into a stairwell that wound down into darkness. As he took the light with him, Hunter was unable to see any more of the strange tower they were in, and she hurried to follow. Her mother came up close behind her. She heard a rustling noise from Jack at the rear, and then his flashlight came on behind them. He shone it down at their feet, so that their shadows would not be obscuring their view of the steps. Hunter heard their guide chuckle once again to himself, as they continued down the stairs. "Must you always see where it is that you are going?" his voice drifted back to them.

"Better to be prepared, than to walk blind," Hunter said softly.

"Better to be blind and heading into the darkness, than to have sight without vision," Finnvarr's smooth, mocking voice floated up to her.

Hunter sighed. She was beginning to get very annoyed with him, whoever he was. "Why won't you tell us your name?" she asked.

Without turning, he replied, "As the Druid said, names have power."

"But what if I need to get your attention?"

"You already have my full attention," he said airily as they wound down the dark stairwell. Hunter rolled her eyes and gave up trying to get any further information from him.

Abigail hefted a large sigh behind her. "I don't understand. Why did we climb this hill, only to head back down it, albeit on the inside?" she asked.

"The hollow hills," said Jack reminded her.

Their guide's voice floated up towards them. "One must have to work, if one is to receive the reward."

"Utter prick," she heard her mother mutter beneath her breath. Hunter smiled, and continued on into the darkness of the hill.

***

Eventually they reached the bottom of the stairwell, and found themselves in a small room flooded with pale light. *Moonlight*, Hunter noticed. She looked around, and saw that it came shining through the high windows.

"I'm *not* going to enjoy going back up those stairs," Abigail said morosely.

"Is it much further?" asked Hunter. She was becoming very conscious of time. "Do you know what time it is, in our world?"

Their guide simply shrugged his shoulders. "Time is a strange beast, Hedge Witch. You can't depend on it."

"I thought time moved slower here, than in our world. Is that wrong?"

The Fae man sighed. "It does, and it doesn't. I don't have the time to explain it all to you right now. For the most part, yes, time moves slower here. But not always. And speaking of time," he said, looking pointedly at Hunter, "I think we best get moving, before we lose the cover of darkness."

Hunter nodded, and didn't push the point any further. Their guide pulled open a door, and they walked out into the moonlight. A gentle slope fell away before them. In the distance, they could see another tower, looming above the treetops. "Is that where we need to go?" asked Hunter, pointing.

"It is indeed, Hunter."

She hated it when he used her name, as she didn't know his. It was a powerplay, and she knew it. "It's miles away; we'll never get there before dawn." Already the sky had lightened considerably, even as the moon began to set in the west.

"Have no fear, you will be there shortly," the Fae man said. "Come this way." He moved off the path and around the base of the tower. Hunter turned back to gaze upon it, realising that it was the same tower, just now in a different place. The Otherworld was full of surprises.

They all walked around the tower, and then down a small path to a circle of stones. Nine tall, slim stones jutted out from the earth, each around twelve feet tall. They sparkled with quartz, and Hunter admired their beauty. She turned to see Jack's reaction to the stone circle. He smiled at her, acknowledging the grandness of it all.

"Enter through here," their guide said, and stood to one side. He waved at them to walk through the stones and into the centre. Hunter was suspicious, of course, but the tug of the thread that connected her to her father told her that they were still on the right track. She strode into the circle, while the others followed.

"Good luck," she heard their guide say, before everything suddenly shifted, and they found themselves in front of an entirely different tower. "You will need it," the Fae man's faint voice echoed softly around them.

The stone circle must have been another type of portal, Hunter concluded, as she looked around and tried to gain her bearings. She was becoming used to this sort of travel, but as she turned to face the others, she saw that it was still difficult for Jack. He wobbled where he stood, and Hunter went to him and held onto his arm. It took a few more moments before he steadied. "Thanks," he said softly.

"Where are we?" asked Abigail.

"And where is our guide?" asked Jack, looking around.

Hunter knew that they were now alone. "He's played his part. Now it's up to us to find my father." She looked at the second tower before them. "I guess he's in here, somewhere." The large tower doors stood open.

"So, we just go in and get him? That seems far too easy," said Jack softly as he studied the structure.

"It is," said Abigail. "Lanoc must *want* us inside, if it is this easy. But we don't have a choice."

Hunter was reminded of their luck potions as she thought about the Fae man's warning. "Okay, I think it's time for a little luck," she said, resting her stang on the ground and then reaching into her pack, pulling out the luck potions. She handed one to Jack and Abigail each, and then opened her own bottle. She looked to her mother. "Do we drink it?"

"Yes, Poppet. Over the lips, through the gums, look out stomach, here it comes!" She tipped her head back and emptied the bottle.

"I only hope that it goes well with the eyebright potion," Jack said with a rueful grin, before downing the contents.

Hunter smiled as she drunk hers, and then put away the empty bottles in her pack. "Okay, well, here we go." She walked through the tower doors, and into a dimly lit room. Jack's flashlight turned on behind her. As he shone it around the room, Hunter noticed a hallway that led deeper into the tower. "That's probably where we should go," she said softly. "Everyone have their protection amulets, talismans, and such?"

A soft chorus of assent answered her. She then turned and headed into the corridor. It only took a few moments before they came out into another room, a rather grand and impressive chamber. "Whoa," breathed Hunter as she gazed about the opulent space.

The circular chamber was lit by an unseen light source that gave the entire area a soft glow. Hunter assumed that this was Fae magick of some kind. She looked at the round, stone walls which were covered in beautiful tapestries, depicting all manner of mythological creatures. At one end of the space was a large stone throne, draped with sumptuous fabrics. There were wide steps that led up to the throne, and all around them more steps angled away in all directions, steps that led to row upon row of seating. Whoever sat on the throne could address their subjects easily, and be seen by everyone. Behind the seating, at the very top row in the back, were alcoves. Some held statues, some were empty. As they walked around and took in their surroundings, their footsteps echoed in the empty chamber.

Hunter pursed her lips, wondering what they should do next. She closed her eyes, and focused once again on the thread that led her to her father. Suddenly, she heard a voice behind her.

"I am here, my daughter."

Witches of the New Forest

Chapter Eleven

Hunter turned at the sound of the voice. She saw a mist flowing in an alcove, and slowly the form of a tall, dark-haired man appeared.

"Aedon!" her mother cried, and rushed towards him.

A bolt of lightning shot out straight at her from the throne, and struck her hard. Abigail went flying the last few steps to the feet of one of the statues, near where Aedon's form was held in the mist.

"No!" cried Hunter. "Mom, no!" She began to run to her mother, but another bolt of lightning shot out. This one just missed Hunter, passing harmlessly in front of her. She stopped dead in her tracks, her arms circling wildly as she fought to stay on her feet. She heard Jack chanting off to one side:

Victorious Brigid
The living one of life
And the courage of Maev the great Queen,
Brigid the strong
Be with me now!

The room began to glow with a blue-white light, and then a pulse of energy shot out from Jack's staff towards the throne. Lanoc stood there, tall and angry next to it, and didn't flinch as the magick came towards him. He simply raised his hand and said in a commanding tone, "*Bás.*" Jack's magick disintegrated into tiny motes of light, before fading away.

Hunter pushed the stray tendrils of hair out of her eyes and continued on to where her mother was lying on the ground. "Mom! Mom! Please, Mom, can you hear me?" She dropped to her knees by her mother, who moaned softly where she lay. Hunter's stang clattered on the floor beside them.

A low, evil laugh filled the room. Hunter ignored it, reaching down to pull her mother towards her. Holding her by the shoulders, she cradled Abigail and said, "Mom, Mom – are you alright? Please, oh please, by all the gods, be okay." Tears streamed unchecked down her cheeks.

The misty figure in the alcove shifted, and seemed to glow a bit brighter. "You will pay for this dearly, my brother," said the man trapped in the mists.

Jack ran up to Hunter and Abigail, placing himself between them and Lanoc. Hunter could feel Jack drawing energy from deep within the earth as he stood, fists down and clenched. "Mom," said Hunter, "Mom, please, answer me."

Abigail opened her eyes. "Poppet," she said softly. She blinked a few times, and groaned. "I – I'm okay. I'll be okay. I – I am just winded, I think," she said, starting to move. It was then that Hunter realised that her mother was still clutching her walking stick.

"You were thrown a good seven feet," Hunter said, not wanting to let her go.

"And I can feel it," her mother answered ruefully. "I'm lucky nothing was broken. Go and stand with Jack. I'll see to Aedon," she whispered with a small smile.

Hunter gave her mother the barest nod, and released her. She grabbed her stang and stood up slowly, heat and anger rising within her. Her uncle, Lanoc, had caused them all such pain and worry, starting with the loss of their mother when they were just children, and then attacking them when they had come to the

New Forest. For her mother and father, he had caused equal pain, for nearly two decades during their imprisonment. "This ends now," she said softly.

Lanoc laughed softly to himself. "Look at the little Witch and her pet Druid. Really, what do you think you can achieve here?"

Hunter decided to try and keep him talking, so that she and Jack could gather up as much strength and energy as possible, and also to give her mother time. "Why? Why do you delight in causing us pain? What have we ever done to you?"

Lanoc's ice-blue eyes flashed. "You should never have been born, half-breed. You are a vile abomination. I have spent many years preventing your kind from mixing with mine. You are nothing but animals."

Shocked at this new revelation, Hunter's mind reeled. "Are you kidding me? All this, because you're a racist?"

Lanoc smiled an evil smile. "This goes beyond anything you humans could ever have dreamt of with your narrow, animal minds. You are a danger to our kind. Our blood must be kept pure. And I will see to it that it remains so."

Hot fury leapt in her heart. "So, you're a racist then, plain and simple." Hunter fed on that anger. Her inner compass told her that certain kinds of anger were useful, and necessary. In this situation, it was rightfully justified. Holding her stang in her left hand, she reached with her right and touched Jack's arm, their hot, burning energy rising to a full crescendo. "Now," she simply said, as a brilliant bolt of green-golden light shot across the throne room and into Lanoc.

**

The Witch's Compass

Abigail moved silently towards Aedon, while Lanoc's attention was focused on Hunter and Jack. She could see his form, held within the mists in the alcove recessed into the wall. "How can I free you, my love?" she whispered to him.

"There is only one thing that can overcome all obstacles, my heart," she heard him say from within the mists. "Now that you are free, only this can release me."

Abigail immediately understood, and closed her eyes for a moment, centring herself and taking a deep breath. She then opened her eyes, and walked into the alcove, into the mists.

***

Lanoc was thrown across the room from where he had been standing next to the throne. He smashed into the wall, and slowly sagged down. For a moment, Hunter felt an awful dread at the thought that she had just killed a man. But then her heart sank even further, as he opened his eyes and gracefully rose to his feet. "Pitiful," he said menacingly.

Hunter whispered to Jack in a rising panic. "What do we do now?" Her heart was racing, even as she felt physically depleted after throwing that much energy around.

"I don't know, Hunter," Jack simply said. He looked at her for a moment, considering.

"Can we call upon Brighid again?"

Jack shook his head. "I already have. She gave me what power she could in that moment. I don't feel her close to me any longer."

Hunter shot a look at Lanoc, who was now smiling and walking towards them, before turning back to Jack. "Mom needs more time," she whispered.

"Well," said Jack with a wry smile, "when magick fails, blood, sweat, and tears prevail." Hunter looked at him quizzically. "You distract him, and I'll jump him," he explained softly.

"Got it," she said. She turned and ran away from Jack, feeling slightly dizzy from the loss of energy after throwing magick at her uncle. She kept close to the wall of the circular chamber, her hand running along the smooth stone, helping to keep herself upright. Jack, Hunter, and Lanoc now stood in a triangle, which meant that Lanoc could only attack one person at a time.

"You're the one who is pitiful," Hunter shouted at Lanoc. "Causing all this pain, because you can't handle the fact that people just want to live and love as they please. You're scared, Lanoc. You're afraid of losing the power that you have, each and every day, and this is how it manifests."

Lanoc smiled and turned towards her. "I am doing what is right for my people," he said, raising his hands.

"You're doing what is right for yourself!" shouted Hunter, raising her staff and trying to summon some more energy to defend herself. She was utterly depleted however, and when the wave of magick came towards her, she had no choice but to dive to the floor and roll away, bruising her elbows and knees on the hard stone floor in the process.

"Your kind are a blight upon all the worlds," said Lanoc, marching towards her.

"You are pathetic," Hunter sneered at him, all the while battling the growing weakness and sick feeling inside her.

Furious, Lanoc raised his hands once more. Hunter had nowhere to go, as she was still on her hands and knees. Suddenly Jack was there, and he threw himself upon Lanoc, taking him down with his sheer physical strength. They wrestled on the floor for a moment, before Lanoc suddenly shimmered out of existence.

Jack found himself splayed on the floor, with nothing underneath him. He quickly rose, and looked around the room.

"Where did he go?" asked Hunter.

"I have no idea," said Jack.

***

Abigail moved through the mists, and came into a separate space. Behind her was a window out into Lanoc's throne room. Before her was a wall of even thicker mist. Fear crept up her spine, as it reminded her of her own imprisonment for nearly twenty years, held within the mists. But she knew that she could now free Aedon, with the one thing that could never fail.

True love.

"Aedon!" she cried out. "I am here, my love! Come to me, and I will lead you out!"

She saw a form coming towards her in the mists. Her heart pounded, as hope leapt in her heart. Her love was coming to her, and soon they would be free.

But the man that emerged from the mists was not Aedon. It was Lanoc. Abigail raised her small staff, and pooled her energy.

"No, Abigail, don't!" Lanoc shouted.

But he shouted with Aedon's voice.

It was yet another trick. Abigail shuddered, realising that she had nearly blasted her love. Then, her suspicions returned with full force. "If you are Aedon, prove it," she said.

The man stopped, and spread his hands wide. "I love you, Abigail. I always have. Ever since the first day that I saw you, in the beechwood, by the yew tree. When I heard you nearby, and turned to see your beautiful face watching me, your red hair tumbling around your shoulders, I knew, right then and there, that you were the woman for me. We were meant for each other, dear heart. Now and forever, forever and always."

In that instant Abigail knew it was Aedon, and reached out to him. As she took his hand, the illusion that Lanoc had cast dissipated, and she was swept up into Aedon's arms. She held onto him tightly, tears spilling down her face. "I'm so sorry," she kept repeated.

"My love," Aedon said, running his hand down her long, red curls. "It's not your fault. It was never your fault."

Abigail sniffed, and gently pulled away. "Come, we must leave here immediately. I don't know what danger Hunter and Jack may be in, right now." She turned to the window, and took Aedon's hand. The words that she needed to free him came to her mind, and she chanted, just before she pulled them both through:

"I release you, Adeon of the Fae
By the power of the Lord and Lady
Return to your world immediately
By the power of the World Tree."

Tugging his hand, she went through and into the throne room. Aedon was pulled out from his misty prison behind her.

"Mom!" Hunter cried, stumbling towards to her mother from where she stood with Jack near the throne.

"Hello, Poppet," Abigail said, taking Hunter into her arms. Abigail looked around the throne room. "What happened to Lanoc?"

"We don't know," said Jack, coming up to them. He eyed Aedon warily.

"He must have shimmered elsewhere," Aedon said. "If we are to get out, we should move quickly, before he summons his strength again."

"Shimmered?" asked Jack.

"With his magick. The Higher Fae able to move from location to location in that manner."

Hunter pulled away from her mother's embrace to study her father. He was tall, with dark hair and dark eyes. He looked upon her as well, and Hunter could see the resemblance in the shape of the nose, the mouth, and the eyes. "Hello, Father," she said, a little uncertain.

"Hello, Daughter," he replied, a warm smile upon his face.

Abigail clapped her hands. "Let's go, quickly, as Aedon said. We might just make it out of here before Lanoc recovers."

"Hang on," said Jack, reaching into his pack. "Hunter and I released a lot of magick. We need to eat or drink something." He pulled out two electrolyte drinks, and handed one to Hunter. They drank them down, and then he handed Hunter a protein bar.

"Let's go then," said Hunter, chewing on the snack as she led the way out of the throne room and towards the tower entrance.

***

Everyone was now on their feet and watchful. It was after midnight, and Ryder began to yawn loudly. Elspeth turned at the sound and smiled, even as she shook her head. "The Witching Hour is coming," the older woman said. "We must be vigilant."

Ryder was instantly intrigued. "The Witching Hour? I thought that was, like, midnight, or something."

Elspeth nodded. "Many people nowadays do think that, but in the old lore it was the time around 3am, when everyone was in their deepest sleep, before slowly resurfacing back to a wakened state. It is the time when Witches were said to be able to work their greatest magicks, in peace and relative safety."

"Huh," said Ryder. "You learn something Witchy every day."

***

The group retraced their steps to the tower entrance. The light of dawn was shining through the open doors. They jogged out into the early sunshine and stopped, waiting for their eyes to adjust to the light coming from the rising sun. Suddenly, a mist rose from the ground all around them.

"Oh no," said Hunter, her heart dropping to her toes.

Out of the mist strode Lanoc, with a long, heavy two-handed sword in his grip. And he was not alone. Fae warriors in silvery plate armour surrounded them, in ranks five fighters deep.

"Oh no, oh no," Abigail moaned behind Hunter, her hand coming up to her heart. Hunter turned to see Aedon standing next to her. He put his arm around Abigail's shoulders.

Hunter felt Jack moving up from behind her, and he took his place next to her. He held Hunter's hand as they stood in silence, surrounded by these Fae warriors. There was no escape.

A strange sense of calm filled Hunter. *If this was where we are to meet our end, then so be it*, she thought. She turned to look up at Jack's handsome face. He smiled down at her, his green eyes full of love. "At least I have known your love in my lifetime," Hunter said, her heart full.

"If this is where our adventure ends, I will find you in the next life," Jack said, pulling her towards him.

"How endearing," Lanoc sneered. "This has gone on for long enough. You have vexed me to no end, you and your little friends," he said, looking at Aedon. "My brother, this ends now."

The warriors around them lifted their swords and shields. Aedon held onto Abigail, and Jack pulled Hunter into his arms, shielding her with his body as much as possible. Time stood still, until a new, mocking voice cut through the crowd.

"I rather doubt it."

Finnvarr strode towards the knights that had encircled the group, a slim longsword in his hand and his own band of warriors fanned out behind him, ten times the number of Lanoc's small army. They had suddenly materialised in the mist behind Lanoc's warriors. With a wave of his hand, Finnvarr directed his fighters to encircle Lanoc's band of warriors. With long spears and swords now pointed at them, Lanoc and his band found themselves surrounded.

"My *King*," said the strange Fae man to Aedon. Hunter watched as he bowed slightly to her father. With the rising sun behind him, his blond hair shone in a halo around his head. His grey clothing was paler than usual, being almost, but not quite, white. "I am glad to see that you have returned."

Aedon inclined his head towards their rescuer, but said nothing.

Lanoc erupted in anger. "Now! Kill them all!" he shouted. "Do it!"

Lanoc's fighters charged into action, coming directly towards Hunter and her group. Finnvarr's warriors followed, cutting them down from behind. Finnvarr himself ran forwards and leapt acrobatically over the heads of the men in front of him, to land within the circle with Hunter and her party. He went straight for Lanoc, and Hunter gasped as they exchanged blows.

The strange Fae man whom she had known to be arrogant and annoying was fighting with a speed and precision that took her breath away. Lanoc matched him, his two-handed sword again and again defending against his opponent's thrusts and slices.

A sword suddenly swept down right in front of her nose, and Hunter was abruptly brought back from watching the battle before her, to find herself in the midst of her own. Jack moved from her side and stepped in front of her, his staff raised and deflecting blows from the swordsmen around them. Hunter turned and saw her mother and Aedon move quickly up to them until they all stood back-to-back. A sword was hurled over the heads of the attackers, which Aedon deftly caught, and then he began his own attack. Abigail poked her walking stick into the belly of a man who was approaching, thinking she was an easy target. He doubled down in pain, and she then whacked him on the side of the head with her stick, knocking him aside. Looking around she saw Hunter watching, and she gave her daughter a smile. She then turned back to her opponents and swept out her hand, muttering something Hunter could not hear. The three men moving towards her suddenly tripped and fell.

Seeing her mother's bravery rallied Hunter, and brought her out of her shocked state. If her mother could battle these strange warriors, well then, so could she. She pulled up her energy, and raised her staff. Out shot a golden light that blinded the two men who leered at her as they approached. They shouted and covered their eyes, but they were too late. Following her mother's cue, Hunter bashed them both in the stomach, before turning to see how Jack was doing.

Jack spun and fought with a wild, green fire in his eyes. "*Faugh a Ballagh!*" he cried. He then began to sing as he fended off the sword blows with his staff, splinters flying everywhere.

*"Oh the night fell black, and the rifles' crack
   made perfidious Albion reel
In the leaden rain, seven tongues of flame
   did shine o'er the lines of steel
By each shining blade a prayer was said,
   that to Ireland her sons be true
But when morning broke, still the war flag shook
   out its folds in the foggy dew."*

The song seemed to weave a new energy into their fighting, rallying them all with the tune. Hunter, who had heard this song being sung many times at folk nights, added her voice to Jack's, hoping to increase their strength.

*"Oh the bravest fell, and the requiem bell
   rang mournfully and clear
For those who died that Easter tide
   in the spring time of the year
And the world did gaze, in deep amaze,
   at those fearless men, but few,
Who bore the fight that freedom's light
   might shine through the foggy dew."*

As she sang, she pulled up the energy of the Witch's Compass within her. She drew in the energies of the four directions, of the four seasons, above, below, and centre, and raised her arms above her head, her stang in her hands. She kept drawing energy until she felt herself vibrating with it, and when she could no longer contain it, she then thrust the stang downwards, hitting the ground as hard as she could with the bottom of the small staff. A shockwave of energy rolled out, knocking most of the combatants off their feet.

As the wave of energy rolled towards where their rescuer and Lanoc battled, Hunter saw the strange Fae man look up at her for a split second, before leaping up once more into the air to avoid the magick. As the wave of energy rolled towards them, it knocked Lanoc to the ground. The Fae man landed on his feet like a cat, with his sword poised before him, right where Lanoc lay sprawled. All around them, the fighting suddenly ceased. As Lanoc's warriors stepped back, waiting to see what would unfold, Hunter's party did the same. Jack moved towards her, his breath coming hard and sweat beading down his forehead. He took up his place beside her, to protect her, whatever would happen. They were both decidedly unsteady on their feet. Hunter saw Aedon draw her mother towards them, and they stood together, watching the two Fae men.

Finnvarr towered over Lanoc, who lay on the ground before him. Both were breathing hard. Finnvarr held his sword to Lanoc's throat, a murderous look in his eyes. "I should have done this a long time ago," he said in a low, menacing voice.

"Wait!" cried Hunter. She saw that the Fae man was about to kill Lanoc, and something within her desperately sought to stop the violence. "Please, wait!" she said, as she stumbled weakly towards them, with Jack, Abigail, and Aedon at her heels.

"This is not your decision to make, Hedge Witch," the Fae man said through gritted teeth as Hunter came up to them.

"Neither is it yours," Aedon said behind her.

"Please," pleaded Hunter. "Hasn't there been enough violence already?" Her heart twisted as she looked around at the dead and the wounded warriors from both factions around her. "Look around you! Whatever vengeance you wanted; you have had."

The Fae man never took his eyes off Lanoc, who lay on the ground before him. There was hatred and fear on Lanoc's face.

Aedon moved up to them, but still stayed at a safe distance, outside of the reach of the Fae man's sword. "I believe it *is* her decision to make," he said softly.

"And how have you come to that decision, *my King*?" he asked, with a bitterness resounding on the last two words.

"Because Lanoc has hurt her most of all. It was he who took away her father, and then her mother. It was he who attacked her and her friends time and again. It is she who had been our hope for many long years. I say she is the one who has been the most impacted by his behaviour, and so it is she who should decide his fate."

Hunter's heart pounded in her chest as everyone looked at her; everyone, that is, except the Fae man holding the sword to her uncles' throat.

"I – I, no, I can't make this decision," she said, panic rising in her chest.

"Yes, my daughter, you can." Aedon's soft, measured voice cut through her fear to some degree, but still she felt paralysed and unable to move, let alone think. A heavy silence hung over the area, as everyone awaited Lanoc's fate.

Hunter looked at the Fae man, who had been her ally in so much of this. She was certain he was still hiding things from her, but without his help she could never have found her father so quickly. However, the look in his eyes was clear: he would murder her uncle in a heartbeat.

Feeling her gaze on him, Finnvarr flicked his eyes towards her for a moment, before looking back down at the man who lay on the ground before him. "Very well," he said softly. "As you have brought about his downfall, I shall abide by your decision."

He kept his sword at Lanoc's throat, while Hunter tried to decide what to do.

"What will it be, daughter?" asked Aedon, turning to Hunter.

Full blown panic rose in Hunter. She couldn't make this decision. She was not a part of this Fae world. She didn't know all the facts, the politics, the reasons why they were all here. She didn't know who truly were the good guys, or the bad guys. There was no way she would be able to make any sort of informed choice.

She felt a hand on her shoulder, and turned around to see Jack standing behind her. He nodded silently at her, and she could feel his green energy supporting her. He had always believed in her, especially when she had no belief in herself.

Her mother came up and took her hand. "Go with your heart, my love, and you can never go wrong." Jack squeezed her shoulder gently, before letting go.

Tears sprang up in Hunter's eyes. She closed them, and the tears fell down her cheeks. She pushed down the panic, and took a deep breath. She called upon the Witch's Compass, to help guide her. She felt its glowing, golden light, and she centred herself within it. She saw all that was good, and all that was bad within her. She saw this reflected in everyone around her at this moment. There was so much pain. So much sorrow. And enough violence for a lifetime. She did not want Lanoc's death on her hands, or anyone's hands. But what other choice did she have?

She heard a woman's voice speak gently in her mind. *Banishment, Daughter of the Forest, is always an option.* Hunter pondered this. She knew the voice to be the goddess, Brighid. Could she banish Lanoc, and avoid further violence? How?

An image of three staffs, crossed together, flashed through her mind. Suddenly, it all made sense. And there was a certain poetic justice to it as well, that Lanoc would be punished by the very means he had punished her mother and father for nearly twenty years. Nodding, she thanked Brighid. "Lady of the Sacred Flame, Lady of the Holy Well, I thank you," she whispered softly.

She opened her eyes, to see her uncle still lying on the ground, held at sword point. Her Fae ally's blade never wavered, and there was steel in his grey eyes, even as there was steel in his hand. She turned to look at her mother, and squeezed her hand once, before letting go. "Jack, please join us," she said.

With her mother to her right, and Jack now on her left, she lifted her stang. "Cross them," she said softly, holding hers straight out. Her mother moved and crossed her walking stick diagonally across Hunter's stang. Jack did the same on the other side. Suddenly, seeing the crossed staves before her, Hunter realised that they formed the rune, *Hagall*. This rune, meaning 'hail', represented chaos and disruption symbolised by violent storms which brought about hail. On the other hand, hail, though damaging, was extremely short-lived, and melted away within minutes, turning to nourishing water. This symbolism struck a deep chord within Hunter, and she poured her own energy into the rune that they had created in front of her. The image of the World Tree flashed before her eyes, and she realised that the configuration of the three staffs were also symbolic of this great vehicle for journeying to other worlds. She now knew what she had to do.

Gathering her power to her, and drawing more from the vision of the World Tree that she had seen when she first discovered the Witch's Compass, she felt her stang warming in her hand before her. She opened her eyes, and saw that now all three staves were glowing with a golden light. She pushed out that power as she spoke the words that came to her mind:

"I banish you, Lanoc,
From the human world
And the world of Faery.
I banish you, Lanoc,
By the powers of the World Tree."

As she looked at Lanoc, she saw his eyes widen in fear. He opened his mouth to say something, but the golden light shot out from the staves and struck him with a low, reverberating wave. He flashed once, and then disappeared, the golden light of the staves fading into nothingness.

Finnvarr slowly lowered his sword, and then turned his gaze to Hunter. Hunter returned his gaze, a little unsure as to what exactly was going on in the strange Fae man's mind. He nodded once, and then turned and walked away, his warriors following, disappearing into the mists that rose up around them once more.

Hunter watched him go, and then looked around her, horror growing once again in the pit of her stomach. The sight of the fallen, broken, dead, and dying warriors lay around them. She had never witnessed death like this, up close and violent. She broke out in a cold sweat, fell to her knees, and began to heave. Jack was immediately right there next to her, his hand on her back, trying to soothe her. With his other hand, he held back her long, red hair that had fallen free of the plait as she brought up all that she had ingested not so long ago. After she had finished, she sat up shakily and murmured her thanks to Jack, before everything went dark.

Chapter Twelve

"Do you pledge your allegiance to me, your rightful King, and foreswear any former allegiance to my brother?" Aedon asked quietly. The warriors around him nodded, and as one, they said, "Yes, My Lord."

Aedon nodded. "Good. Take your wounded, and bring the dead to the lake, where the Washers will prepare them." The fighters picked up their wounded first, taking them to the healers, before coming back for their dead. There was sorrow on many a face at the death of some of their comrades, but there was also an underlying hope.

Hunter came around from her faint in a short amount of time, after Aedon had sent her some healing energy. She had been completely depleted, after banishing Lanoc. She now rose and stood beside Jack, who held an arm around her protectively. Hunter looked around in awe. "Is - is that it? Just like that, it's over?"

Aedon smiled at her. "Yes, my daughter, it is over. Our people know their rightful King."

Hunter was astounded. "But, who appoints you? You don't have elections, or anything? How –"

Abigail put her hand on her daughter's arm. "There will be plenty of time for all that, Poppet," she said with a smile. "Right now, we must get home as soon as we can."

"Right," said Hunter, looking at Jack. He leaned on his splintered staff, weary, but still he smiled at her. She blushed slightly. She had no idea that he could fight like that, and wondered where he had learned those formidable skills. She pushed those thoughts aside for the moment, as a new worry surfaced. "Um, how do we get back without our guide, though?" she asked, turning back to her mother and father.

"We will use the portal here in my tower," said Aedon. He held out his arm to Abigail, and together they moved towards the tower.

"Okay," said Hunter, unsure of what was going on, but deciding to go with it. Jack came up to her and held out his arm. She gave a little laugh and took it, walking into the tower which now bustled with Fae, busy on various errands. Hunter leaned in close so that only Jack would hear. "Does this feel totally weird to you?"

Jack grinned. "We're in the Otherworld, fought off an evil Fae King, helped to reinstate the proper King, or so it seems, and you're asking if it feels weird?" He shook his head and looked at her with dancing eyes. "Yeah, it's totally weird."

"I'm glad I'm not the only one," Hunter smiled as they followed her parents through the tower. They walked back into the throne room, and Aedon swept out a hand in front of him, revealing a glowing door on the opposite wall. "Here we are," he said, turning back to look at Hunter.

"Just like that?" she asked again, incredulous.

"Just like that, Daughter," he said, smiling at her. "This will take you to the path that leads to the clearing in the wood, where you came through the other portal leading back to your world."

"But – how? I don't understand. How can you just wave a hand and a portal appears? And how did you know where we came through?"

Aedon laughed softly. "Whoever rules has access to the portals that are spread across this world. There are many, many portals, so that we can keep track of what is going on, and to help our people. Distance is not an issue. I'm sure that some, like my brother, abused this power and used it to garner more people to his opinions about humans, to move troops across to where there was resistance, and so on. It's a privilege that the rulers have, and one that should not be abused, but instead, be used to help. A full investigation will come. As to your other question, I could feel it when you three came through. We are linked, as you well know."

"Oh," said Hunter, taking in all this new information. "So, others have these powers too, using portals. Like our guide, who used the one in his tower to get us to this tower."

"That's correct. He does have access to some of the portals, but not all."

"He never told us his name," Hunter said, exasperated. "Can you tell us?"

Aedon shook his head with a sad smile. "I'm afraid not, Daughter. Names have power. If he chooses to give his name to you, then that is all well and good. If he chooses not to, that is his prerogative."

"But he knows mine," said Hunter with a grumble. She looked up at this Fae King, who was her father. "Um, you can call me Hunter, if you wish, instead of 'Daughter', you know. I guess that would be alright."

Aedon smiled and held out his hand. Hunter reached out, and he clasped her forearm with his hand. She did likewise, assuming that this was some sort of Fae handshake. "Very well, Hunter. You may call me Father, or Aedon, as you choose."

"Okay."

Abigail interjected, gently laying her hand on Hunter's shoulder. "Come, Poppet, we must go. We have no idea how much time has passed in our world. We need to get back as quickly as we can."

Hunter looked at her father, studying him carefully for a long moment. She wanted to take in as much as she could, not knowing if he would come with them or not. He seemed able to read her expression. "There is much to do here, Hunter. I will visit as soon as I can."

"How did you know who I was?" Hunter asked.

"We know our own," Aedon said softly.

Hunter remembered hearing that before, from other Fae. It was all still so strange. But she felt a tug towards the portal, and sensed that they were needed back. "Well, it was nice to meet you," she said awkwardly.

"And you, Hunter."

Abigail went to Aedon and hugged him. "Visit as soon as you can. We have much to talk about."

Aedon looked at her, sadness in his eyes. "Much time has passed since we last walked in the beechwood together," he said.

Abigail nodded, her eyes welling with tears. "We will deal with all that, when we have the time to do so." She turned to Hunter and Jack. "Come, my lovelies, let's go." She wiped her eyes, and resolutely turned away and walked towards the portal, waiting for Hunter. Hunter took one last look at her birth father, and then walked through the portal. Abigail went next, with one last sad smile for Aedon. Jack then moved up to the portal.

"Take good care of my daughter, young man," Aedon said.

Jack simply nodded, took a deep, steadying breath, and went into the portal.

Hunter came out onto the path that led to the clearing, and waited for her mother and Jack. This time, she didn't feel dizzy, and smiled as she waited for the others to come through. Her mother came out and laughed when she saw Hunter's smile. "You've gotten used to it quickly, my dear!" she said, pleased.

Jack then came through, and he stumbled as he found his feet. He looked pale, and swayed slightly. "Unlike your man here," Abigail said, and reached out to steady him. Jack gave her a small smile of thanks, while looking decidedly queasy. It soon passed, and after a few moments he nodded at them to continue. They wearily jogged down the path and soon were back in the clearing, where the first portal waited. They walked across the open space, and one by one went through, back to the New Forest.

***

It was 3am when a sharp wind suddenly blew across the clearing, nearly blowing out the flames of the fire with its intensity. Ryder whirled around, trying to see if anything or anyone was coming. The wind died almost as soon as it had arrived. A feeling of dread settled upon Ryder, and she clenched her fists. "I have a feeling that shit's about to get real," she said softly.

An owl screeched in the darkness and the silence, causing Ryder to jump. She turned to face the noise, Harriet by her side. She saw a movement in the trees, and her body tensed. "Incoming!" she shouted, as a large, pale owl shot out, straight towards her.

At the same time, from beneath the trees two dark, shadowy creatures emerged, snarling and growling. The wards that had been placed around the perimeter of the clearing flared, and the beasts were thrown back. The owl, however, managed to pierce through the energy field with another cry and dove at Ryder, with its long, sharp talons out. Ryder ducked and threw her hands up instinctively to cover her head. She felt searing pain as the talons raked across her arms.

A bolt of white energy flew from Harriet's hands to hit the owl. The owl screamed once again, this time turning on her. It dove, the sharp beak open and hissing. Harriet threw herself to the ground and rolled just in time, and the owl swerved to one side, its silent wings pumping.

A knife flew out from the darkness and struck at the owl's wing. Ryder spun around to see Thomas running towards them, his knife now laying upon the ground not far from where they both were. "Ryder, stay down!" he cried as he ran.

Ignoring the order, Ryder turned back to Harriet, to see if she was okay. Harriet looked a little shocked, but she caught Ryder's eye and quickly moved to stand with her friend. Ryder remembered that she had her knife as well, and drew it out to protect them.

A flash of light blinded them all for a moment. Blinking, Ryder looked around, trying to get her vision back. She could just see the shadowy figures had broken through the wards, and were now stalking towards Elspeth and Dougal who were by the fire with their collection of bags. "Behind you, Elspeth!" she cried.

***

Dougal and Elspeth turned to face the threat that was coming up from behind. "What in the name of all hell are those?" Dougal said, as he frantically rummaged through his work bag in the firelight.

"Chained Black Dogs. Hell hounds, if you will," the Witch said evenly. "Dougal, stand back, away from the fire, please."

Dougal took a couple of steps back, and pulled an axe out of his bag. Elspeth lifted her left hand, and the fire suddenly leapt up to twice its height, illuminating the entire clearing. "Fucking hell!" Dougal swore, as he moved further away from the roaring flames. He then turned to face the creatures that were growling and stalking towards them. "Ugly bastards, aren't they?" he asked, hefting his wood axe.

Dougal was right. The dogs were three times the size of a normal dog, with long, matted black fur, red eyes, and huge teeth that made them drool. A strong smell of sulphur emanated from them. Long, heavy chains dragged from their spiked, metal collars, but they did not seem to care one bit. Still they stalked forward, towards Dougal and Elspeth.

***

"Oh shit," Harriet said softly beside Ryder.

Ryder tore her gaze away from Elspeth and Dougal, to see the owl's form shift and change as it landed on the ground nearby. Bones snapped and tendons cracked, until a woman's form emerged, clothed in a tattered, white robe. Her dark hair fell across her face, and her left arm was bleeding. She straightened, throwing her hair back, her fingers curling in like claws as she drew up energy. Ryder recognised her instantly.

It was Courtney.

"You will pay for that," Courtney hissed, and raised a hand towards Thomas. A bolt of dark energy shot out towards him. He knelt down to avoid the brunt of it, and held onto a pentacle necklace that he wore. The energy mostly missed him, but he still reeled silently from the impact.

"Thomas!" cried Ryder. She grabbed Harriet's arm, and pulled her towards where Thomas knelt on the ground, swaying. He put a hand down onto the earth to steady himself.

"Run, little girls, run. This will certainly be fun," Courtney said in a singsong voice behind them.

Ryder shot a glance towards Elspeth and Dougal. The blazing fire threw their long shadows across the clearing. The dogs still stalked forward. Slowly, Elspeth raised her hand towards the fire. Ryder could see the energy of the fire being heightened by Elspeth's hand. She then closed it into a fist, turned, and made a throwing motion at one of the dogs.

A tongue of flame shot out from the fire, exploding in a large fireball against the head of one of the dogs. A piercing howl rang through the night. The smell of sulphur increased, along with the scent of burning hair and skin. The dog shook its head, half of its face scorched. It then growled low and long, and resumed stalking towards Elspeth and Dougal.

Ryder turned her gaze back to Courtney. The woman gave her an evil smile, and began to close the distance between them. Ryder held her knife out, pointing it at the Witch, expecting a bolt of energy to shoot out as when she had previously used it in a similar situation with Lanoc.

Nothing happened.

***

Wearily, Hunter emerged from the portal, back in her own world and into the clearing. It was still night, and the fire burned high and bright. She heard a growl nearby, and turned to see a large, chained, Black Dog looking at her. "Oh crap," she said, and stood in front of the portal to shield her mother and Jack, who had yet to come through. She realised that she ached all way to the very marrow of her bones, but nonetheless she raised her stang and stood her ground. She tried to pull up energy from the earth, but she felt that she didn't even have enough of her own energy to root herself, let alone draw up more.

She was totally empty.

Abigail came through, and immediately saw the danger they were in. Hunter scanned the area, trying to find Ryder, but was unable to see her. "Ryder?" she called out, panic stricken. "Ryder!"

"Over here, Hun!" she heard her sister call out, and Hunter nearly cried in relief. The Black Dog was still looking at her and growling, and began to move towards her. Hunter turned to see where her sister had called from, and froze. There, across the clearing, stood Ryder and Harriet, with Thomas kneeling on the ground beside them.

And then there was Courtney.

Jack came through the portal, and fell onto his hands and knees, still slightly ill from the previous journey. Hunter didn't know what to do. Her sister was in grave danger, but then, so were the three of them by the portal, with Jack out of action until he recovered. "Mom, I've run out of juice – I don't have anything left. And we're in trouble," Hunter said, pointing at the Black Dog that was moving towards them.

"Yes, I see. Alright then. Let's see what we can do." Her mother closed her eyes, and Hunter assumed that she was gathering energy and power. Hunter stood protectively in front of her mother and Jack, her stang in her hands, facing down the Black Dog with renewed fear in her heart. Behind them, the portal flickered once, and then faded from sight.

***

"Shit," Ryder swore, looking down at her knife. "I can't make it work."

"It's okay," said Harriet. "I've still got a trick or two up my sleeve."

Thomas slowly stood, and took them both by the arm. "Get behind me, both of you."

Ryder shook off his hand. "Sorry Thomas, no can do. We're in this together."

Courtney gave them a smile of pure malice as she approached them. Ryder's heart was in her throat. The memory of the last attack she had been through, the pain and terror, flashed through her, making her unable to move, to think, to do anything. Her breath quickened. Thomas moved in front of her, blocking her view of Courtney. He turned and placed hands on her shoulders, and in a calm, quiet voice, said, "Ryder, look at me."

Ryder looked up into his blue eyes. "Breathe slowly, three-count in, three-count release." Ryder did, and instantly felt better. His blue eyes calmed her mind and body, and she nodded to him that she was okay. He held her gaze a moment longer, and then nodded in return, before facing Courtney. His arms were stretched down towards the ground, and Ryder knew that he was drawing up energy from the earth.

"Oh, how sweet," Courtney said, her voice dripping like honey. "Aren't you all just too cute. Do I scare you, Ryder?"

"Go to hell, Courtney," Ryder replied.

Courtney glanced down and saw the blade that had wounded her lying at her feet. She reached down and picked up Thomas' knife. Letting out a cry of pain, she instantly dropped it.

"That does not belong to you," Thomas said evenly.

"You will pay for that," Courtney threatened.

"Guys, let's pool our energy together," Harriet said softly, so only they could hear. "Like at Elspeth's. Direct it to me. I can harm, as well as heal."

It took Ryder a moment to understand, before she nodded. Thomas did the same, and they both took one of Harriet's hands in their own, and channelled energy into her. Courtney saw what they were doing, and frowned. She turned to face the treeline, and made a waving motion.

As Ryder was pouring energy into Harriet, she looked in the direction that Courtney was gesturing towards and saw Alice, standing at the circle's edge. Alice had her eyes closed, and Ryder knew that she was feeding Courtney with energy. With no time to tell her friends of her plan, Ryder pushed out a last pulse of energy towards Harriet, and then raced off across the circle towards Alice. The woman stood just outside the wards. Ryder ran towards her and straight through the wards, closing her eyes briefly. Alice opened her eyes as she heard Ryder's approach, and the flash of white light from the wards blinded her. Ryder kept going, tackling her to the ground.

"No!" shouted Courtney, her face livid.

"Hey, Courtney," said Harriet, her eyes now glowing white. "It's payback time."

Harriet threw a bolt of white-hot energy at Courtney. Just before it hit her, a red wall of energy rose up, shielding Courtney from harm. Harriet's energy clawed up the red barrier, trying to find a way through, but not succeeding. Finally spent, it sizzled out. "Damn," she said. "I didn't know she could do that."

***

Elspeth saw that one of the dogs had focused on something new. She followed the path the dog was taking, and saw that Hunter, Abigail, and Jack had just returned through the portal. She gave a huge sigh of relief, until she saw that Jack was unsteady, and the Chained Black Dog was coming closer. She heard Hunter call out for her sister, and Ryder replying. There was nothing that Elspeth could do for them, and she swore softly. The other Black Dog was nearly upon her and Dougal, and the Witch ground her teeth in frustration.

Dougal stood beside Elspeth, his wood-axe in his hand, and a look of determination on his face. He quickly glanced over to where Ryder, Harriet, and Thomas stood, facing off Courtney. His eyes were drawn back to the immediate threat before him, as the beast crouched, growling, ready to leap at them. Dougal found himself doing the same, ready to meet the beast head on.

"Dougal, wait," Elspeth said, and reached out towards the fire once more. She closed her fist once again, and directed a spout of flame to hit this dog. It was as yet uninjured, and when the flame shot out towards it, it leapt forwards. The flame passed along the side of its body, and it yowled horribly, even as it came down in their midst, teeth snapping and wild, red eyes rolling.

Dougal wasted no time and brought the axe down upon the creature. It sank into its shoulder, and was then yanked out of his hands as the beast whirled upon him, howling. He saw Elspeth now behind the creature, with her eyes closed, and he assumed that she was gathering more power. He needed to keep the beast's attention. "Come on, ya wee beastie. Tongue my fartbox, you fucking walloper!" he shouted. The Black Dog snarled, a long strand of drool dripping from the side of its mouth. "Your mother was a poodle, ya little shite."

Without warning, the beast leapt at Dougal. The Scotsman reached out and grabbed either side of the creature's head, trying to stop the snapping jaws from ripping his head off. Where he touched the creature, his hands burned, and he yelled even as he held on. A blast of energy suddenly hit the beast from behind, and threw it off and over Dougal, who lay on his back upon the ground. He panted for a moment, before getting up and facing the beast once again.

"Thanks, darlin'," he said to Elspeth.
"Think nothing of it, Dougal," she replied.

***

Hunter clutched her stang with trembling hands as the beast approached. It quickened its pace, and began to run towards them. "Incoming!" she cried in warning to Abigail and Jack behind her.

Abigail swept past her and went down on one knee, her hands thrust out before her. A gust of wind roared towards the Black Dog, and the creature slammed into it as if hitting a wall. Abigail began to make circular motions with her hands, and closed her eyes. Dirt and debris began to fly around the beast in a mini tornado. It tried to escape, but couldn't pass through the wall of air. "Hunter! Jack! Go to Elspeth, now!"

"I'm not leaving you, Mom!" Hunter cried above the wind.

"I'll be right behind you – go!"

Jack, having now recovered from the portal journey, grabbed Hunter's hand and half-dragged her across the clearing to where Elspeth and Dougal stood. He looked behind to see Abigail rise up from her kneeling position, and begin to follow them, still circling her hands in an ever-increasing motion. The beast was suddenly lifted off the ground, and Abigail threw her hands up high. The Black Dog shot up thirty feet in the air, and then suddenly Abigail threw her hands down to the ground. The beast plummeted to the earth, and lay still.

Jack and Hunter reached Elspeth and Dougal, who were facing off with the other Black Dog. It growled, an axe stuck in its thick hide and huge burn marks down one side of its body. The stench of burnt hair and flesh, combined with the smell of sulphur, was sickening. Hunter turned to see her mother running wearily towards them. Behind her, the other Black Dog began moving weakly, trying to rise after smashing to the ground.

"Well, that's me done," her mother grinned as she approached them. She stopped and swayed on her feet as she reached the group. Hunter grabbed her mother by the shoulders to keep her upright.

"Nice to see you again," said Elspeth calmly, her eyes still focused on the menacing dog before them. "Did you have a nice trip?"

"I wasn't made for portal travel," Jack said wryly, before closing his eyes and energetically reaching out to the trees around them for power. Hunter saw him begin to glow with that green light, but it was much dimmer than before.

"Jack, be careful," she said softly.

Jack opened his eyes, lifted his staff, and sent a blast of green energy at the Black Dog. It hit the thing smack in the face, and the beast was thrown backwards. It quickly jumped to its feet, shaking its head and growling.

"That's one tough dug," said Dougal, looking over at Jack.

Now it was Jack's turn to sway, and he suddenly fell down to his knees. Hunter cried out, but couldn't leave her mother, worried that she too might fall.

"He will be fine, Hunter," Elspeth said. She closed her eyes, and whispered some words that Hunter could not hear. She thought she heard the word, *coven*, though, and after a moment or two the Witch opened her eyes. They were glowing with a red fire.

***

Ryder pinned Alice to the ground. She had her knees upon the woman's shoulders, so that she couldn't move. She was sorely tempted to punch her in the face, but restrained herself, instead grabbing the woman's blonde, coiffed hair to help keep her pinned to the ground.

"What are you doing?" Alice screamed at her. "Get off me!"

"Not a fucking chance," said Ryder through gritted teeth.

Alice's vision was returning, and she glared at Ryder. "You are making the biggest mistake of your life, you little shit. Do you know who I am?"

"Yeah," said Ryder lightly. "You're Courtney's bitch."

Anger flashed in Alice's eyes. "You are *nothing*, you pathetic little whore. My family will destroy you."

"I'd like to see them try," said Ryder conversationally.

"You are nothing but a liar and a cowan," Alice spat.

"Nope, and I have no idea what that other thing is, but probably nope as well."

"You will pay for this, bitch," said Alice.

***

Elspeth raised her hands which were now glowing with red fire, and blasted the Black Dog before them. It flew across the clearing and hit the wards, where they flashed again with a white light. It landed in the bushes beneath the trees, and didn't rise again.

"That's givin' it laldie," said Dougal with a low whistle.

Hunter looked around at their little group. Everyone was spent. She then cast her gaze over to where she had last seen Ryder, Harriet, and Thomas. She could see Harriet and Thomas, but not her sister. She then saw Courtney, pulling out an evil looking blade from beneath her tattered robe. "Where's Ryder?" Hunter whispered, fearing the worst. "Oh my god, where is she?"

Abigail grabbed Hunter's shoulder and pointed off to one side of the clearing. "There she is," she said. They could see Ryder, sitting on top of someone lying on the ground.

"Oh dear," Elspeth said, focusing the group back on Courtney.

Behind her, three more Black Dogs appeared. Courtney smiled an evil smile, and raised her dagger. They saw Thomas grab Harriet's arm, and they both ran towards Ryder, trying to get clear of whatever it was that Courtney was about to throw at them. Hunter knew that she could never reach them in time. Her heart fell, and she went numb.

Courtney glowed with a dark red energy, surrounded by roiling shadows. Sparks flashed in the shadows; claws and ghostly faces could be seen, as if trying to escape.

"By the Lady," Elspeth breathed. "She's given over to the darkness completely."

Hunter looked at the older Witch, panic in her eyes. "What does that mean?"

Jack had recovered somewhat and rose, coming up behind Hunter and putting his arms protectively around her. "It means, *mo grá*, that this is probably the end for us. We are out of energy, and unable to do anything more."

Hunter turned to look up at him. His face was calm, but sad. "No," she said, twisting to look back at the scene unfolding before them. "No, it cannot end like this."

***

A heartbeat passed, then two, and suddenly a loud roaring came from the dark woods. It made Hunter's knees tremble, and she was glad Jack was holding on to her. There was a rustling in the bushes near to them, and suddenly Police Constable Hart appeared. He had a shotgun, and as he came into the clearing, he raised it and aimed at Courtney.

She laughed, and shot her hand out towards him, even as he fired his gun. A bolt of dark red energy raced towards him. He fired and then rolled, the blast just grazing him. Ignoring his seared uniform, he took aim again and fired once more.

Both shots hit Courtney, but they barely slowed her down. "David!" shouted Elspeth. "You can't hurt her, step back!"

Instead, PC Hart broke open the shotgun, flicked out the spent cartridges and reloaded it, snapping it back in place with grim determination.

The loud roar sounded again, and this time Courtney slowed, her eyes darting this way and that, trying to find out where the new threat came from. Behind her, a large figure emerged from the forest.

"Oh my goddess," breathed Abigail. The little group were stunned into silence as they took in the strange creature.

A huge, lion-shaped beast, twice the size of a normal lion, with a blazing red mane and large, glowing yellow eyes appeared in the clearing. A huge rack of antlers, the size of a small tree, flowed from the top of its head. It bellowed again, and this time Courtney turned to look at it, fear in her face.

"What the hell is that?" Hunter finally managed to say, her body rigid with fear.

Elspeth's voice was filled with wonder. "That, my dear, is the Stratford Lyon."

The beast's eyes flashed, and then it charged at Courtney. She raised her hands, trying to fend it off, the faces in the roiling smoke around her screaming. The three Black Dogs hurled themselves towards the Lyon. It barrelled through them all, heading straight for Courtney.

It lowered its head, and hit Courtney with full force, impaling her upon its antlers. She screamed, and the sound, combined with the screams of the strange faces in the smoke around her, caused everyone in the clearing to cover their ears.

The Lyon threw Courtney up into the air, and she came smashing down with a sickening thud. The smoke dissipated around her, as did the three Black Dogs. Silence descended upon the clearing.

The Lyon slowly walked up to the broken and bleeding form of Courtney. It picked her up in its massive jaws, and strode towards the mound of earth. Without a single glance at those who stood in stunned silence, it leapt up into the air, its prize still in its jaws, and dove down towards the mound of earth that lay next to where the portal had been. The earth opened up, and the beast disappeared into the ground. The earth swept back in and covered the hole, and then two large antlers sprouted from the ground, forming into branches like some strange tree in the middle of the clearing.

Chapter Thirteen

Hunter's knees finally gave out fully, and Jack lowered her gently to the ground, kneeling down beside her. She felt like she was going to pass out again. "Breathe, my love," said Jack softly in her ear. Her vison swam, and Jack moved to her side, putting her head in his lap. Hunter closed her eyes as Jack stroked her hair softly, calling her name gently.

Eventually, the feeling passed. She opened her eyes and looked up to see Jack's worried face. "Jack – my sister – Ryder, where is she?"

"I'm right here, Hun," she heard Ryder say, before her sister's head popped into view above her. "You look white as a sheet."

"Thanks," Hunter said, trying to rise up onto her elbows.

"Stay down for another minute or two," Jack said gently, pushing down on her shoulders. Hunter gave in and closed her eyes again, trying to process everything that had happened.

"Let me go!" she heard a shrill woman's voice scream nearby.

Hunter opened her eyes and turned her head, to see PC Hart holding onto Alice Hardwick's arm. He twisted it behind her back, and she screamed again, this time in pain. Deftly grabbing a pair of handcuffs from his belt, David slapped them on Alice's wrists, and then pushed her down onto her knees. "Stay there, and be quiet," he said, anger lacing his voice. Alice looked up at him, her anger turned to fear, and nodded.

David approached the group, concern on his face. "Is Hunter alright?" he asked, as he leaned to one side, trying to see her as she lay upon the ground.

"She's fine," Jack said softly. "Just a bit drained and overwhelmed."

Hunter slowly rose up into a sitting position. "What in the world was *that*?" she asked. She couldn't believe what she had just seen.

"There will be time for full explanations later," said David, relief upon his face at seeing her rise. He looked over the whole group. "I think you all should clear out of here immediately. The noise may have been heard from a great distance, depending on the wind. While we can pass off the noise as deer-hunting in the hour before sunrise, it's best if you all make yourself scarce, in case any other officers or park rangers are called to the scene." He looked around at the clearing. "Any more of those Black Dogs around?"

"No," they heard Thomas say, as he approached the group. "I just went to check and dispatch any that were still alive, but their bodies have disappeared."

"Good," David said, nodding.

Elspeth reached out her hand towards the fire, her palm facing downwards. She slowly lowered her palm, and the fire died out.

"Wow, neat!" said Ryder. "That is so cool! So, Elspeth, are you, like, a firestarter or something?"

"There is time enough to discuss this later, as David said," replied Elspeth calmly. "Right now, we must get back without being seen."

"I will eradicate any traces of the fire, and take Alice back to the Hardwick Estate, to face her father. Go now. I will be in touch," said David, before he strode away and began to throw dirt upon the now dead fire.

"Do as he says," Elspeth said. They gathered up their belongings and began the weary walk back home, even as the darkness in the sky began to recede in the pre-dawn light.

***

They made it back to the cottage, all of them tired and weary. Harriet, however, still had sufficient energy left over, and healed the cuts along Ryder's arms from the owl's talons before healing the burns on Dougal's hands. As they stood in the driveway, Harriet bid them farewell, saying that she would call them tomorrow. She then got in her car and drove off. Elspeth too made her goodbyes, and drove back the short distance to her cottage together with Jack and Dougal, offering the Scotsman her couch to sleep on. After bidding them to sleep well, Thomas drove away, leaving Abigail, Hunter, and Ryder to enter their cottage, and go straight to bed.

***

When Hunter woke later that morning, she could barely move. She was sore all over, and her mouth was dry. She groaned as she turned over, and lifted her head to gaze blearily around the room. Ryder was still in bed, snoring softly as she lay sprawled on her back, arms outflung to either side.

Quietly, Hunter rose from her cot. She was still in the clothes from the night before, and she slowly stripped them off, bundling herself into a bathrobe. She didn't have the energy to do anything else before she made her way downstairs. She could smell coffee, and as she entered the kitchen, she saw her mother standing by the sink, looking out the window.

"Mom?" Hunter croaked. Abigail did not answer, and Hunter shuffled over, worried. "Curly Wurly," she said softly in her mother's ear.

The trigger word worked, and Abigail came back to herself. "Oh, hello, Poppet. My, you are feeling it today, aren't you?"

Hunter nodded. "Mom, are you okay?"

"Yes, of course. Though I didn't hear you come in."

Hunter eased herself into a chair by the kitchen table. "Mom, I think you were hedge riding."

Abigail poured a cup of coffee for her daughter, and placed in on the table in front of her. "Was I? Hmm. I was just thinking about your father. About Aedon."

Hunter poured milk from the little jug on the table into her coffee, and took a long sip. The warm liquid felt good on her raw, dry throat. She took a few more sips, before putting the cup down. "What will happen now, with him?"

Abigail sat down next to her. "Honestly? I have no idea, my love. It was… it was so nice to see him again. It was just like old times. But it could never be like old times. I moved away. I got married. I had another child, with another man. I cannot ignore all that, nor ignore the fact that I am still married to Daniel. That poor, sweet man. I love him for everything that he has done for us, and more."

"Mom, I don't think you are married to him anymore," Hunter said, reaching out. "Dad remarried many years ago now. He's moved on, remember?"

Abigail looked over at her eldest daughter. There was sadness in her eyes, even as there was hope blossoming. "Oh, yes, I suppose you're right. I'd forgotten. There's been so much information to take in, since I came back. It's difficult, sometimes, to remember all that has happened while I was trapped."

Hunter patted her mother's hand. "It's okay, Mom. I get it. You should go to Aedon."

Abigail sighed. "I don't know if that's a very good idea, Poppet. He has a kingdom to settle right now, many wounded and even some dead because of what has happened. He has to learn about all that has gone on since he was trapped, and figure out probably a whole host of other things I can't even begin to fathom. I doubt he will have any time for me."

Hunter smiled. "Mom, I saw the way he looked at you. The way he held you. He hasn't forgotten, nor have his feelings changed, from what I can gather."

"Perhaps," Abigail said, shrugging. "We will see what comes."

Hunter could well understand her mother not wanting to get her hopes up. They heard Ryder coming down the stairs, and when she entered the kitchen she stood before them, rubbed her eyes, and simply said, "Fuck me."

"That about sums it up," said Hunter.

Ryder shuffled over to the coffee machine, grabbed the largest mug, and poured herself a cup. She sat down at the table, and motioned for the sugar pot. Hunter passed it to her, and Ryder proceeded to dump four spoons of sugar into her coffee. No one said anything. They understood.

They sat in companionable silence for a few minutes, before Ryder finally came up for air from her coffee. "So, that was crazy, wasn't it?" Heads nodded around the table. "Tell me what happened when you guys went to the Otherworld, and I'll tell you what happened over on this side."

Abigail made them all some toast and eggs, while Hunter relayed what happened. By the time she had finished, they were halfway through eating their breakfast. Ryder then took up the tale, and described what had happened in the little clearing by the portal. When she finished, Ryder looked at her mother and sister quizzically. "So, what's the deal with Courtney? What the hell was she? And where did the Strutherford Lion take her?"

"Stratford Lyon," Abigail corrected her. She looked at her youngest daughter, her hair sleep-rumpled and matted on one side. She reached out and brushed her hand softly down Ryder's long, straight blonde hair, tidying it up somewhat. "I don't really know what Courtney was. All that I can say is that she let the darkness take her over fully."

"What does that even mean, letting the darkness take over?"

Abigail shook her head. "I think it's best if we wait until Elspeth is here. She can probably explain it better than I can. All I can say is, that it's not a route any sane person would take."

"But where did the Stratford Lyon take her?" Hunter asked softly.

Abigail leaned back in her chair. "I have absolutely no idea." She thought about it for a moment. "Remember when Elspeth came near the portal, and said something about old magick? Well, I'm guessing that it's all related to the myth and legends of the Stratford Lyon. But just what it is, and what it can do, I don't know. Perhaps even Elspeth doesn't know. All I know is that it showed up when PC Hart did."

"Yeah," said Ryder, perking up. "He was totally badass, with that shotgun."

Hunter shook her head in warning. "I don't think shooting anyone, even Courtney, is badass in any shape, or form."

"Says the woman who brought two small armies to their knees, or so she tells me," said Ryder with a grin.

"Yeah, and who promptly threw up afterwards."

Ryder shot her sister a sympathetic look. "Aw… don't worry about that. Did Jack hold back your hair?"

Hunter put her head in her hand. "Yes, Ryder, he did. My boyfriend saw me throw up."

"And he held back your hair. That's true love. Right there."

Hunter then lowered her head onto her arms on the table, suddenly very tired. "I feel like shit after throwing around all that magick yesterday."

Abigail stood and began clearing the table. "Go back to bed, both of you. Now that you've got some food in your bellies, you'll sleep better." She ushered them up from the table, and shooed them out the kitchen. "Go! If I hear anything, I will let you know."

***

Hunter woke again late in the afternoon. She rose up from her cot, saw that Ryder had already awoken, and had left her to sleep in peace. She quickly checked her messages, and saw one from Jack.

Good morning, beautiful. I hope you slept well. I miss you.

Good afternoon, Jack. Sorry I didn't get in touch earlier. I felt like hell, but am much better now. I miss you too.

Will I see you tonight?

Of course. I look forward to it.

Hunter then rose and went to have a shower, and was brushing out her long, wet hair when her sister returned.

"You're looking more human now," Ryder said.

"Thanks, Ry."

Her sister sat heavily on the bed, watching Hunter in the mirror work serum through her curls. "I don't get it," Ryder said, throwing her hands up in the air. "Everyone's got these amazing powers, and what do I have? Zilch. Nada. Nothing. A big, fat, zero."

Hunter looked at her sister in the mirror's reflection. "I don't understand. You've got power, Ry."

Ryder heaved an enormous sigh, and looked down at the floor. "I have *some* power, yes. But it comes and goes, and I have absolutely no control over it. And when I needed it the most last night? Nothing."

"I thought you channelled energy, and sent it to Harriet," Hunter said, turning around to face her sister.

"Yeah, yeah, that's not a problem. But when I tried to use my dagger, to shoot out energy like I had before, nothing happened. And the worst thing about it? That puts me on par with Alice, who was just a big, dumb, battery for Courtney."

Hunter stood up and went over to her sister, sitting down on the bed next to her. "That's not true, Ry, and you know it. You are so much more than that. Just because you couldn't summon your magick the way you wanted to last night, doesn't mean anything, or make you less than anyone else. You *have* power, we've all seen it. Perhaps it just takes some people a little more time to understand how it works. I'll bet it works differently for each person too."

Ryder looked up at her sister. "Yeah, but you're throwing it around like you were born to it."

Hunter gave her a small smile. "Ry, I kind of *was* born to it. Don't forget, I'm half Fae."

Ryder looked down again. "Oh, right. Yeah, I keep forgetting that."

Hunter put her arm around her sister's shoulder. "It's so weird, isn't it? All this time, we had no idea who we were. And now we're in the midst of all this... craziness."

Ryder nodded. "I still wouldn't ever leave. This is where I want to be, crazy or not."

Now it was Hunter's turn to sigh. She still hadn't decided what she was going to do. She had her mother to worry about, and wondered how she was going to be able to live any sort of life, while technically being thought dead these last twenty years. Could they all really stay here in Burley? How would that work? And what about her house, and her own career back home?

Ryder put her hand up. "Jeez, Hun. You're practically yelling your thoughts at me."

Hunter let go of her sister's shoulder. "Whoops – sorry. I didn't realise I was doing that again."

"Yeah, well, when you're stressed, it kind of leaks out everywhere. Plus, you're right next to me."

"Sorry."

Ryder waved her hand. "S'okay, We've still got time, you know. It's still only August, and you took that extra month sabbatical for September. You've got time to think about it."

Hunter sighed. She wasn't sure there was enough time in the world to process everything that had happened, let alone what might happen in the future.

***

As the sisters came downstairs, Abigail came in from the back garden. "Oh good, Hunter's up. How are you feeling, Poppet?"

"Much better," said Hunter. "Still a little tired, but at least I don't feel like I did earlier."

Abigail nodded. "Go and have a nice lunch. I made a cheese and onion quiche. And there's a nice, big salad to go with it."

"Thanks, Mom," said Hunter, moving towards the kitchen.

Just then the phone rang. Ryder jumped up, and ran to it. "It's so weird, this whole landline thing!" her sister said, as she raced for the phone. Hunter stopped to listen in. Ryder picked it up, and answered. "Oh, hey David! How are you?" There was a pause, before Ryder turned to her mother. "David wants to know if we are okay to have a chat tonight, with everyone."

Abigail nodded. "Yes, that should be fine. We will get everyone here, say, 7pm?"

Ryder relayed the news over the phone. "Okay, cool. See you then!" She put the phone down, and looked at her mother and sister. "I guess we're going to get the low down tonight. I can't wait!"

***

Ryder was practically bouncing around the cottage as 7pm neared. Hunter heard a vehicle in the driveway, but Ryder was at the door before she could say anything. She flung it open, and Hunter moved up behind her to see Elspeth and Jack coming out of Jack's jeep.

"Hey, guys!" Ryder said cheerily.

Jack looked over and smiled at her, while Elspeth smoothed out her long, dark grey dress and adjusted a black shawl around her shoulders. "Hello, Ryder," she said with a smile.

Jack waited for his sister, and followed her up the little path to the cottage. "Come on in!" said Ryder, cheerfully. Elspeth nodded, and entered. "Can I get you anything?" asked Ryder, following the older Witch into the living room.

"Tea, please, if you wouldn't mind," said Elspeth.

Hunter stayed by the door, and looked up at Jack as he stood in the porch. He smiled at her, and said, "Hello, beautiful."

Hunter felt her face flush at the look in his eyes. "Hi, Jack," she managed to reply.

Jack pulled her out onto the porch and closed the door to the cottage to give them some privacy. He then swept her up into his arms, and gave her a searing kiss. When he finally let Hunter come up for air, he smiled down at her again. "There is nothing more beautiful than a woman who owns her power," he said, looking deep into her eyes. "You were amazing, last night."

At his words, Hunter felt a wave of love wash over her entire body. No one, ever, had said anything like that to her before. She looked at the tall, handsome Druid before her, and his green eyes held a wealth of emotion, including desire, pride, and respect. She didn't know what to say.

"I love you, Hunter. For all that you are, and with all that I am, I love you." He leaned down again, and kissed her.

Another vehicle pulled into the driveway, and they heard Dougal's voice as a truck door slammed. "For pity's sake, get a room," he said, as he and Harriet walked up the path.

Jack gently pulled away, and the look in his eyes made Hunter's toes curl in delight. She pushed her feelings down, however, and tried to get her brain back in gear. Still held in Jack's arms, she turned to face her friends. "Hi, guys. How are you?"

Harriet smiled cheerfully. "I'm good. Dougal gave me a lift, as he was in the village, picking up some groceries after work."

Hunter looked at him in shock. "You went to work today?"

"Aye," Dougal said, rubbing the back of his neck. "I thought Jack here might be pulling a sickie today, so I covered for him."

Hunter turned to Jack, who nodded at her. "I felt pretty shite this morning, I must admit," he said, smiling at her.

"Well, you're feeling your oats now, it seems," said Dougal with mock annoyance.

Hunter gave a small laugh, and pulled away from Jack. "No Mackenzie tonight?"

Dougal shook his head. "His car broke down, and he's been trying to get it fixed all day."

"That's a shame." She opened the door, and waved them through. "Please, go in. Mom did some baking this afternoon."

Dougal's face perked up immediately, and he bustled into the cottage. Harriet stopped by the door, and put her hand on Hunter's arm. "How are you, today?" she asked, her dark eyes searching Hunter's own.

"I'm okay," Hunter replied. "I still haven't even begun to process everything yet."

Harriet nodded. "Me neither. It was… a lot, last night."

"It sure was," said Hunter with a smile. "Are you okay? You look chipper."

Harriet smiled back. "Yeah, I'm fine. You look tired though. Ryder messaged me, and told me that you threw down some big magick in the Otherworld." Hunter nodded silently. "I'll bet you had a hell of a magickal hangover this morning, then."

"That I certainly did," admitted Hunter, and waved her inside. Jack followed them, closing the door behind him. He placed his hand on the small of Hunter's back, and directed her to the sofa, where he sat down next to her, putting an arm around her shoulders. Dougal sat on a chair next to Harriet, who had taken a spot on the edge of the sofa. The Scotsman was currently stuffing a scone into his mouth, while Harriet rolled her eyes at him.

"You're dropping crumbs everywhere, you big lummox," she said, picking them up from the floor.

"Sorry," Dougal said, putting down his plate, which looked tiny in his big hands, and bent over to help. He accidentally head-butted Harriet in the process.

"Ow!" she said, raising herself up and glaring at him.

Concern was evident in his blue eyes. "I'm so sorry, Harri! Are you okay?"

"No thanks to you," she muttered, rubbing her head.

Elspeth crossed her legs as she sat in the armchair, with a cup of tea in hand. "And how are we all this evening?" she asked.

"Good!" said Ryder. "Did Jack tell you what happened in the Otherworld?"

The older Witch nodded. "Yes, he did indeed." She turned to Hunter. "That was an incredible thing that you did, Hunter, with the staves. Well done."

Hunter swallowed, a little uncertain under Elspeth's gaze. "Um, thanks. It just came to me, what to do, that is. An image flashed in my mind, and I just went with it."

Ryder interjected. "What, like, no thinking, no deliberation, et cetera, et cetera?"

Hunter shook her head. "Nope. Ever since I've found the Witch's Compass within, I've felt more... free to just go with what is in my heart, rather than in my head."

"The Witch's Compass? You never told me about that." Ryder looked hurt.

"I'm sorry Ry, I truly am. Things have been so busy, and truthfully, I only just discovered it a couple of days ago." Ryder pouted, and sat back on her chair with arms crossed. "Really, I honestly just forgot to tell you. I haven't told anyone properly yet, except Mom."

Jack spoke up. "She hasn't really told me yet either, Ryder. Just mentioned it, but we haven't had time to discuss it further."

Ryder looked at him for a moment, and then softened. "Well, okay then. But I want to know all about it."

"I'll tell you, Ryder. I promise."

"And me too," Jack said with a squeeze of her shoulder. "I want to hear everything."

"Well, I was going to tell you, Jack, but then we ended up in the circle behind Elspeth's cottage…" Hunter's voice drifted off, and she blushed profusely as she realised what she had nearly said in front of everyone.

Ryder grinned from ear to ear, enjoying her sister's embarrassment. Just then, another knock at the door sounded, and she popped up to answer it. It was Thomas, and she waved him inside. "You got our message, then," she said.

"Yes, sorry. It's been a busy day, and I didn't have any time to reply." Thomas smiled down at Ryder, his tall, slim frame next to her.

Ryder looked up at him, and smiled back. "No biggie. Come, have a seat. Care for a drink?"

"Tea, please." Ryder led him into the living room, and motioned him to the dining table. "Grab a chair and I'll bring it out to you," she said. Thomas nodded, and Hunter noticed his eyes linger on Ryder as she walked back to the kitchen, before he pushed his glasses back up the bridge of his nose and went to fetch a chair to bring into the living room. She smiled to herself.

"Perhaps it would be best to recap what happened, for the benefit of everyone," said Elspeth, bringing the focus back together. "Before PC Hart arrives."

Hunter and Abigail nodded. Hunter began the tale, Abigail and Jack allowing her to speak for them. When she was finished, Elspeth was nodding, silently.

"Interesting," she said. "There is so much more happening that we realise. I only hope that the machinations of the Fae do not spill out into our world."

Abigail straightened in her seat. "I'm sure Aedon has everything under control. He is not the same person as his brother, Lanoc."

Elspeth smiled at Abigail. "I'm certain that is true. But there are many other Fae, whose motivations we do not know, and possibly never will."

Like our strange Fae guide, thought Hunter.

Elspeth's gaze went straight to Hunter, as if she read her thoughts. "You mentioned you had a guide. What was his name?"

Startled, Hunter could only shrug. "He never told us his name."

"He was certainly a cagey fellow," Jack said.

"An arrogant prick," muttered Abigail.

"Describe him to me," Elspeth said.

Hunter was unsure why the older Witch was being so insistent, but still she was willing to comply. When she tried to bring his face to mind, however, it was all hazy. "Um... that's odd. I can't really remember."

"He had..." Jack's voice drifted off. "Damn. I had a picture of him in my mind, and now it's gone."

"He doesn't want you to remember," said Abigail softly. All eyes turned to her. "It's a Fae thing. Aedon warned me about that, when we first got together. Some of the Fae were very interested in me, as I told you before, and were quite friendly, before Lanoc changed their minds. After that, I couldn't remember who was friendly towards me, and who was not. It's like their faces were wiped from my mind."

Elspeth sighed. "They most likely were. It's part of the Fae glamour that they can use on us."

"Much as I still don't trust him, he has been a great ally," Hunter said.

"I've no doubt," Elspeth agreed. A knock on the door sounded, and Hunter went to answer it. She opened to door to find PC Hart standing there, in uniform.

"Hello, Hunter," said David, smiling at her.

"Hi David. Please, come in. Tea?"

"Yes, please." He moved his tall frame into the cottage, and took off his hat. "Hello," he said to everyone.

"Hey, David!" said Ryder, bouncing up to him. She gave him a great big hug, and after a moment of surprise, he cautiously hugged her back, a little unsure. Ryder pulled away, and looked up at him in admiration. "You were so awesome last night," she said, her eyes shining with respect.

David looked away and cleared his throat uneasily. "Um, thank you, Ryder. I was just doing my job."

Ryder led him into the living room, and offered up her chair. "I've never seen anything like it. You were suddenly just there, and bam, bam!" she mimicked the shotgun that he had fired.

"Yes, well, let's just keep that between us, shall we?" asked David, looking uncomfortably around the room.

Elspeth reassured him. "Have no fear, David. We will not tell a soul." She held everyone's gaze for a moment, while Hunter came back with David's tea. "Perhaps we should start at the beginning," the older Witch said.

David pulled up another chair from the dining room, and sat down. He took the tea from Hunter with thanks, and had a sip. He then put the cup and saucer down, and ran a hand through this short, brown hair. He looked tired, and there were dark circles under his eyes. Hunter took in his appearance, and knelt down beside his chair. "Are you okay, David? You look really tired. And you've been working today," she said, worried for him. "Did you get any sleep at all?" Across the room, Jack shot them both a look, but remained quiet. Ryder, who was now sitting on the floor by his feet, nudged him softly. When he looked down at her, she simply mouthed, *she loves you.* He nodded, and then smiled, the worry lines on his forehead easing.

David smiled down at Hunter, and nodded. "Yes, I'm fine. I got in a couple of hours before my shift started. Thank you for the tea." Hunter remained for a moment, studying him.

"Take care of yourself," she said softly, patting his arm before rising and then walking over to where Jack sat on the sofa.

David cleared his throat, before addressing them all. "Well, I think we should begin with why you were all in the forest last night," he said, taking command of the conversation.

"Very well," said Elspeth. "Abigail, Jack, and Hunter were going to the Otherworld, in order to try and find Hunter's father." David looked at Hunter quizzically, but remained silent. "There is a portal there, that Hunter's familiar identified for her to use. We remained behind, to guard the portal and ensure that they would be able to return, safely." Elspeth leaned forwards in her seat, and gave PC Hart a hard stare. "But it would appear that there is another portal there," she said.

David nodded, unfazed by her look. "Yes, there is." He looked around the room, and sighed. "I guess I cannot keep it from you all any longer, not after what happened last night." He took another sip of his tea before he began. The room was silent, waiting to hear his story.

"My ancestor is John Stratford. He was a normal man, who inherited land from his grandfather in 1401."

"Holy shit. That's a *long* time ago," said Ryder softly.

David nodded. "Yes, it is. We are descended from the de Stratford family line, who were around at the time of Edward II, back when the New Forest was still called the Ettinwood. John Stratford, upon receiving his inheritance of land, went out one day to survey his estate. Some say that the land was in South Baddesley, but actually, it was in the South Burley area. John came across this clearing in the forest, early in the morning when the mist lay thick upon the land. A shaft of sunlight shone through the mist, and fell upon a strange, twisted tree in the centre of the clearing, or so the story goes." David paused for a moment, collecting his thoughts.

"Some say that John Stratford was guided to the clearing by a horned man, others by a deep and magickal intuition, while others say that he was simply lost." At the mention of a horned man, Ryder and Hunter looked at Jack, whose eyes flashed briefly in knowing.

"I have seen the Horned Man in the New Forest," he said softly.

David looked up at Jack for a moment, before nodding. "So, that part is true then, I take it. I still don't really know how much is truth, and how much is conjecture. I was only recently made aware of my heritage in this respect last year, after I had taken up my post here." Nods around the room urged him on with his tale. "When John Stratford took a closer look, he saw that it was not some strange, twisted tree, but upon reaching out to touch it, found that it was actually an enormous set of antlers, seemingly buried in the ground.

"He pulled on the antlers, wanting to drag them loose from the soil and hang them in his manor. However, they held fast, and so he pulled and pulled. It is said that John Stratford was a very strong man, and suddenly the antlers were torn from the ground. And what John saw there both amazed and terrified him.

"The head of a great beast had been pulled out, attached to the antlers he still held. It had huge yellow eyes, a flaming red mane, and great, pointed teeth. It was the head of a lion, crested with a rack of antlers. It roared, but John kept pulling, and then eventually the entire beast was freed.

"The Lyon tossed its head, and threw John across the clearing. It then charged him, but John jumped aside and grabbed onto the antlers, swinging himself up onto the beast's back. It howled and roared, and then ran three times around the entire the New Forest, trying to free itself from the man who now rode it. After it circled the forest three times, it stopped, and lowered its head in submission. And from that day the Stratford Lyon has pledged itself to the descendants of the Stratford line, to aid them at times of great need, and to protect the land and its inhabitants."

There was a long pause as the story sunk in. Everyone was stunned, and simply looked at David in astonishment. Finally, Ryder broke the silence. "Well, damn, David."

David gave her a small smile. "While the Stratford family line does not have magick like the five families here in Burley, we do have this special ability to summon the Lyon which we can use to protect this place in times of great need."

"That's incredible, David," said Hunter. "And you've had to keep this secret, I'm guessing?"

David nodded. "While everyone in the New Forest knows the tale of the Stratford Lyon, no one really believes it, unless you're from the magickal families scattered throughout the area and perhaps have caught a glimpse of it. And after so many centuries, the Stratford family tree became terribly convoluted, so it is hard to trace just who could possibly control the beast. But, just as my grandfather before me, and his father before him, I have taken up my position here in Burley as a guardian of sorts, alongside the Lyon, of both the place itself and the secrets within the magickal families that reside here."

"That's just – wow. I mean, really – wow," said Ryder, still wide-eyed.

David shrugged, and picked up his tea, taking a sip. "For centuries we have never needed to call upon the Lyon. I myself wasn't even sure that it was real, in all honesty, until I went to the clearing where my grandfather told me the Lyon can come through. This was right after Ryder had been attacked. I didn't want anyone else injured while we tried to deal with this mess, and so I pulled up the Lyon. And it came."

"That was extremely brave, and extremely well done," said Elspeth. David simply nodded at her, drinking his tea.

"So, this Lyon saw Courtney was about to unleash all kinds of hell upon us in the clearing, and then it just went for her," surmised Ryder, looking at David.

He put down his tea, and nodded again. "Yes. You all belong to the New Forest. You are not evil. The Stratford Lyon knew that, from its connection to me. It knew what to do. I was only there buying time, before it found us."

Dougal spoke up. "You were pretty handy with that shotgun," he commented.

David flushed a little. "Well, I'm not an authorised firearms officer," he said, "and so I don't, and can't, carry a gun. But I do have my grandfather's shotgun, and a licence for it. And we hunt pheasant all the time."

"But even your shotgun didn't stop one particular crazy bird," said Ryder grimly.

"No," agreed PC Hart. "So, can you tell me just what all that was, and what happened to change Courtney Peterson? I've never seen anything like it in my life."

"And I hope you never do again," said Elspeth grimly. All eyes turned to her. "Courtney is, or was, a rogue Witch. She came here about ten years ago, and made friends with Alice Hardwick. It seems that she had some magickal powers, though where they came from we do not know. It may be in her blood, or she may have learned some skills and techniques from other magickal practitioners. It is believed that shortly after she met Alice Hardwick, she turned dark."

David studied Elspeth for a moment. "Do you think she influenced the Hardwicks, or was it the other way around?"

Jack ran his hands through his dark hair, and blew out a long breath. "Honestly, David, we don't know. Alice was always difficult, even before Courtney came into the picture."

"And her brother, Xander, is a total arsehole too," Harriet added.

Elspeth set down her cup of tea. "It's hard to say whether the Hardwicks have gone down that route as well, but I would like to believe that Geraint Hardwick would not allow it. However, I cannot be one hundred percent certain." She sat back in her chair and studied David. "I, for one, believe that Courtney possibly had intentions, or at least tendencies to go dark before she even came here, and was using Alice Hardwick to boost her own magickal powers. But I may be wrong."

Ryder nodded, and looked up at David from where she sat on the floor. "She was! I saw Alice, standing at the edge of the clearing, and Courtney was waving to her for something. I then figured it out: Alice was sending her energy, much like we can send energy to boost each other's powers. That's when I went and tackled her, so that she would stop feeding that bitch with magickal power."

"And that was extremely well done," Elspeth said with a smile at the young woman.

Ryder scowled. "Well, it was all I *could* do. My magick wasn't working."

"Maybe that was the best thing you could have done, magick or no," Elspeth reassured her. Ryder still did not look convinced.

"So," said David, "Courtney had become... evil, you say?" Elspeth nodded. "And those things around her? The large Black Dogs, the faces in the mist?"

"Demons, most likely," said Elspeth. "Summoned by her from whatever pact she had made with an evil entity."

David sat back and took this in for a moment. "All those animals that had been killed in the area, their bodies mutilated, the reversed pentagrams, all that was her," he said softly. "I had my suspicions, but I really didn't think it could be true."

Elspeth nodded. "Yes, it would seem that is the case. She was gathering more power to her, in those ritual sacrifices, using the animals that both roam freely and are kept on other landowners' properties." The look of disgust upon her Elspeth's face was unmistakable.

"And the stone circle," Jack said softly. "She used my stone circle too."

Hunter reached out and took his hand. "Brighid cleared it, Jack. It's fine now." Jack simply nodded, looking away. Hunter could understand his conflicting emotions. Courtney had played him for a long, long time, and had seriously messed with his life. She squeezed his hand, and smiled at him warmly. "It's over," she said.

"So where did the Lyon take Courtney?" asked Ryder. "And what will happen to Alice, then?"

David shrugged. "I honestly don't know where it took Courtney, or whether she is still alive after having been attacked by it – I just don't know. But she's gone, and I trust in the Lyon."

Ryder nodded. "And Alice?"

"Alice, well, I took Alice back to her family after I cleared away all traces of you being in the Forest," said David with a sigh. "I can tell you that Geraint Hardwick was fuming, because I brought her handcuffed to his door."

"Really?" asked Ryder. "How can he dispute what you, an officer of the law, saw with your own eyes?"

David studied the floor for a moment, before addressing the room. "The Hardwicks do not believe that Alice, or her friend, Courtney, ever attacked you, or Hunter, or Jack even. And they certainly don't believe that Ryder was injured a few weeks ago either. They believe that your two families are trying to set them up."

Hunter was absolutely shocked. "How can they think that? After everything that's happened, and after all the evidence against them?"

David looked at her sadly. "That's just it, Hunter. There is no evidence. Only hearsay. It's your word against theirs. Alexander had already told his family that he saw Ryder in the pub the other day, pretending to walk around on crutches when she didn't need them." He held up his hand. "I know, I know – you did a healing ritual for Ryder, and I believe you. But, the Hardwicks do not. Alice had a story ready for them when I brought her home. She told her father that she was spying on your ritual, because she felt like you all were up to something. She told Geraint that you and Ryder had summoned some sort of demon, and it got out of control and attacked everyone."

"You've got to be kidding me," said Ryder with disgust.

David continued. "Faced with her version of events, or mine, Geraint Hardwick decided to go with his daughter's story. Combined with what Alexander had said about Ryder, he was ready to believe it. In my opinion, it's easier for him to think that, than to admit that his children are dabbling with the dark arts, and possibly out of control."

"But you're an officer of the law, or whatever they say over here in England," Ryder said.

"That means very little to a man like Geraint Hardwick, it would seem," replied David with a sigh.

"But what exactly do the Hardwicks think we have to gain from starting a conflict with them?" asked Hunter.

"Because Geraint Hardwick, like all the Hardwicks, believes that they are superior to us in every way," Elspeth said with disdain. "His family have always been that way, for generations. They fought long and hard to climb to the top of the social ladder, and are always thinking that others want to do the same. They come from a long line of people with wealth and privilege, and it shows."

Dougal, who had just picked up another scone from the table, dropped it accidentally. "Sorry," he muttered. "Again." He picked it up from the floor, and put it aside on the table.

Abigail smiled at him, and handed him another one. "No worries, Dougal. Please, eat." Dougal thanked her, and ate his scone in silence, even as Harriet glared at him.

"But you were there, and you saw what Courtney and Alice were doing, with your own eyes. Your own, *police* eyes," said Ryder.

David shook his head. "That doesn't matter to Geraint Hardwick. He believes his son and daughter. And as all this is outside of official police jurisdiction, my word carries as much weight as yours."

Elspeth sighed. "I only hope that the youngest, Eleanor, has managed to stay out of all this."

David looked at her. "I believe she is living with her mother, and has been for the last year or so," David said. "At least, that's what Geraint told me when I asked him about his current household."

"Let us hope that is true," said Elspeth. "Did Alice mention seeing Abigail?"

David shook his head. "No, I don't think she even registered that there was an extra person there."

Ryder chimed in. "She spent most of the time on her back, pinned to the ground beneath me," she said with a sardonic grin.

Abigail spoke up. "So, what happens now? The threat of Courtney, it seems, is now taken care of. But what of the Hardwicks? What will they do?"

Everyone looked to Elspeth. She took another sip of her tea. "It would seem that is the question. If Geraint does indeed think we are out to besmirch his name, as well as being up to no good, then we have quite the problem on our hands. He was always a hard-headed fool."

David leaned towards Elspeth. "Do you, Elspeth, think that Geraint Hardwick has become, or perhaps has always been, evil in some way?" he asked.

Elspeth thought this over for a few moments. "No," she said slowly. "He was always a pompous arse, and an arrogant prick, but no, I don't believe he is evil. But then again, I haven't seen or spoken to him in years."

"Perhaps you need to pay him a visit," said Abigail softly.

"Perhaps," said Elspeth. Silence fell upon the room for three, long, heartbeats.

David shifted slightly in his seat. "The Petersons have filed a missing persons report earlier this evening. There may be other police officers coming around to question people." He looked directly at Jack. "I think you, Jack, should be prepared, as you recently had a relationship with Miss Peterson."

Jack sighed and ran his hands through his dark hair. "Damn. You know that's not really true, don't you, David?"

David nodded slowly. "I had figured as much, from what Hunter has told me. But still, you should be prepared, with strong alibis." David looked at them all, before he said, "I think everyone should have clear alibis, in case of questioning."

Heads nodded in silence around the room. Tears came to Hunter's eyes, as fear filled her heart for Jack, and for everyone. "We've started a Witch War, haven't we?" asked Hunter in a small voice. "And we could be in real, serious trouble with the police as well."

David looked to her with sympathy. "I'm sure you all will be fine. Just keep your alibis and your stories simple, and everything should be fine. I will do all that I can to minimise the damage."

Elspeth joined in. "And no, my dear, *we* haven't started a Witch War. But Courtney and Alice certainly have."

Abigail spoke up. "You are not to blame, Hunter. Neither you nor your sister have done anything wrong. If the Hardwicks won't see the truth that's right in front of them, then it's their own fault."

Elspeth cleared her throat. "I will do what I can," she said with determination. "I know we all would rather avoid such a situation. I will go and see Geraint tomorrow."

"I will go with you," said Jack.

Elspeth shook her head. "There is no need, Jack. It would be better if I went myself. It would be less confrontational. I will be fine." Jack looked at his older sister dubiously, but remained silent.

"So," said David, breaking the silence after Elspeth's words, "tell me what you did in the Otherworld last night."

***

PC Hart took his leave of them shortly afterwards. He said that he would be keeping a close eye on both Xander and Alice Hardwick. Hunter saw him to the door, and told him to get some rest. He looked completely worn out. He nodded and thanked her, before getting into his police car and heading off into the night.

Dougal said that he would drop off Harriet at her place, and wished them all goodnight. He clapped Jack on the shoulder and said, "I'm going to sleep all weekend, now. Don't call me." Jack grinned and gave him a hug, slapping him gently on the back. Dougal turned to look at Hunter. "Is it okay if I tell Mackenzie everything that's happened?"

"Please do," replied Hunter.

"It's time for us to leave too," said Elspeth, rising from her chair.

"Elspeth," said Hunter, "what did you do, to save us after we were empty of energy? I heard you whispering, and saying the word, 'coven'."

Elspeth studied Hunter for a long moment, before looking away. "I drew energy from the coven, Hunter. And I did so, without their permission." Everyone looked at her in shock. "I know, that goes against all protocol and etiquette, but there wasn't any time. As a coven, we are bonded together, and so I drew energy to save us all. And I will bear the burden of the consequences of doing so as I did not obtain their permission first. I'm sure they will understand, and I will make reparations as needed."

"I still want to know about that fire thing that you did," said Ryder.

Ryder's comment reminded Hunter of what she had seen her mother do, which she had completely forgotten about. "And the tornado that Mom summoned."

"What?!" cried Ryder. "I must have missed that. Damn!"

Elspeth sighed, and sat back down again. "I'll need more tea," she said. Ryder ran to grab the teapot.

"It's not much, really," said Abigail, sitting down on the sofa next to Hunter. "All Witches have an element or two that speaks to them, that works for them above all the others."

"How come you never told us? Or showed us those powers?" asked Ryder, coming back into the room.

Abigail shook her head slowly. "We didn't want to influence you. Your element should show up on its own, without other people's preferred elements overriding your own natural affinity. This usually happens when the Witch is very young, but as you girls have come into your power later in life, we wanted to make sure that we weren't going to muddy the waters, so to speak."

Hunter spoke up. "So, the elements: do you mean earth, air, fire, and water?"

"Yes," Elspeth said. "I have an affinity with the element of fire. Your mother, with air. Your aunt, Ivy, was earth."

"The gardens," said Hunter softly, understanding dawning on her.

"My main element is air," said Abigail, "but I also have an affinity for earth, as you can tell."

"I'll bet earth is yours too, Hun," said Ryder.

"And air," said Elspeth. "Academia is related to the element of air."

"I wonder what mine is?" mused Ryder.

Elspeth sipped at her new cup of tea. "Well, that depends. What do you feel, in your heart?"

Ryder scrunched up her face in concentration. "Um... nothing really."

"She's a practical girl, from what I can see, so perhaps her main element is earth," said Abigail.

"She's passionate, so maybe she's fire," said Hunter.

"She's free with her emotions, so perhaps she's water," said Jack.

"She always talking, and asking questions, so maybe she's air," said Elspeth with an amused look.

Ryder sighed. "So, how do I figure this out?"

Elspeth sipped at her tea once more. "Time will tell," she said.

***

Jack brought Hunter outside, while Elspeth finished her tea. "Well, that was something, wasn't it?" Hunter said, as they walked out into the back garden.

"Burley always has new secrets to uncover, that's for sure," said Jack. He stopped, and swung Hunter into his arms. "I'm so glad you came here," he said, with a piercing look.

Hunter's heart began to race. "Even though our presence here has caused all sorts of upset? And now possibly a Witch War? You could be in real trouble, Jack."

Jack pulled her close to him, and she lay her head on his chest. "Something would have happened anyway, it would seem, whether you were here or not. You must know that. You are not to blame for any of this."

Hunter sighed, and accepted Jack's statement. It was true. She needed to stop blaming herself for things that were beyond her control. Courtney and Alice had started brewing trouble long before she and Ryder had even inherited their aunt's cottage.

"Hunter, look at me."

Hunter lifted her head and looked up into Jack's green eyes. The moon hung above them, lighting up the darkness with its silvery light. "Spend the night with me," he said.

Desire welled up within Hunter's heart. "I think I know just the place," she said with a smile. "The old yew tree, where you first kissed me." Jack smiled at her, even as his eyes flashed with that uncanny green fire, when the leash he kept on his powers was loosened. She pulled out her phone, and sent a message to her sister, mother, and Elspeth. She then took Jack's hand, and headed down the garden into the beechwood behind the house, the crickets chirping softly in the night.

Chapter Fourteen

Abigail was kneeling in the soft earth of the back gardens, amongst the flowering pumpkins that Hunter had planted months before. It was early morning, and a week had passed since their adventure in the Otherworld.

She ran through the events of the week in her mind, as she knelt down in the garden. She had slipped out the back door and hidden in the woods behind the house when the police had come to question Hunter and Ryder five days ago. Everything seemed fine, and the police were content with the story of their whereabouts the evening that Courtney went missing. Jack had been questioned too, and the police seemed satisfied with his alibis, though they told him he was not to leave the country until they had finished their report. Hunter had been sick with worry the entire time, but was feeling much better now that it seemed that they were all safe.

Aedon's face kept coming to her mind, but she pushed it aside, trying to focus on keeping the weeds at bay so that they would not choke their pumpkin harvest.

Seeing Aedon again had ignited a passion in her soul. Abigail had longed for Aedon ever since the day they met, when she was just eighteen years old. And when he disappeared, she had to keep it together for the sake of her newborn daughter, Hunter. She eventually moved away and married, starting her life over in Canada. When she had returned to the New Forest many years later, searching for Aedon to tell him of his daughter, she found herself surrounded by the memories of their time together in the forest where they had met. And when she had been trapped between the worlds, with Lanoc using Aedon as bait for his trap, she still had felt a thrill run through her at the sight of him, caught between the worlds as they both had been for many long years.

For even in their imprisonment, they had still managed to find a way to see each other, every evening as the sun set. In this liminal time, their love found a way for them to be together, even for a few brief minutes. They could not touch, nor be close, but at least they could see each other from across the barrows, knowing that the other was alive, yet stuck in a magickal limbo, in a world of mists.

Those few minutes each day were what had kept Abigail going. That and her conviction that her daughters would find her. She knew her daughters. They were strong and smart, and they were also descended from a long line of Witches. They would find a way.

But right now Abigail found that she was missing seeing Aedon every day, even though she much preferred her newly won freedom. She wondered what he was doing in the Otherworld, and what upheaval he was facing as he retook his throne. She hoped that the people of the Fae kingdom were happy to have him back, as she could not imagine Lanoc having been a particularly good ruler. He had always hated humans, and being King for nearly two decades could have turned the ear of many to his way of thinking.

Aedon was the complete opposite of his brother. He was warm and loving, compassionate and caring, where Lanoc was cold and calculating, always seeking power. She hoped that Aedon was happy, back where he belonged in his world. She knew that time ran differently in the Otherworld, and that she might not see him again for many, many months, even though only a few days may have passed for him on the other side of the veil.

Abigail sighed, and bent down to focus again on her work. She emptied her mind, and began to hum a little tune. As she did, she felt something shift in the air around her. "Oh no," she breathed, fear rising in her throat. "Curly Wurly, Curly Wurly, Curly Wurly."

A mist formed around her, and she knew then that she was not hedge riding. Someone, or something, was coming through the veil. Abigail stood, her garden trowel in her hands, pulling up energy from the earth, and calling upon the winds to aid her.

"Hello, my love," a soft voice came from behind her.

Abigail whirled around and saw Aedon standing there, tall and handsome with a delicate, small silver crown upon his head. Her heart flipped over in her chest, and her mouth went dry. She swallowed, and managed to find her voice. "Hello, Aedon."

The tall Fae King closed the distance between them, and swept her up into his arms. He held her gently, and Abigail burst into tears as she rested her head upon his shoulder. "There, my love, be at ease," he said, stroking her long, red hair.

After a few moments, Abigail ceased weeping, and pulled away gently. She wiped her face with the back of her hand, her palms still covered in the soil from the garden. She then wiped them on the jeans that she wore, and took a deep breath, looking up into the Fae King's face.

"It's nice to see you," she admitted.

"And you, my love," he said with a small smile.

"How goes everything in the Otherworld?"

Adeon's smile widened. "It goes very well. Though there is a faction that still shares Lanoc's views, they are the minority, and they have accepted my rule nonetheless. I will allow them their viewpoint, for I've no wish to be a dictator. But it is hard, and I am constantly trying to educate them on their skewed bias against humans."

Abigail gave a small, bitter laugh. "That can't be easy."

Aedon shook her head. "No, it is not. But I think there might be a way to change their minds, more quickly than anything I could ever do myself," he said, looking deep into her eyes.

"What's that?" Abigail asked, her heart thudding in her chest.

"Come with me."

A few moments passed between them, before Abigail could speak. "I'm sorry, did you say-"

"Come with me."

"But, I –"

"Come with me."

The trowel dropped out of Abigail's stunned hands. Aedon closed the gap between them, and took her hands. "For too long have we been separated, my love. I ask that you rule by my side. With your kindness, your open heart, and your love for life, you would make an excellent queen, and also make me the happiest man ever."

Abigail felt completely numb. "But – but so much has happened since we were together. I had no idea what you had been through; only that you had stopped coming to see me. I searched for you, but could not find you. Then Hunter came along, and I lived with Ivy, trying to hide my co-called 'indiscretion'. I then moved away when I had the opportunity, across an entire ocean, with a man who loved me and promised to take care of us. I married. Many years later I came back to the New Forest, to try and find you, to tell you about your daughter."

"Do you love him?" Aedon asked, his face unreadable.

"I – well, yes, I did."

The Witch's Compass

"You did?" he asked, with a strong emphasis on her love for Daniel being in the past.

Abigail searched within her heart. Yes, she had loved Daniel, that kind, handsome young man who had taken care of them when her world fell apart. And all that was in the past now.

"Dad has moved, on, Mom."

Abigail spun around at the sound of Ryder's voice, to see both her daughters standing by the back door, overhearing their conversation.

"Everyone back in Canada thinks you are dead," Hunter added in softly. "Perhaps it's time you got on with your life."

Abigail didn't know what to say, even as the thought of new opportunity filled her heart with hope. "But, could I really do it? I couldn't bear to leave you two, now that we have been reunited. You girls are my world."

Hunter and Ryder moved forwards. Hunter reached out and took her younger sister's hand, looking at her for a moment as something passed between them. She then turned back to her mother, and said, "Mom, you can't live for us. You must live for yourself."

"We will be here, whenever you want to see us," Ryder said.

Abigail's eyes widened. "Does that mean you are staying, my loves?"

Hunter nodded, smiling at her mother. "Yes, Mom, we're staying here."

Abigail turned to Aedon, who was now smiling openly at her. He squeezed her hands as he said, "You can visit them whenever you like. You can come and go as you please, between the worlds, my beautiful Hedge Witch. And we can finally be together, now and forever, forever and always."

Tears once again welled up in Abigail's eyes. This was the answer to so many of her problems, for how she would live while still trying to remain hidden all the time. She could have a freedom in the Otherworld that she could not have here. But she dearly loved this world too, and there was still so much she wanted to do. "On one condition," she said, smiling at Aedon.

"Anything," Aedon said.

"That you and I both spend time together in this world as well, so you can get to know your daughter. Your *daughters*," she said, emphasising that Ryder too, would be his daughter.

"There is nothing I would like better," he said, smiling, before he drew her in for a long, sweet kiss. Hunter and Ryder looked at each other, huge grins on their faces, and Ryder let out a loud cheer.

***

Elspeth walked up to the manor door. She took a deep breath, before she reached for the large, brass knocker. She tapped it firmly three times, and stood back, waiting.

An older gentleman answered the door. "Hello, Jeremy," said Elspeth, with a small smile. "I am here to speak to Geraint."

The butler's bushy eyebrows raised, but he said nothing. Instead, he waved her in and directed her to one of the hall chairs. Elspeth sat down, as he went to speak to the head of the household. The manor was Georgian, with large, open spaces. Elspeth could appreciate the architecture, even if it wasn't to her tastes. She preferred smaller, cosier spaces. She sat with her hands calmly folded in her lap, and waited.

Eventually, she heard footsteps coming down the long hallway just outside the waiting area. Geraint Hardwick appeared, standing in the archway. He was tall and slim, and was wearing an expensive, tailored pin-stripe suit. "Elspeth. To what do I owe the pleasure of this visit?" he said, his tone making it clear that it was anything but pleasant to see her.

"I am here to talk about Alice," Elspeth said evenly.

Geraint Hardwick stared down at her with a stern expression. He was of similar age to Elspeth, with a shock of silver hair that was swept back from his forehead, and dark eyes that bored into hers. He was a good-looking man, and he knew it. However, today he was certainly not exhibiting his usual charm. "Come," he said gruffly, and waved for her to follow.

Elspeth bit her tongue at his rudeness. The head of a Witch family should always treat another head with respect, and Geraint's manners were borderline rude. But she steeled herself against his behaviour, needing to speak to him for the overall good of all the magickal families.

He led her into a small day room, just off the hallway. He took a seat by the unlit fire, and Elspeth settled herself in the other chair across from him. She smoothed out the folds of her long skirt, and crossed her legs calmly. Manners dictated that he should offer her some refreshment, however, she knew this would not be the case, and so she dove straight in.

"Alice helped Courtney Peterson to attack us, not long ago, while we performed a ritual," she began. "She was directing energy towards Courtney, who then used it to unleash dark magicks upon us. I am afraid that your daughter has been poorly used by her so-called friend, and that she may be heading down a dark and dangerous path herself."

Geraint Hardwick steepled his hands before him, as his elbows rested on the arms of his chair. "And what were you doing in this ritual?" he asked with suspicion.

"Nothing that would harm anyone or anything," Elspeth said. Her business was her own.

"I see," said Geraint, his handsome face showing obvious signs of disbelief. "And how is the young Williams girl? This... Ryder, is it?"

Elspeth controlled her temper. "She is very well, thank you."

"David told us that she had been attacked and badly injured by Miss Peterson nearly a month ago, and yet, here she is, walking around and pretending to still be injured. It's a very curious thing, is it not?"

"We did a ritual to heal her, shortly afterwards. She had to keep up the pretence of being injured, so that the non-magickal folks in Burley would not be suspicious."

Geraint's eyes flashed. "I see," he said, his countenance still stern. "So, you would have me believe that my own daughter, the eldest of my children, is working evil magick against other Witches in this community."

Elspeth took a deep breath. "Jack found traces of rituals on your estate, rituals performed by Courtney and Alice. These were dark magicks, used to try to control and coerce both him and the elder Miss Williams."

"Ah yes, Hunter Williams. Where do they come up with these names? But at any rate, you still have no evidence. Anyone could have done those magicks. PC Hart told us about them, but there is still nothing to link these practices to Alice, or Miss Peterson, except for the fact that your so-called evidence was found on my property. I have heard that similar incidences have been occurring all over the area, and not just on my estate."

Elspeth remained silent, for there was nothing to say.

"Your brother, Jack, he also lives on my estate," Geraint said, with a dark gleam in his eyes.

Elspeth felt her power rise within her at the insinuation. "My brother does not work the dark arts."

"How can you be sure?"

"I know my brother."

"And I know my daughter."

"Not as well as you might think," said Elspeth, trying to tamp down the flames of anger that flared in her heart.

"Until I have solid evidence, Elspeth, I will not turn against my daughter. I would suggest that you keep a closer eye on those newcomers, as I do believe that they are the ones bringing trouble to the area, and to the families. That ritual that you did recently in the forest with them only confirms my suspicions that they are trouble. You would do well to stay away from them, to protect the five families that have resided here for hundreds of years."

"And you don't think that it's possible that your daughter has made up this story, to cover for her own culpability?"

"Alice would never do such a thing. She knows our reputation means everything."

Elspeth sighed. "It's clear that nothing I can say will change your mind on this matter. Despite telling you what I have seen with my own eyes."

Geraint leaned slightly forward in his chair. "My dear," he said, condescendingly, "I know that you have these pretensions of greatness, these illusions of grandeur with your little coven. But you are nothing more than a shopkeeper, who has grand designs of making a name for herself in the magickal community."

"How dare you," said Elspeth, gritting her teeth. "You know me better than that. We grew up together, here in Burley."

Geraint leaned back into his chair. "Yes, we did, at that. And you were quite the interesting young Witch. But things have changed, Elspeth, and the cards that you are playing are plain for all to see. I am giving you this one warning, my dear. Stay away from my family, and cease all of these ridiculous allegations immediately, or you and those newcomers will face the consequences."

"Are you threatening me, Geraint Hardwick?"

"I am making myself perfectly clear, Elspeth Caldecotte."

***

Hunter and Ryder helped their mother to pack the few belongings that she had accumulated in the months since she had returned to them. Though it pained Hunter to let her mother go, she was still very happy that her mother would get the fairytale ending, after all that she and Aedon had been through. With many promises to return as often as possible, Abigail kissed both her daughters farewell in the back garden with a smile of pure joy on her face. "I will be back tomorrow, which may be a few days from now in this world, but I won't be long. Make sure you have some chocolate ready for me," she said with a wink. "And don't worry about the police. I'm sure PC Hart has everything under control. Just know that you can go to Elspeth for anything, do you understand?"

"Sure thing, Mom," said Hunter, her eyes tearing up.

"Have fun, Mom," said Ryder, similarly holding back tears.

Aedon came up to Hunter. "May I?" he asked, holding out his arms.

"You may, Father," said Hunter, stepping into his embrace. Though it still felt strange, it also felt right. "I look forward to getting to know you better."

"And I you, Hunter," he said, kissing the top of her head. He let her go, and looked to Ryder, who without hesitation flung herself into his arms.

"Take care of my Mom," she said, squeezing the Fae King.

"With all my heart and soul," Aedon said softly, hugging her back.

Ryder released him, and went to stand with Hunter. The two sisters looked at each other briefly, before smiling at Abigail and Aedon. "Goodbye," said Hunter. "We will see you soon."

"Goodbye, Poppet. Goodbye, Peanut. Be good, and stay safe."

A mist rose around them, and Abigail and Aedon slowly disappeared from sight, their eyes on each other and warm, loving smiles upon their faces.

***

The next day, Elspeth and Jack came to visit. They all explored the garden, enjoying the late August sunshine. Hunter and Jack walked hand in hand, followed by Ryder and Elspeth. Hunter showed off her pumpkin patch, of which she was very proud. Tiny pumpkins had formed from the flowers in the last few days. As they ambled around the gardens, they spoke of Abigail and Aedon. Naturally Jack and Elspeth were pleased for both of them, even though Elspeth looked a little sad. "We had become friends in the short time that she was here," she said. "I will miss her."

"She said she will be back in a few days."

Elspeth nodded, knowing how time could shift and change in the Otherworld. "They will be good together," she admitted. "It was the right decision."

Jack turned to Hunter, and squeezed her hand. He looked at her with those gorgeous green eyes of his, and asked, "So have you come to a decision, Hunter?"

"Well, I think I need a lot more time," said Hunter. "There's still so much to do."

Jack's face fell, and he looked down, even as Hunter continued. "I want to open up a more formal garden here in the back, and extend the vegetable patch so that we're pretty much self-sufficient. I was also thinking of creating a ritual circle of sorts towards the bottom of the garden. What do you think?"

Jack's gaze shot back up and looked at her intently for a moment, his green eyes flashing with that uncanny light as his magick rose within him in response to his heart's longing. "Does that mean you are staying, *mo grá?*" he asked.

Hunter looked at her sister, smiling. "Ryder and I discussed this yesterday, before Mom left. We had a big heart to heart. And before that, I had a talk with myself, using the Witch's Compass to help guide me. By that, I mean that I came to my decision using not just my head, but my heart. I looked at where my life has led me, at my past and the choices that I have made. I have also thought about the future, and the possibilities that await me. No longer will I allow my past to dictate my present or my future. I have let all that go, and am willing to trust in my heart, and in what gifts and opportunities are placed before me, right now, here in this moment. I have learned that everything that we think, everything that we do, is a spell. And so I am making a conscious effort here, to create the world that I want to live in. There is still so much to consider, but I have made my choice."

"And?" Hunter could feel Jack's energy shimmering in anticipation.

Hunter smiled at him. "Yes, Jack. Yes, I am staying. This is where I belong. With you."

Hunter felt Jack's energy envelop her, and her own energy responded. A golden-green light surrounded them both, shining brightly. Jack swept Hunter into his arms, twirling her around and laughing with joy. He finally set her down, where they kissed with a passion that only few people knew.

Ryder and Elspeth had stopped, watching them. "I'll bet those two are married by the end of next year," whispered Ryder with a grin.

"My money is on Lammas, the first harvest, next year," replied Elspeth softly.

Ryder looked at the older Witch. "Are you using your mojo to get an insider's information on that bet?" she asked.

Elspeth laughed. "No, my dear, just my feminine intuition. A love like theirs will not wait long."

Ryder studied them, a winsome smile on her face. "I wonder if I'll ever know a love like that."

She felt Elspeth's hand on her shoulder. "I'm sure you will, my dear. When you are ready, which is usually when you least expect it, love comes to you."

"I'm ready now," said Ryder with a grin. "Bring it on!"

Epilogue

Aedon stood on the crest of the hill, looking out over the forest. Abigail was still fast asleep in their warm bed, and he had silently left her sleeping peacefully. He strode through the portal gate to one of his favourite places. It had become a habit of his, to come to this place first thing in the morning, to sort through his thoughts and prepare himself for the day. He took in a deep breath, the scents of the forest and the dew upon the grass filling his senses.

A faint mist crept up behind him, and he knew that someone had appeared. Reaching out with his mind, he knew instantly who it was. "Hello, Finnvarr," he said softly in the early morning light.

"My *King*," the smooth voice replied from behind him. Aedon remained where he was, looking out over the view. He heard the Fae man move up to stand beside him. Only then did Aedon turn to look at the lithe, blond man beside him, as ever dressed in shades of grey.

"And what can I do for you?" Aedon asked.

Finnvarr looked out across the forest that stretched before them. "What I want is something that you cannot give me," he said bitterly. "And you are perfectly aware of that."

Aedon sighed, and turned his gaze back to the view. "That is correct." Heavy silence hung between them. "It was your own actions that brought this about," Aedon said simply.

"That it was, my *King*."

Aedon sighed. "Things will never be the same between us, will they? I have lost your friendship, though that was not my intention. I had no say in this. I did what needed to be done."

"You are a fine and noble *King*," said Finnvarr, his lip curling up in distaste.

"I thank you for aiding my daughter, and for your timely rescue. I know that couldn't have been easy for you."

"I did what needed to be done," Finnvarr replied, echoing Aedon's earlier words.

"And what will you do now?" asked Aedon, with a heavy heart. There was a short pause, before Finnvarr answered.

"Whatever I must."

The adventure continues!

***Smugglers and Secrets*, Book 4 of the Witches of the New Forest series**

Samhain is approaching, and that can only mean one thing: ghostly, paranormal activity is ramping up in the little village of Burley! Join Ryder for her new adventure, alongside the usual cast of characters including Hunter, Jack, Elspeth, Harriet, Dougal, Mackenzie, and of course, Finnvarr, in the fourth book of the Witches of the New Forest series. The New Forest awaits you!

If you enjoyed this book, please do leave a review. It is the best thing that you can do to help an author continue writing and creating wonderful worlds to explore.

Thank you for reading, and I hope you enjoyed being in Burley with its magickal community as much as I have! And as a special thank you for joining me on these adventures, head on over to my website at www.joannavanderhoeven, where you will find bonus content relating to this book and all the previous books in this series. Enjoy musical playlists that reflect the adventures and emotions of the books themselves in this bonus content. I hope you'll join me in Burley again soon!

Author's Note

Thank you so much for spending time with me again in the little magickal village of Burley, in the New Forest. I have always loved this area with its myths, legends, and magick aplenty. I hope to write many more books in this special setting, with its engaging and interesting characters. The characters actually write the books for me, and it's a pleasure to spend time in their company. I can't wait to find out what they will do next!

Burley is a real place in the New Forest, England. It does indeed have Witchcraft shops, an antique shop, two pubs, a community centre and a hotel among other amenities. It really is a tiny place, nestled in wooded dell. The witch, Sybil Leek, did actually live there, with her jackdaw (a member of the crow family), Mr Hotfoot Jackson. She was flamboyant, and caused a great media stir in the village until her landlord evicted her, when she then moved to the US. The famous New Forest Coven is legendary, and I advise anyone who wants more information to read Philip Heselton's *In Search of the New Forest Coven*.

You may have noticed some of the spells and incantations in some of the books in this series. Many of these, especially Jack's Druidic magick, are drawn from the *Carmina Gadelica*: a collection of prayers, songs, charms, blessings, incantations and more that were collected from the Gàidhealtachd regions of Scotland between 1860 and 1909. This material was recorded and translated into English by Alexander Carmichael (1832–1912). Though much of the recorded lore has a gloss of Christianity, it would appear that it stems from a much older Pagan oral tradition that has been passed down through the centuries. For the purposes of this series, I took out the Christian references and substituted them for a modern Pagan context. As well, Jack, with his Irish heritage, uses Irish Gaelic words and terms throughout the books, such as *mo grá*, meaning 'my love'. Finnvarr too uses Irish Gaelic words, such as in his encounter with the White Hind, whom he calls *Bán Fianna*, meaning 'white deer'.

Also, in this book, when Jack calls upon the goddess Brighid (also known as Brigid, Bride, Brigantia, Ffraid, and many other names) he says the words: *Adjuva Briggitta!* This is a phrase that is found on several ancient Irish manuscripts, and is a call for help to the goddess, Brighid.

The 'phallic broomstick' is a topic that is still hotly debated by Witches and Pagans alike in the community today, as to its veracity and authenticity. I will leave you to do your own research on that matter, should you so wish! As well, the lightning struck oak is indeed a powerful magickal tool, and using some of the wood can create very potent amulets and talismans.

The rune that Hunter used to banish Lanoc is *Hagall*. This rune can look very different, depending upon which time period you are referring to and which system you are using. Hunter used the Norse Younger Futhark rune for *Hagall*, which would have been used during the Viking Age. There is an Elder Futhark, as well as other runic systems such as the Anglo Saxon Futhorc. Therefore, the same shape of the rune in different systems can have a different interpretations, such as "beaver" or "harvest". As well, the rune for hail in other systems such as the Elder Futhark can look totally different and more akin to our modern "H".

Alison uses the term, "cowan" for Ryder. In Witchcraft, this term refers to someone who is not a Witch. It is used as a derogatory term in Witchcraft. The original meaning of this word stems from the Freemasons, where it was used to denote someone who was pretending to be of the Order, but who didn't have the knowledge or the skills, and who wasn't initiated.

In all the books of this series, the myths and legends that have been spoken about Burley and the New Forest are all derived from local folklore. For instance, in Book 1 when Jack described some of the creatures that he had come across in the New Forest, those are actual beings that are said to live, or did live, in the New Forest. The giant, Yernagate, is a folkloric legend which does indeed actually relate to the local site, called Yernagate's Nap. Also, in Book 1 the bedraggled pony that caused Jack's jeep to swerve in the road before being pushed into the ditch by the hummer is the Colt Pixie, a creature that leads people astray and into danger. There are tales of Black Dogs in the New Forest, just as there are spread out across the entire country. Some of these dogs in folklore are protectors, others are omens of death. When the Black Dog is chained, it is most definitely not a beneficent force. The horned, humanoid creature Jack spoke of seeing when he was younger is related to and described in the tales of the Red King, Rufus, as well as appearing in the tale of the Stratford Lyon. And speaking of such, the being with the yellow eyes, a red mane, and huge antlers from the end of Book 2 and throughout Book 3 is the Stratford Lyon itself, as revealed at the end of this book. It is a protector of the New Forest who is loyal to the de Stratford (now just 'Stratford') line and who aids them in times of need. Though this myth comes from the South Baddesley area, I used creative licence to move it closer to Burley for this book. More myths and legends of the New Forest will find and weave themselves into future books in this series.

And on a final note, if you are interested in learning about modern Hedge Witchcraft or Druidry, please see the books listed at the beginning of this work.

About the Author

Joanna van der Hoeven has written many non-fiction books exploring the traditions of both Druidry and Hedge Witchcraft. Joanna has worked in Pagan traditions since 1991, and has published many books, articles, blogs, and videos on the subject.

Born in Canada, Joanna has lived in England since 1998. She now lives on the Suffolk Coast in a little village nestled in the heathland, with the forest and the sea near to her door. To find out more, please visit her website at www.joannavanderhoeven.com, or see her author's page on Amazon.

Printed in Dunstable, United Kingdom